Safe In His Arms

Cover by Shannon Passmore at Shanoff Designs.

Editing by Paper Poppy Editorial and Free Bird Editing

SAFE IN HIS ARMS

ALEXA RIVERS

To every woman out there
who's had to be her own white knight.
You're amazing. You got this. Keep on rocking.

1

Tione Kingi bolted upright at the warning bark. Laying his book on the pillow, he extended a tattooed arm to scratch his Chihuahua, Pixie, behind the ear.

"What is it, girl?"

Pixie yapped again, her tiny body vibrating with nerves. She scrambled to her feet and jumped to the floor, landing on light paws. Trevor, a bull mastiff, lifted his massive head to watch her dart toward the cabin door. Bella, the border collie, perked her ears up, and Zee the rescue pup stretched and circled before settling back onto her bed. It seemed that Trevor, Bella, and Zee hadn't heard anything, but that didn't mean much. Pixie was the most sensitive, and she reckoned something was out there. Tione sighed, scratched his bearded chin, and slipped from the bed. Chances were that all she'd heard was a possum in the trees but it was worth checking. As Tione yanked his sneakers on, Pixie started to growl.

"Yeah, yeah. Be patient, will you?" he muttered. Maybe she needed to do her business. Wouldn't be the first time one of them had disturbed him under false pretenses.

Switching on the security light, he opened the door. Pixie shot through the gap like the proverbial rocket and raced down the slope toward the lodge—his place of employment. She vanished from the illuminated patch of garden and into the shadows, barking and snarling like the *mata kai kutu*—warrior—she believed she was. Something had really set fire to her tail. A flurry of yaps ensued. The kind she made when she'd locked sight on her prey. With a reluctant glance back at his bed, Tione closed the door to keep the warmth inside and then followed her into the dark.

A moment later, he heard something that gave him pause. The squeak of a rusty hinge. There was no way a possum had made that noise.

Someone is out here.

In his backyard. Trying to get into the lodge.

Whoever it was, they had a prime view of him silhouetted against the forest by the security light. The barking continued, and his shoulders stiffened with tension. Moving out of the light, he padded along the strip of lawn between the flower beds. Slowly, his vision adjusted and he could make out a figure at the lodge's back entrance. The person tried the handle, then paced over to a window and pried at it.

Seriously? Who would want to break into the lodge at Sanctuary? And why?

It didn't matter. Fact was, they were.

"Oy!" he shouted, hoping to catch them off guard. "What the hell do you think you're doing?"

The figure jerked around, their face hidden beneath a deep hood. They froze for all of two seconds and then broke into a run. He gave chase, closing the distance quickly. The would-be thief was slower than he'd expected, and moved awkwardly. He reached out and grabbed a fistful of the thief's jacket. The guy was smaller than he'd seemed from a distance. Perhaps a teenager out for a thrill.

And then the thief took him by surprise. He'd assumed that once caught, he'd see he was outgunned and stop. Maybe cuss for a while. Instead, the kid fought like a fucking hellcat. Small and slight, but no less fierce for it. Arms flew, limbs twisted, and a kick landed solidly in his nuts, but within a matter of seconds, Tione had him pinned to the ground, struggling to break free.

"Let me go," a voice hissed. "I won't let you hurt me. I *won't*."

Tione went rigid. That voice. The soft, petite body beneath his. Not a teenage boy.

A woman.

"Bloody hell, I'm not going to hurt you," he growled, his guilt over manhandling her growing by the second. "Why were you trying to break into the lodge?"

She whimpered. "Break in? I just wanted—" He shifted his weight, and she cried out. Shit, he couldn't have hurt her that badly. They'd tussled for only a few moments. Was she playing him?

She sniffled. Damn, she was convincing. Real sobs wracked her body as she whispered on repeat, "Please don't hurt me, please don't hurt me, please don't hurt me."

Disgusted with himself, and with her, he reared up and yanked off her hood before she could retreat. Then his stomach hardened and his mouth dropped open.

"*Motherfucker*."

His gaze swept her face, inventorying injuries. Purple cheek, left eye swollen shut, split lip encrusted with blood, a deep wound at her temple that was weeping fluid. Dark smudges ringed her neck and looked an awful lot like impressions from someone's fingers. Big, male fingers. Like his. But he hadn't grabbed her by the neck. None of this was his doing. Someone had worked this woman over with as much finesse as a bulldozer.

Her eyes squeezed shut, and even though they weren't touching, he could feel waves of fear emanating from her. She was terrified. Completely and utterly scared shitless. Jesus, who was she, and what the fuck had happened to her?

He didn't recognize her. Although to be fair, with her face how it was, he couldn't be sure. He guessed she might be blonde, but in the dim light, with blood set into her hairline, it was impossible to tell for certain. She scuttled back, drew her knees to her chest and winced, her mouth contorting in pain. His chest constricted. Her injuries must extend beyond her face. Who knew how battered the poor thing was beneath that oversized jacket?

Taking a mental step back, he tried to remain calm. Yeah, she'd been searching for a way into Sanctuary, but he didn't know it was for a nefarious reason. Fact was, she looked like a woman who desperately needed help. Exactly the type of woman that Kat, his employer, was notorious for taking in.

"Why are you here?" he asked.

MEGAN HAD BEEN SO *CLOSE*.

So damn close to escaping Charles. She'd given it her best shot and the bastard's goons had still managed to track her down. She hadn't been sure if she could survive another beating, and she couldn't fight her way out because the guy on top of her was big. Not tall, but stocky and muscular. Worse than that, he'd had angry eyes.

She couldn't budge him.

Now she was weak. Judging by the pain that stabbed her every time she moved, she'd guess her ribs were broken, and she could barely see out of her swollen eye. She was in worse shape than a hunk of tenderized steak. Closing her eyes, she rested her pounding head on the cold ground. Was this how it all ended for her? In the dirt, miles from home. No one would even know where to look. How long would it take before her family noticed she was missing? She'd quit her job months ago, when she moved in with Charles, so nobody would expect to see her at work in the morning. As for her friends, well, she'd hardly seen them lately.

Tears still burned in the backs of her eyes. Was there any point continuing to plead with the bearded rock of a man hovering above her? She swallowed, her throat aching. It didn't matter if begging was useless. She had nothing to lose.

She forced her lips to move the way she wanted them to. "Please don't hurt me."

Her voice was husky and raw, nothing like usual. She repeated herself. The man's black brows drew together and he pulled back. Even though every damaged part of her body screamed in protest, she hauled herself out of his reach. If she tried to run again, he'd catch her, but the distance helped her think. She noticed his lips were moving, but with her pulse drumming in her ears, she couldn't hear a word he said. His dark eyes scanned her face, some of the lines around them easing so they seemed wary rather than angry.

His lips moved again.

"I can't hear you," she rasped. Why was he bothering to talk at all? Why hadn't he thrown her over his shoulder and tossed her in the back of his car? Charles would want her returned immediately, before anyone noticed anything was amiss. His professional future depended upon it. She made an effort to slow her breathing and tune out the furious hammering of blood and adrenaline through her veins.

The man scowled and said with exaggerated patience, "Who are you, and why are you here?"

"You don't know?"

"If I knew, would I be asking?"

She laughed. Only once, and her ribs paid the price, but it felt good. "You don't know."

A statement this time. This man wasn't here to drag her back to Charles. She'd misunderstood. Now he was looking at her like he suspected she wasn't right in the head. And who knew, maybe she wasn't. But she was so wonderfully relieved, she didn't care if she sounded like she had a screw loose.

"I've got no fucking clue who you are," he said. "I live in a cabin behind the lodge and as far as I can tell, you were trying to break in."

"You live here? At Sanctuary?" She hadn't screwed up so badly after all. Maybe she was safe, at least for now. "Do you work here?"

He nodded. Tears streamed down her puffy cheeks, stinging her injured lip. She'd made it. She wasn't going to be returned unwillingly to Auckland to live out the rest of her life as a captive trophy wife.

She'd done it. She'd escaped.

Turning her gaze heavenward, she stared up at the thousands of twinkling stars interspersed with the twisting ribbons of pink and purple that were the Milky Way. For the first time in months, she was a free woman, beneath a starry sky. The skies in Auckland were never like this. She eased back onto the ground and let all the tension seep from her body.

She was tired.

She was sore.

But goddamn it, she was *free*.

Something wet nudged the top of her head. The dog's nose. It had stopped barking, but pranced around her body, sniffing curiously.

"Are, uh, you okay?" the man, who still hadn't told her his name, asked.

"I am," she replied, with feeling.

"Looks like you need a doctor."

"No." The word flew from her lips before her brain had fully processed it. She got to her feet, cringing at how much it hurt. "No doctors."

"Okay, okay." He held his palms up in a gesture of peace.

"Can I—" She swallowed her nerves, and wiped her gritty palms on her thighs. "Can I see Katarina? I'm here to stay at Sanctuary." Stringing so many words together brought more tears to her eyes, but she powered on. "I've heard wonderful things about her, and I wasn't trying to break in, I promise. I was just checking whether anything was open, or if I'd have to sleep in my car."

His eyes widened in disbelief. "You'd have slept in your car in that condition?"

He scrubbed a hand over his dark beard, then bent and scooped the dog up with one arm. His bicep bulged and a fresh wave of relief overcame her because he had no intention of hurting her with his powerful body, even though he definitely could if he wanted. He must have twenty pounds on Charles, who'd managed to knock her around just fine.

"Fucking hell." He pinned her with a look. She couldn't tell the color of his eyes, but they were black in the moonlight. "You're going to be trouble."

"No I'm not," she said, shrinking away from him. "Please, take me to see Katarina. I won't do anything to cause a problem." She'd promise him almost anything at that point.

"Fine." He sighed. "I'll need to wake her up. She's probably in bed. I'll dig out the first aid kit, too. Even if you won't see a doctor, we need to do something about that cut on your forehead."

She touched a finger to the gash and hissed. With her fight or flight reflex fully engaged for the past hours, she'd forgotten about it. Head wounds bled a lot, so she must look a fright.

"Thank you," she whispered.

He shook his head. "What happened to you?"

She didn't answer, and he didn't ask again as he led her to one of the doors she'd tried to open earlier and fished a set of keys from his pockets. Casting a glance over her shoulder, she searched the shadows for movement but didn't see anything.

She prayed that meant nobody was out there.

2

Once he'd unlocked the foyer entrance, Tione waited while their unexpected guest limped up the stairs with Pixie on her heels. He wanted to help but he'd seen the way her eyes followed him, like she was waiting for him to lash out, and he didn't want to frighten her. Instead, he closed the door and led her to Kat's apartment, where he knocked softly. Something rustled, low voices murmured, and then the door cracked open.

"Tee?" Kat asked, opening it wider and shoving hair out of her eyes. "What's up?"

"You've got a problem." He spoke quietly so the woman behind him wouldn't hear.

She frowned. "What is it?"

"Come out here and see."

Stepping into the hall, Kat's gaze traveled to the mystery woman but in the dim light she hadn't yet noticed the extent of her injuries.

"*Kia ora*, sweetheart. I'm Kat. How can I help you?"

"I found her outside, trying to get in the garden entrance," he said.

Kat glanced at him irritably. "*Arohamai*, sorry, but I was talking to..." She trailed off, waiting for the woman to fill the gap.

"Hope," she rasped in that gravelly voice he suspected had more to do with the bruises ringing her neck than anything else. "You can call me Hope."

Interesting choice of phrasing. She hadn't actually said her name was Hope, just that they could call her that. It didn't slip past him, and he was pretty sure it didn't get by Kat either. His friend came closer, offering her hand, but it froze in midair.

"Oh, my God." With that, Kat hip-barged Tione to the side and stared at Hope in horror. "You poor thing! What happened? Wait—don't tell me now." She turned to him. "Take Hope to the pink bedroom. I'll be there in a minute."

Just as he'd feared, she was ready to take the girl in, no questions asked. This was exactly why she needed him around. But he'd wait before he raised his concerns. Right now, Hope needed tending to.

"Come with me," he ordered, leading her to the guest room with pink decor. The door stood ajar and he switched the light on before letting "Hope" in. She went straight to the bed and settled on the edge of it. The artificial light cast her vicious facial bruising into sharp relief. Her left cheek was a map of mottled purples and blues, and the wound at her forehead was still bleeding. Her eyes were downcast, and she wore a baggy black jacket and loose pants. It was easy to see how he'd mistaken her for a boy. Dark blonde hair was tied in a tail at the nape of her neck, but a few strands hung around her face, sticky and red.

"You're a mess," he said, bending to stroke Pixie's

trembling body. "What happened?" She kept her head down and didn't reply. Crossing the room, he bent to study her wound more closely. "This might need stitches."

She shivered. "Tape will be fine."

"You're cold?" It had been brisk outside, and her body was probably putting all of its energy into healing.

"No, I'm fine."

"Liar." He switched on the heat pump that was mounted on the wall. "There you go."

"Thank you."

Kat bustled into the room carrying a bucket and a large plastic container, and closed the door. The scent of disinfectant followed her, and Pixie backed away, put off by the strong antiseptic odor. Laying the container at the foot of the bed, Kat sat on the bed beside Hope and lifted a steaming cloth from the bucket, then wrung the water from it.

"Let's get you cleaned up. This might sting a bit."

"I can handle it," Hope mumbled.

With painstakingly careful movements, Kat dabbed the dried blood from Hope's upper lip and down the side of her face, where her head wound had been trickling for long enough to cake it on thickly. If Tione were the type to faint at the sight of blood, he'd be a goner, but true to her word, Hope didn't make a sound. Before long, the water in the bucket had turned red and her face was clean.

Kat turned his way. "Tee."

He jumped to attention. "Yeah?"

"Can you fix Hope a hot meal? We need to take a look under her jacket and take some photos, and I doubt she'll agree to that with you looming in the corner."

"Yeah, sure. Be back in ten." Leaving Pixie with the women, he went to the kitchen and grabbed a portion of pumpkin soup from the freezer. He doubted Hope would be capable of eating anything that involved much chewing. He heated the soup, cut fresh bread and slathered the slices with butter, then poured enough soup into a bowl for two average-sized meals. He suspected she might need a good feed.

When he returned to the bedroom, Hope's outer layers had been stripped off, and she was propped up in bed wearing a t-shirt he recognized as one of Kat's. She took the bowl from him, and he noticed bruises up her forearms, as though she'd been trying to ward her attacker off. Hot fury knifed through him. Whatever she was involved in, it wasn't right for someone so slender and helpless to be victimized like that.

"I think she has a broken rib," Kat said. "Maybe several."

His jaw clenched. No wonder she'd been in pain when he landed on top of her. But what had happened? A car accident, or was something more sinister at play?

"Thank you for the soup," Hope said, but didn't meet his eyes. "It's very kind of you to make me a meal at this time of night. I'm sorry for causing a fuss."

He shrugged, a little uncomfortable with her gratitude after he'd contributed to her pain. "No problem."

She took the spoon between shaking fingers and tried to ladle the soup into her mouth. When it became apparent she couldn't manage it, she ripped a chunk off the bread and dunked it.

Tione turned to Kat. "She can't stay here. Something serious has happened to her. We should take her to hospital. She needs more care than you can give."

Kat sighed. “You’re probably right, but we can let her sleep and take her in the morning. There’s not much anyone can do about busted ribs. Trust me, I know.”

“What if there’s more damage than we can see? We need to call the police.”

“No.” Hope, who’d been eating ravenously, now spoke. She dropped the bread and put the bowl down. Her uninjured eye was wide, her skin pale. “No, no, no, no, no. I don’t need a hospital—except for the ribs, I feel okay—and I won’t talk to the police. Not under any circumstances.” She started to ease the covers back and swing toward the edge of the bed, her face crinkled with effort. “If you don’t want me here, I can go. Don’t call them, just let me get my things and I’ll get out of your hair.”

If Tione had been suspicious of her before, this cemented it. Kat, however, was not of the same opinion.

“Hold on, slow down. No one said we don’t want you here, honey.” She sat on the end of the bed and gestured for Hope to get comfortable again. Or at least, as comfortable as she could be. “If you don’t want the police involved, that’s okay. We won’t force you into anything.”

Hope’s shoulders were stiff, her expression wary. She didn’t trust them. That was all right with him. He didn’t trust her, either. What kind of person turned up in the middle of the night, black and blue, and insisted no one call the authorities? Someone who was in trouble with those very authorities, that’s who.

“Tee?”

He grunted. “Yeah.”

“You can head back to bed now. I’ve got this.”

He was reluctant to leave, but her tone brooked no challenge. “Fine.” He scooped Pixie into his arms and, instead of returning to his cabin, went to the room Kat shared with Sterling, where he rapped on the bedroom door. "Sterling, wake up."

Kat's boyfriend groaned. "What?"

"I need to talk to you."

"*Now*?"

Tione didn't reply, and after a moment, a light appeared beneath the door and it opened. Sterling wore gray track pants and a blue t-shirt. His blond hair was tousled, his jaw stubbly, eyes bleary.

"This better be good."

"It is. I caught a woman trying to get into the lodge. She's beat up pretty badly. Kat is with her at the moment, but the girl refuses to talk to the police or go to hospital. I don't trust her, and I think she lied about her name."

Sterling sighed. "I'm not going to get back to sleep, am I?"

"Just take a look and let me know what you think. I'm going to make them both hot chocolates, then go home. I won't be making any ground with Kat tonight, but you might."

He nodded. "What room?"

"The pink one."

The two men paced out to the hall, where Sterling went left and Tione turned right. He put Pixie outside, then heated milk and dark chocolate in a pot, mixing until they combined. He inhaled the rich aroma and gave into temptation, pouring a small mug for himself as well as two for the women. He added marshmallows to each, drank his, then carried the remaining mugs to the pink room. The door was ajar and he pushed it with his foot. When Kat glanced between him and Sterling and narrowed her eyes, he handed her a mug and kept a blank expression.

"Hot chocolate." He placed the other on the wooden cabinet beside the bed. "One for you, too."

"Thank you," Hope said.

He bit the inside of his lip to keep quiet, waved at both women, and went into the hall to wait for Sterling. A moment later, the other man joined him.

"Well? What do you think?"

They walked down the hall together and paused outside Kat and Sterling's room.

"I think she's had a rough day," Sterling said.

That much was obvious.

"And I agree, she's hiding something," he continued. "But if Kat trusts her enough to let her stay here, that's okay with me."

Of course it was. Sterling was absolutely smitten, and Tione shouldn't have expected anything different.

A furrow formed between Sterling's brows. "Strange thing, though. I could swear she looks familiar."

"Huh." Now *that* was interesting. "But you don't know from where?"

"No, but I'll think on it."

"You do that." With a racing mind, Tione left the lodge, wandered across the garden to his cabin, brushed his teeth and went to bed. Whatever "Hope" was up to, he'd figure it out.

"THANK you for not calling the police," Megan said to Kat as the other woman peeled back the blankets and rubbed anti-inflammatory lotion into her multi-colored torso. To distract herself from the licks of pain dancing up her side, Megan applied the lotion to her forearms, breathing in the familiar menthol smell. She closed her eyes and rested her head on the pillow, feeling like her limbs had been infused with lead. Everything was heavy and sore. But the weariness was more than physical. It was soul deep.

"No problem." Kat probed her ribcage with firm fingers and Megan hissed in pain. "Might be broken."

"Or bruised." She'd known as soon as Charles's foot had connected with her body that he'd done some damage but she wasn't convinced they were broken.

"This isn't from a car accident."

Megan didn't want to reply, but she also didn't want to get kicked out. It had been so long since anyone had touched her with as much kindness as Kat did. Since anyone had smoothed a hand over her skin with the intention of healing rather than hurting. Charles had isolated her from anyone who might fill that role, and she hadn't even realized it was happening until she was alone.

She cleared her throat, and winced when it burned. "No, it's not."

The other woman nodded. "Is this the first time?"

"No."

Kat made a sound of distress in the back of her throat. A moment later, she said, "You'll tell me when you're ready."

Thank God. Kat wasn't going to push her. She wasn't going to force her to voice what had happened. Hot tears prickled in her eyes and she tried to contain them, but they slid from the corners and rolled down the side of her face, soaking into the pillowcase.

"Thank you," she said, her tongue thick in her mouth. "A… friend… told me that Sanctuary is a good place to start over. That's what I want. A fresh start."

Was that too much to hope for?

"Look at me, Hope."

Megan opened her good eye, guilt pulsing through her at the lie about her identity. The jig would soon be up, but the longer she could be anyone other than Megan Talbot, the better. She wanted to make it as difficult as possible for Charles to find her. Then, once she had her life under control, she'd reach out to her family.

"Listen to me, sweetheart." Kat's expression was gentle. She sat on the edge of the bed and took Megan's hand in hers. "I don't know your story, but I can tell you're *wahine toa*—a warrior woman. You stay here and we'll do everything we can to give you that fresh start."

Megan swallowed, afraid to let herself be happy yet. What if everything came crashing down? Kat didn't know her, and the man she'd called Tee certainly didn't trust her.

"Your friend doesn't want me here."

Kat waved a hand. "He'll come around. Tee doesn't like new people, and he wants to make sure no one takes advantage of me."

"He's a good friend, then."

She smiled softly. "Yeah, he is." She squeezed Megan's hand once, then released it. "I'm going to get you an ice pack and some painkillers. Be back in a minute."

While she was gone, Megan studied the room. Pink walls, white curtains, and a small wooden desk in one corner. It was in the style of buildings from the early 1900s, but recently renovated. The room was charming. She could be happy here. Footsteps padded down the hall, then the door eased open and Kat came back in. She had a bundle of ice cubes wrapped in a towel, and pressed it into Megan's side. In her other hand was a water bottle.

"There you go. It won't help as much as it would have when the damage was first done, but it might slow the bruising a little." She set a pair of tablets and the bottle on the nightstand.

Watching her, Megan did her best not to cry again. Most days she was self-contained, but at the moment, she felt like a faucet that had finally burst under pressure.

"Why are you being so nice to me?"

Kat's hands stilled.

She continued. "I could be a fugitive for all you know."

"Don't be silly. You're a good person who's come upon rough times. Everyone needs help sometimes, and I built Sanctuary to be a place where people could get that, whatever their situation may be." She reached up and, ever so gently, stroked a hand through Megan's hair.

The tears started to fall again. Such a simple, sweet touch. Charles had stopped bothering to be gentle with her a while back, and these days, she rarely saw anyone else without him around. He wouldn't let anyone near enough to her to discover his secret. *Their* secret. She couldn't even visit her family without him tagging along or monitoring her calls.

"Thank you." Shuffling up in the bed, she took her hot chocolate in hands that trembled. Her split upper lip throbbed as she drank but it was delicious. Rich and creamy. She'd been cold and hollow on the inside, but together the soup and hot chocolate had warmed her.

When she'd drained it, she set the cup on the nightstand and lay down again.

"Will you be okay here until morning?" Kat asked.

"Yes," she murmured, already well on her way to falling asleep. "Lock the door, please."

"Okay. Sleep well, Hope."

3

The following day, Tione didn't see their new guest. He didn't know whether she even left her bed, other than to visit the bathroom. Kat collected food from the dining hall for her and disappeared into the pink room with it. She also carried a black suitcase from the ancient car in the parking lot—which he assumed belong to Hope—to the guest room. The second day after her arrival, Hope hobbled into the dining hall, her head ducked low. She'd showered, so her hair was no longer matted with blood, and the swelling on her cheek had gone down, her bruises now in hues of blue, green, and yellow. The family of four eating breakfast at one of the round tables stopped and stared.

The little girl pointed and asked, "What's wrong with that lady's face?"

Her dad hushed her, but if possible, Hope's head ducked lower and her shoulders hunched. He watched her slink to the hot water urn and fix herself a cup of tea. While the tea brewed, she scanned the room, her eyes settling on him. Taking her cup, she headed his way, her gaze skittering to the exits.

"Hello," she said when she stood across the counter from him.

He leaned forward on his elbows and she glanced at his inked forearms. He wondered what her opinion of tattoos was. She seemed the type to find them intimidating. Up close, he could see her eyes were brown. It had been impossible to tell until now.

"*Kia ora*," he replied.

"I, uh…" She swallowed, drawing his attention to the ring of purplish-brown around her throat. Definitely finger marks. Whatever her situation, no woman deserved to have someone bigger and stronger choke her. No *person* did, ever. "I wanted to thank you. For helping me the other night." Her voice was less scratchy than it had been. Softer. More feminine. "I know it must have looked bad when you caught me trying to get in. Thank you for stopping to listen rather than just kicking me out."

Frowning, he tried to think of something to say. Her gratitude had caught him unaware. Especially when he'd done nothing to deserve it. He'd chased her when she was already frightened, and hurt her when she was injured—even if it had been unintentional.

"Don't mention it."

She looked down, her lips pressed together. The tear in her upper lip had scabbed over. "Okay. I'm heading back to my room in a moment. Thank you again."

He watched her go to the breakfast table and slather jam and cream cheese on a croissant before carrying it out, wondering how much courage it had taken for her to approach him. She reminded him of a puppy who'd been kicked one too many times. In the case of a dog, it took a lot of patience, positive reinforcement and love before they stopped being skittish and trusted a person again. He had no doubt Kat would appoint herself the chairperson of the Let's Fix Hope Club and begin a campaign to erase the shadows from her chestnut eyes.

He still thought they ought to call in the professionals. She needed real help. The kind Kat couldn't give her. The woman was clearly in trouble, and they weren't equipped to deal with it. Across the dining hall, the mother of the family rose and came over to him.

"Who is that poor young lady?" she asked quietly.

"Her name is Hope," he told her. "She arrived Friday night."

"What happened to her? Is there anything we can do to help?"

"No idea what happened, she won't talk about it. At least, not to me. As for helping, you'd be better off asking Kat."

She nodded. "I will. Thanks, Tione."

As she returned to her children and husband, he stared at the exit Hope had passed through and, for the first time in years, his fingers itched to scramble over a keyboard. To enter the strokes that would bring up her whole life story for his viewing pleasure. He didn't like not knowing. Clenching his fists, he shook his head. Even if a bunch of gangsters turned up looking for her—not that he thought they would—he wouldn't return to his old ways.

He couldn't.

EVERYONE AT SANCTUARY was so *nice*. Katarina was everything Megan had hoped and more. She'd taken it upon herself to be Megan's personal savior, keeping her warm, comfortable, and fed. She even had her friend Brooke visit so she had company. Brooke was an ethereal blonde with a penchant for quirky t-shirts and an unending amount of good cheer. When she'd turned up on Sunday morning and walked in with a bright "good morning, gorgeous," then beamed at Megan with no hint of shock or caution as she took stock of the assorted bruises and injuries, Brooke had earned her eternal affection.

The only person who seemed less than thrilled by her presence was the gruff guy who worked in the kitchen. Tione. Since he clearly didn't want her there, she hadn't talked to him after that first breakfast. She'd collected her meals and refilled her mug as quickly as possible, and tried to make herself small and inconspicuous so she didn't attract his ire.

She could understand his concern. In his shoes, she'd be suspicious, too.

But he didn't worry her. Not too much, anyway. Behind his inscrutable expression and rough exterior, she got the impression he was a good person. After all, what did external appearances matter? Charles gave every impression of being an upstanding gentleman when nothing could be further from the truth. Unfortunately, by the time she'd realized that, it had been too late.

No, appearances didn't mean a thing. People should only be judged by their actions.

Shifting her weight, she brushed up against Brooke, who was sitting beside her while they watched a cupcake-baking reality TV contest.

"That one looks good," Brooke said as the camera zoomed into a cherry cola cupcake frosted with vanilla and topped with a glace cherry.

Megan shook her head. "It's undercooked, and the frosting is too soft; it'll slip right off." Sure enough, a moment later it oozed over the sides, losing its shape.

Brooke turned to her, mouth agape. "How could you tell that?"

"Experience."

"You like to bake?"

"You could say that." Up until she'd moved in with Charles, she'd worked in a high-end bakery, and before that, she'd apprenticed under a world-renowned pastry chef in Paris. But Charles had convinced her to quit her job, because why would she need to work when he could afford to take care of her?

Fool.

"You should use the kitchen while you're here. I'd love to eat something Tione didn't make."

Megan frowned. "His food is perfectly tasty."

Brooke grinned. "Yeah, but he doesn't have the widest repertoire."

She considered this. She missed being in the kitchen. Except for the pulse-pounding days when she'd taken on private commissions while Charles was at work so she could raise money to leave—which she'd spent constantly in fear he'd turn up and demand to know what she was doing—she hadn't had an outlet for her creativity. The menus for his parties had been elegant but simple. Nothing to excite her. Besides which, it was hard to enjoy herself when she was afraid he'd decide her efforts were subpar and make his disapproval known as soon as they were alone.

She shivered, an icy sensation sliding down her spine.

No, don't think of that. Think of strawberry cupcakes and delicate pastries.

She nibbled on her lip. "Do you think he'd let me? I don't think he likes me very much."

Brooke waved a hand. "Pfft. That's just Tee. He's growly around everyone. It's his way. Trust me, it will be no problem at all."

Megan rested against the headboard. She wanted to believe it. But she couldn't shake off the shadow that had descended on her. Even when Charles wasn't here, he managed to ruin her mood.

"Are you okay?" Brooke asked.

"Yes, I am."

At least, she would be, once she was certain she'd made a clean break. Two and a half days had passed with no sign of him, so maybe he couldn't find her. Or perhaps she'd misjudged and she wasn't important enough for him to bother coming after her. He'd said his promotion depended on her—that his boss loved her—but perhaps he'd exaggerated. She clung to that thought and burrowed into the blankets, but she couldn't quite get warm again.

MEGAN WAS WATCHING *World's Best Cake Makers* and scribbling notes when someone knocked on the door. Everything inside her stilled, as it did whenever someone visited.

"Who is it?" she called.

"Sterling."

Swinging her feet off the bed, she eased her weight onto them. She was healing, but it was slow, and moving hurt. Especially her torso. She unlocked the door and cracked it open.

"Hi."

"Hi," he replied, his blue eyes locking on her face, something lurking in them that made her anxious. *Knowledge.* "Can I come in?"

"Please do." Politeness was so ingrained in her that she found herself stepping aside and indicating for him to take the seat in front of the desk before she'd even made a conscious decision to do so. Damn it, she needed to work on that. She couldn't very well invite Charles into her room if he came to collect her.

"What can I do for you?" she asked, untucking the hair from behind her ear so it fell over her face and obscured her features. She'd tried to keep her distance from him over the past few days in the hopes he wouldn't recognize her, but the way he was looking at her made her think that her grace period had come to an end. Would he spill the beans, or would he keep her secret?

"Megan, I know who you are."

She squeezed her eyes shut and exhaled between clenched teeth. He'd called her by her real name. There was no point in pretending anymore. Slowly, she backed over to her bed and sunk onto it. "What are you going to do about it?"

"Look at me."

She forced her eyes open, willing to do whatever he said if he'd keep quiet for a few more days. Another week, maybe. Enough time for her to figure out her next step.

"Mark is my friend," he said.

She nodded. "I know."

It was because of her brother's friendship with Sterling that she'd heard of Sanctuary in the first place.

"He'd be beside himself with worry if he knew what happened to you. How long do you think it will take before your family notices you're not in Auckland anymore? Do you really want them to wonder where you are, and whether you're all right?"

"I'll call them soon," she said, desperation creeping over her. "I promise. Please, just let me go on being Hope for a while longer."

His expression didn't flicker when her voice cracked. Sterling was a cool customer. Always had been. Mark's total opposite.

"What kind of trouble are you in, Megan?"

"Stop saying my name." Her throat clogged with unshed tears. "I can't tell you. Not yet. I just need a little more time. Please don't mention this to Mark or Kat."

Slowly, he nodded. "Fine. You've got three days to tell your family you're safe, otherwise I'll call Mark. Is that fair?"

"Yes, thank you." She swallowed and the tension ebbed from her shoulders. Three days was more than she would have had if he'd outed her now. "I won't let you down."

"Don't." He stood, and brushed imaginary lint from his jeans. "When you're ready to talk, you know where I am." He met her eyes. "I'd like to help you."

She started to get up as he left, but he gestured for her to stay where she was. The moment the door clicked shut behind him, she got up anyway and flicked the lock. Then she wondered how on earth she was going to explain herself to her family.

4

Tione grabbed a tray of eggs from the fridge and set them on the counter, then glanced outside. The sun streamed through the clouds, giving the appearance of more warmth than was actually there. Trevor and Bella frolicked in the garden and, as he watched, Trevor tripped over his overly large feet and went muzzle-first into the dirt. Tione shook his head. Giant goofball. He cracked an egg into a glass mixing bowl and was about to crack another when the kitchen door opened.

"Hi," a soft voice said. Not Kat.

He turned. Hope hovered in the doorway, looking around the kitchen with interest. Her hair hung loose around her shoulders, a slight wave to it, and she wore light blue jeans and a pink blouse that didn't cover her arms. Her bruises were fading, and the one on her face had turned a strange shade of yellow.

"I look a fright, don't I?"

He realized he'd been staring. "You look a damn sight better than you did."

The edges of her lips curved up. It was barely perceptible, but he noticed. In general, he noticed far more than people expected him to.

"Thank you." She shifted from one foot to the other, sucked in a deep breath, and then made eye contact with him. "Is there anything I can do to help?"

He blinked at the unexpected question. "With lunch?"

"Yes."

Well. This must be the first time anyone had offered to help him cook. It was his job. What he was paid for. Suspicion flared. She'd avoided him for the past few days. Why was she here and offering to help now?

"No, thanks. I've got everything under control."

To his surprise, she didn't lower her gaze and hurry out. Instead, her expression turned earnest. "If you're worried I'll get in your way, don't be. I have some experience in the kitchen, and I promise I won't get under your feet."

She didn't flinch when he appraised her from head to toe. Apparently she wasn't as mousy as he'd thought. Sighing, he went to run a hand through his hair, then remembered he was wearing a hairnet.

What could it hurt? He relented. "Okay."

She beamed, and not even the ugly scab on her lip could dim her smile's brightness. "What are you making? How can I help?"

He washed the egg off his hands and dried them on a towel. "We've got two options for lunch today: quiche and filled rolls. You can finish cracking these eggs and then dice some of the vegetables for the quiche." He gestured to the other counter. "There's a list of quantities over there, and they're all in the fridge. I'll get started on the pastry. Does that sound okay?"

She vibrated with excitement. It was odd, but then he was beginning to think Hope was an odd girl. "Perfect. Where are the hairnets?"

He fished one from the top drawer and handed it to her, then watched as she washed her hands and crossed to the eggs. "Be careful not to drop the shell in."

She cracked the first egg with a deft movement, draining the innards out and setting the remnants aside in a neat pile. His eyebrows rose. She hadn't been lying when she said she was familiar with a kitchen. She cracked a second one and he set to work on the pastry, blitzing together egg, flour, butter and a little water, then dusting the countertop and rolling the pastry out. By the time he'd got it to the appropriate thickness, cut it to size and pressed it into the pie tin, Hope had finished with the eggs, found the chopping board, and was quickly growing a pile of finely diced carrots, which were exactly the right size, and consistently chopped. He was impressed. He was also impressed by the quick, economical movements with which she peeled and cut. There were no hesitations. If he'd wielded a knife the way she did, he'd have lopped off a finger.

"Are you a chef?" he asked.

"No." She didn't so much as falter.

"A cook? A caterer?"

"No, and no." She finished the stack of carrot, laid the knife down, and turned to him. "What about you? Did you apprentice to be a chef, or are you just good in the kitchen?"

He didn't like how she'd turned his questions around on him. "I'm not a chef."

According to his qualifications, he was a software engineer. Funny how life worked out.

Something out the window caught her attention, and he followed her gaze. She'd spotted Trevor, and her entire body had stiffened. Great, she was probably afraid of dogs.

"Whose dog?" she asked. "Does he live here?"

"That's Trevor. He's mine. And yes, he lives here. You'd better get used to it."

He waited for her to freak out. For her cheeks to pale and her tongue to trip over itself, but she just smiled and said, "That's cool. I love dogs, especially big ones. He looks like a lovable goober. Can I meet him later?"

He grunted. "Suppose so."

Shaking his head, he wondered what to make of this woman. She came across as a jumpy, jittery mess one minute, but a warm, competent person the next. Which version of Hope was real?

WAS BEING ATTRACTED to scruffy beards and tattoos a side effect of being abused by a clean-shaven man with virgin skin?

Megan would have to look into that, because she was finding herself impossibly attracted to the surly cook. Everything inside her was so mixed up that she didn't know how to act around him—or anyone else. It was like a tornado had whipped through the emotions she'd contained so carefully over the past few months and sent them spinning wildly out of control. She'd been a brittle pane of glass, and now she was spider-webbed with cracks. Her words felt foreign in her mouth, and when she moved, her movements were jerky, as though there was a disconnect between her brain and her limbs. She imagined this was how it would feel to be a ghost inhabiting someone else's body.

The only thing that made sense was baking. She *needed* it. And heck, chopping vegetables and cracking eggs was hardly what she most wanted, but the rhythm was familiar and for the first time in days, her hands had stopped trembling. So she ignored the way Tione cast sidelong glances in her direction, and the long silences that could have been awkward if she were the type who needed to fill them.

Long silences were nothing new to her.

While Tione blind-baked the pastry, she beat milk and eggs together, then whisked in the vegetables and grated some cheese.

"You know what you're doing," he said, not for the first time. He was probing for information, but she wasn't about to offer any.

"Quiche is delicious but simple." She stood back as he grabbed the pastry, poured the filling into the case, and returned it to the oven. "Have you made the filled rolls yet?" She wasn't ready to return to her bedroom, where there would be nothing more than her thoughts to occupy her. She'd pondered where she'd veered off the tracks enough for one lifetime.

"No. The rolls are in the pantry." He hung the oven mitts from a nail in the wall and pointed. "Can you cut them open?"

"Sure thing." She collected the paper bag of rolls from the pantry and sniffed. The scent of freshly baked bread was one of her favorites, and if she wasn't mistaken, these had come from the bakery this morning. “These look good.”

“Hmm?” He glanced over. “Oh, yeah. They’re from Cafe Oasis in town.”

Cafe Oasis. Perhaps if Charles didn’t come for her, she could find work there. She’d need a job before long. She didn’t have much money—only what she had left over from spending the cash she’d managed to hoard on an ancient car.

With precise movements she cut the bread rolls and stacked them on a tray, then hovered, unsure what to do next. “Um...”

“Shred the lettuce.”

He wouldn’t win any awards for his manners, but she appreciated him directing her. This was his kitchen, not hers. She was playing sous chef. She made short work of the lettuce, and between the two of them, lunch was ready with time to spare.

“Thanks,” he said as he washed his hands.

“No problem. I like to feel useful.” Especially since she was finally able to do something after playing the part of the perfect Stepford girlfriend.

“You’re certainly that,” he said.

Swallowing her nerves, she put a little steel in her back, and looked him in the eye. “What do you usually do for dessert?”

More than anything, she wanted to bake. Cute little cupcakes. Cinnamon rolls. Souffles. Nothing fancy, just comfort food. The kind that wouldn’t have been up to Charles’s standards.

Tione checked a piece of paper stuck to the side of the fridge. “Apple crumble is what’s on the menu for tonight.”

She nodded, then winced at the sharp pain in her neck and head. “Can I help again, please?”

Crossing his arms over his chest, he cocked his head, looking perplexed. “Why?”

She told him the truth. “I need something to keep me busy.”

His dark eyes seemed to see more than she wanted them to. He knew she wasn’t telling him the whole story, but he didn’t press her. “Be back here at four.”

“I will.”

She hadn’t gone more than two steps when he said, “Hope?”

She turned back, dread infusing her. Was he having second thoughts? “Yes?”

“You want to meet Trevor?”

She smiled. “I’d like that.”

“This way.” He opened a side exit she hadn’t noticed previously, and she followed him out. He’d removed his hair and beard nets, which meant she could see a swirl of ink peeking above the collar of his t-shirt as he walked. The glimpses she caught made her curious, and she wanted to tug down the neckline to get a better look, but doubted he’d appreciate that.

He stuck two fingers in his mouth and whistled. The brown mastiff’s ears perked up and he loped over the garden toward them, kicking up dirt and chunks of grass.

She bent over, hands on her knees, and called, “Here, boy. What a good boy!” When Trevor skidded to a stop and nosed her hand, she scratched behind his ear and laughed. “Aren’t you lovely?”

“Don’t encourage him,” Tione grumped. “That’s the last thing we need.”

“Ooh, but he’s got such a cute face,” she cooed,

patting him until his tail wagged so powerfully that he was in danger of knocking someone over with it. She could already tell this was the kind of dog she'd always wanted. Lovable, adorable, and big enough to scare away the bad guys.

"I have to do the lunch service," he said abruptly. "Don't let him walk all over you."

"Okay."

"There are another three of them around here, somewhere," he told her.

"Another three...?"

"Dogs," he explained. "Pixie, you've already met."

She frowned, trying to recall. "The Chihuahua who wanted to pick a fight with me when I arrived?"

"Yeah. The other two are Bella and Zee. A border collie and a bull terrier cross. If you see them, they're friendly."

"Thanks." Sanctuary just got better and better. "You head in, I've got things under control out here." She patted Trevor. "We're going to be the best of friends."

He might have smiled, but it was hard to tell. His expression seemed to change so little. These days though, she was acutely aware of even minor alterations in a person's mood. She didn't think he trusted her, but he didn't dislike her either, and if she wasn't mistaken, he was pleasantly surprised by her reaction toward Trevor. He swung around and returned inside, shutting the door behind him.

She scanned the garden and spotted a chew toy beneath a naked rose bush. She went over and no sooner had she picked it up than Trevor grabbed the other end and yanked hard enough to topple her off balance. She caught herself only a moment before she hit the ground.

Her heart gave a painful thud. Man, that would have hurt.

"Maybe I'm not up to tug-o-war yet," she murmured, and looked for an alternative. There was a tennis ball on the deck of Tione's cabin. She strode over, Trevor on her heel, and grabbed the ball, which she lobbed as far as she could with her right arm. The ribs on that side were less sore. She suspected they were only bruised, not broken. The dog bounded after the ball, but before he could reach it, a shaggy black and white shape darted in front of him and snatched it from the ground. The border collie.

Megan couldn't help but laugh at how disappointed Trevor seemed, big head drooping until his ears brushed the ground. He turned back to her, and she could have sworn his expression was hopeful.

"Sorry, boy," she said. "No more balls over here."

The border collie had stopped on the far side of the garden, and Trevor eyed her as if he were considering giving chase. She dropped the ball, taunting him. Trevor took a step forward, and the border collie took the ball in her mouth and danced backward. Megan was about to go after her when the guttural growl of an approaching car made her heart stop for what seemed like forever. When it started again, it thudded so hard she half expected it to beat right out of her chest. She recognized the sound of that particular engine. It was the rough purr of a flat-plane V8 Ferrari. The kind Seeley James drove.

But what were the odds it was him? Any number of people might drive a Ferrari like that. Still, the coincidence was a little too much.

The engine growled louder, and she dashed behind

the cabin and peered around the end. A moment later, the noise quieted. She started counting and had reached twenty-three when the doorway from the parking lot into the lodge—which she could just see from her vantage point—opened inward, and Seeley James entered the foyer.

5

One minute Tione was watching Hope play with his dogs outside, the next she was ducking for cover behind his cabin like the devil himself was after her. Opening the window, he leaned out and looked around. No one else was in sight.

"Excuse me," a man called behind him, and he turned, spying the guy in the doorway between the dining hall and the foyer. "Does anyone work here?"

Frowning, Tione headed over. The man's shoulders were thrown back, his barrel chest straining against the fabric of a gray suit. The kind of suit he knew from experience cost at least five figures. This was a man who wanted to look important. Was this who Hope was hiding from?

He offered a hand, and noticed the man glance at his tattooed forearms with scorn.

"I'm Tione," he said, squeezing a little harder than required. "Are you here to check in?"

The guy's eyebrows flew up at his abrupt tone. Tione wasn't in hospitality for his social skills.

"Seeley James. Is there somewhere private we can talk?"

"What's this about?"

Seeley James cleared his throat, then checked his gaudy gold watch. "I think it would be best if we took this elsewhere."

Tione wanted to refuse. Something about the guy rubbed him the wrong way, but guests were watching curiously and he didn't want to start any gossip, so he strode briskly past him, indicating for him to follow, and led him to Kat's office. Seeley sank into the chair on the visitor's side of Kat's desk, but Tione remained standing. He wasn't going to be walked over by a guy with a designer watch who'd dismissed him with a glance. Instead, he waited for the other man to talk.

"I'm a member of law enforcement," he finally said, leaning back in the chair, splaying his legs wide, apparently unconcerned by his height disadvantage. "I'm looking for a woman named Megan Talbot."

If he was law enforcement, why hadn't he shown a badge, or identified himself? Tione didn't trust him one iota. "Never heard of her."

"She might be traveling under an alias. She's blonde and brown-eyed, about five-four, slim, twenty-seven years old." His thin lips twisted. "Pretty."

Tione's heart gave a jolt. The age and physical characteristics fitted Hope to a tee—and he'd suspected from the start that she'd been running from someone—but despite that, something about this guy didn't ring true.

"Here, I have a photograph." He reached into the front pocket of his suit jacket, extracted a picture and smoothed a thumb over the glossy side before passing it over. The woman in the photo was Hope, no doubt about it. She wore a pink evening dress, and a man in a tuxedo had his arm around her. He peered at the photograph more closely. Though her lips were curved in a smile, it didn't reach her eyes, and she was leaning away from her partner, as though she didn't like him touching her.

He wanted to scrunch the photograph in his fist and toss it in the bin. His instincts told him that the man in the picture was responsible for how badly Hope —*Megan*, he corrected himself—had been injured when she'd turned up in their backyard. He didn't give in to the impulse though, because that would have told Seeley the picture meant something to him.

He forced himself to shrug. "Never seen her. Remind me why you're looking for her."

Seeley's steely blue eyes glinted, and the set of his face reminded Tione of a bulldog. "She's wanted for questioning."

"In relation to what?"

"I can't share the details of an ongoing investigation."

"So, she's a criminal?"

Seeley reclaimed the photograph and slipped it into his pocket. "I didn't say that."

Yeah, there was a lot he wasn't saying.

"What agency do you work for?"

Getting to his feet, Seeley rolled his shoulders. Something in his back clicked loudly enough for Tione to hear it, and the motion emphasized a bulge at his hip. A gun? But why would he be armed? Firearms were rarely used by New Zealand law enforcement.

"Look," he said, straightening. "All you need to know is that we're searching for Megan Talbot, and she's potentially dangerous. Call me at this number if you see her." He dug a business card out of his pants pocket and handed it over. All it had was a name and a number. No department logo or job title. Not very official.

And Seeley honestly expected him to believe that Hope—Megan—was dangerous? Not a chance in hell. He was full of shit.

Yeah, maybe she was wrapped up in something dodgy, and she'd definitely lied. But the woman was as harmless as a bunny.

"Sorry, man, I really can't help you. I haven't seen Megan Talbot, I hadn't heard her name before you said it, and I have no idea who she is. Or who *you* are, for that matter."

"Thanks for your time." What Seeley James's eyes said was, *Fuck you*. "Seeing as you haven't seen nothing, and don't know nothing, you won't mind if I take a look around."

"Do you have a warrant?"

"No, but I can get one."

"You do that. Until then, I can't let you intrude on our guests' privacy. It would be unethical of me."

Seeley's cheeks were beet red, but he huffed out a gust of air and inclined his head. "I understand."

The angry gleam in his eyes said he understood very well, and that Tione better watch his back.

"Good. I'll see you out." He'd lock the door behind him, too.

"That's not necessary."

His jaw firmed. "I insist."

With that, he escorted Seeley James from the building, and waited on the front porch until the asshole drove away in his pretentious car. He had an uncomfortable feeling that it wouldn't be the last Sanctuary saw of him.

MEGAN LISTENED to the Ferrari rumble off the property, but didn't move from her vantage point behind the cabin. She watched Tione emerge into the garden alone, and searched for any sign that he'd sold her out. She knew he didn't really want her there, but they'd been getting along well enough, and the fact Seeley had left gave her hope.

He crossed his arms over his broad chest. "Megan, you can come out now."

She didn't move. Her skin prickled with awareness as two thoughts crossed her mind simultaneously. One, he hadn't told Seeley she was there. Two, he'd called her by her real name, which meant that Seeley had exposed her.

"Is he gone?" she called, peeking around the corner.

"Yeah." The single word gave away nothing. What had Seeley told him? She knew the private investigator better than to believe it had been the truth.

"Did you mention anything about seeing me?"

"No." His chin tilted skyward and he sighed loudly. "Please come out. I didn't tell the slimy *to raho* you were here."

"*To raho*?"

"Dickhead," he explained. "Come on, Megan. Come back and play with Trevor again."

She forced her feet to take one step, then another. Her legs moved robotically, carrying her away from her hiding place, and into the open. She scanned the yard, but didn't see anyone other than him and relaxed slightly. His arms dropped to his sides and when she was tempted to stop at a safe distance, he urged her closer with a gesture.

"I told him the truth. I've never met Megan Talbot. Do you believe me?"

She nodded. He wasn't the type to bullshit. He'd been straight with her from the beginning. "Thank you. Don't worry, I'll get out of your hair before he comes back." She had no doubt that he would return. Tione might have put him off for now, but Seeley was wily and would have sensed something was up. He'd think up a better plan of attack and the second time around, he wouldn't be dissuaded.

But how had he found her in the first place? She'd been careful. She'd left her phone behind in case it had tracking software installed, and she'd squirreled away money from baking jobs that Charles didn't know about to finance her escape. She'd left behind the credit cards he'd given her and hadn't even brought her own clothing. Instead, she'd made a trip to the Salvation Army store a week ago and stocked up on cheap secondhand outfits. The only things she'd brought from home were her toiletries.

So how had he known to come here? She hadn't mentioned this place to anyone. She'd searched it on the internet once or twice, but she'd wiped her browsing history and never printed any information. She must have missed something when she'd cleaned up after herself.

"Where will you go?" Tione asked now.

She ignored the question because the truth was, she had no idea, but she wasn't about to be a sitting duck. "I don't know how he found me," she said. "But I won't stick around to cause any problems for you. That's the last thing I want."

Tione stared at her with those dark, unfathomable eyes. She shifted, uncomfortable with his scrutiny. In her recent experience, people paying attention to her ended badly. Either she'd upset someone, or she'd garnered unwanted admirers, which Charles would no doubt notice and punish her for later.

"I'll just—"

He extended a hand. She frowned at it. He rolled his eyes and shoved it into his pocket. "Let's talk in my cabin."

She stiffened. The last thing she wanted was to be alone with a man who outweighed her, and whose mood she couldn't interpret. "I don't think that's the best idea."

"Bring Trevor with us if it makes you feel better. I promise I won't touch you."

She nibbled her lip, then decided that if he wished her harm, he could have handed her over to Seeley. "Okay."

He whistled, and Trevor bounded over to them. Megan turned and walked on unsteady legs back up the sloping lawn and onto the cabin's deck. She waited while he opened the door, then followed him in.

The interior wasn't what she'd expected. The walls were bare wood, giving it a cozy feel that made her want to snuggle up in front of the fire with a book—and there were many books to choose from. They were stacked on nearly every flat surface. The desk, the nightstand, the counter, the dresser. Many of them were well-read; the kind found in thrift shops and dusty secondhand bookstores. One or two newer volumes were present, as well as half a dozen on a shelf at head height that looked to be old editions of the classics.

A smile spread over her face. The furniture was wooden too; the lamps ornately carved, giving the impression she'd stepped back in time. There was no computer. No television. Not much in the way of technology. Lamps, a toaster, a kettle, and an ancient brick of a phone on the nightstand, but that was all.

"You done looking?"

Her cheeks flushed. "Sorry, it's just so wonderful in here. I didn't mean to stare."

The corners of his eyes crinkled. "You like it?"

She cocked her head. "Well, yeah. Who wouldn't? All it needs is snow outside and a fire blazing, and it's the dream getaway for bookworms."

His brow furrowed, and she got the feeling he wanted to ask her something, but instead he shook his head and sank into a worn armchair beside the fireplace. "Where do you plan to go?"

Her heart stuttered.

Nowhere.

She didn't want to go anywhere but here. She didn't have a Plan B. But she'd figure something out. "I'm not sure yet, but that's not your concern."

"Huh." He snapped his fingers and something thudded behind her. Her pulse fluttered in fright, and she jerked, but it was only the Chihuahua, Pixie, who trotted across the floor and leapt onto his lap. She'd been curled up beside the pillows so Megan hadn't noticed her. Now the dog studied her with beady eyes that were anything but friendly. She didn't growl, though. So there was that.

"Why is Seeley James looking for you?"

"I'm afraid I can't tell you."

Tione stroked the length of Pixie's body. "Can't, or won't?"

"Won't."

Charles and his family were well-connected. If he and Tione happened to have a mutual acquaintance, she'd be done the minute she opened her mouth. And if they didn't... Well, suffice it to say, she wasn't entirely sure he'd believe her. After all, who'd take her word over Charles's?

He harrumphed. "Look, Megan," she flinched again at the sound of her name, "I can't help you if I don't know what's going on."

She pressed her lips together and remained silent, waiting for him to lose his temper. He was getting impatient, she could sense it.

But he didn't snap or strike out. Instead, he asked, "Have you broken any laws?"

"No, I haven't." Of that, she was sure. "I haven't stolen anything, or hurt anyone either. At least, in a physical sense."

Charles's job prospects were another story. His domineering boss, Glenn, had made it clear that promotions only came when employees lived "the values" of the firm —some old-fashioned concept about supportive wives and two point five kids. As far as he was concerned, Megan perfectly fit the bill. She cringed at the thought. Who wanted to be known as the woman who made the ideal 1950s-style housewife? Especially by the kind of man who thought he could get away with feeling up her thigh beneath the dinner table while her boyfriend sat on her other side.

"Good." He watched her thoughtfully, Pixie's tail beating a rhythm on his lap. "I believe you."

Her lips parted in surprise, and she dipped her head to analyze him from beneath her lashes. Was he trying to trick her into doing or saying something incriminating using reverse psychology? Why would he believe her, just like that? He had no reason to.

"Thank you," was all she said. "But really, don't worry. I'll go pack my bags now and be on my way."

6

Like hell was she going to head out into the world, alone and unprotected. Not on Tione's watch. Jesus, the bruises on her face hadn't even healed yet, and ribs took much longer than a few days to mend. He wouldn't be responsible for putting an injured woman back in the sights of the men who'd hurt her.

He might not trust her—she was squirrelly as shit and there was a lot she wasn't saying—but he believed she was the victim in all of this, and he wasn't about to stand by while a woman was hurt. Not again, and especially not when it came to this woman, with her hair like gold and slim shoulders that looked like they'd buckle under the weight of a backpack, let alone anything else. And yeah, maybe he was a bad choice of guardian angel given how epically he'd failed in the past—how badly he'd let Michele down—but right now, he seemed to be all that Megan had.

"Seeley James," he said, voice thick. "Was he the man who hurt you?"

Her eyes widened. "What makes you think it was a man who hurt me?"

He continued stroking Pixie, who'd settled on his knee, in the hopes it would make him appear less threatening to Megan. With his tattoos, muscles, and beard, he wasn't exactly a pussy cat, but petting the dog could go a long way. It kept his hands occupied so she wouldn't worry about him touching her, it showed how gentle he could be, and it soothed the angry beast inside him that wanted to beat the crap out of some asshole who really deserved it.

"You sure as hell weren't in an accident. Those were handprints around your neck, Megan. Don't think I didn't notice."

The neck in question seemed to shrink into her shoulders. "Did anyone else see?"

He shrugged, and Pixie grumbled when the motion disturbed her. "Don't know. I didn't ask, and I didn't mention it. But people have eyes in their faces. At the very least, Kat would have noticed."

"Oh."

"Please sit down," he said, hating how she seemed to hover uncomfortably over him. She glanced around, then perched on the edge of a stool with her feet on the ground, like she was preparing to run. "Was Seeley James the man who hurt you?"

"No."

The tension drained from him. He hadn't realized how wound up he'd been until now. He tried to speak, but his throat sounded like a rusty gear, so he swallowed and tried again.

"Okay. Good."

He still wanted to kick the shit out of whoever *had*

put that glimmer of fear in her eyes. Was it the man in the photograph? Had he been her boyfriend? Husband? He checked her left hand but there was no pale band of skin to suggest that she usually wore a wedding ring. Why did that please him? It shouldn't make a damn bit of difference.

"Here's the thing," he said. "You're not leaving. You're safe at Sanctuary."

Her bottom lip quivered and she hauled in a deep breath, drumming her fingers on her knee. Her eyes had a glossy sheen. "Why do you even care?"

"I can't stand the thought of you out in the world by yourself. I know you're not telling me everything, but I don't want to wake up in the morning and wonder what happened to you."

"Really?" Her entire face crumpled, and then she was sobbing. Body-wrenching sobs, with tears streaming down her cheeks and her nose turning pink. Tione didn't know what to do. He couldn't hug her—that would either hurt her or freak her out—but he'd never been the kind of guy who was good with words. In the end, he reached over and patted her knee.

MEGAN DIDN'T MEAN to cry, but these days it seemed like all it took was a kind word for the tears to flow. Ridiculous that she could handle being yelled at and slapped around, but simple human kindness turned her inside out. Tione's big hand landed on her knee, imparting warmth. She waited for the fear to follow, but all she felt was comfort. He'd shown that he didn't mean her any harm. At least, it seemed that way to her, although God knew her judgment was flawed.

Sniffling, she watched him surreptitiously. He was big and gruff. Not at all the type of man she was accustomed to, and she could scarcely believe he wasn't leaping at the opportunity to get rid of her. They both suspected that if she stayed here, Seeley—or someone else in the Wentworths' employ—would come back.

"He won't leave me alone," she told Tione. "Next time, he'll probably bring reinforcements. I don't want to make trouble for you."

"He can come all he wants. As long as you told the truth about not being a fugitive, and as long as you don't want to go with him, he's not getting his hands on you." The corners of his mouth tilted wryly. "That would be called kidnapping, and it's illegal."

"Something being illegal never stopped him before." Seeley was the Wentworths' fixer. Not in the terrifying sense of the word, but he made problems go away. She'd never quite understood how, but bribery, blackmail, and extortion were mostly likely involved. Whatever the case, he wasn't a good guy.

She wiped her eyes with the backs of her hands, her crying jag over.

Tione's gaze skittered over her features. "Who is he?"

"I can't tell you." To her surprise, she wished she could. Sharing with him would lighten the load on her shoulders. "And unfortunately, much as I'd like to stay, I really shouldn't."

Never mind that she'd been hanging all of her hopes on a fresh start in Haven Bay, the town she'd learned about through Mark's friendship with Sterling. She still hadn't even seen the ice cream parlor, or the gym-slash-art-studio. She hadn't been surfing, or met the cheeky old ladies from the Bridge Club.

Tione raked a hand through his hair, and she noticed, not for the first time, that the short hair and beard combo really worked for her. He may be rough around the edges, but he was a good-looking man.

"I can't believe I'm saying this, but please don't run off. Especially if you don't have a plan. Take a while and think about it. You'll be safe here in the meantime."

Slowly, she nodded. "Okay, I won't leave without talking to you. I do need a little time to think." Although there shouldn't be anything to think about. It should be a given that she'd leave rather than spread her problems to people who didn't deserve them. But his offer to stay was so tempting.

"We'll have to tell Kat and Sterling," he continued. "So they can be on their guard." He must have misread her expression, because he added, "They won't be mad at the deception. They'll understand."

"Actually, Sterling already knows."

"He what?" Finally, Tione's face showed an emotion, clear as day: shock.

Swallowing, she wiped her palms on her knees. "He's friends with my brother. That's how I found this place."

His lips firmed together. "You mean he's known right from the start?"

"No, no, no." She didn't want him to be angry at Sterling. "I didn't tell him I was coming, and he didn't recognize me at first. It was only yesterday that he realized."

"You didn't tell him?" he echoed.

She could see that none of this was making sense to him, but she couldn't explain herself fully. Not yet.

"I didn't."

"And he didn't mention it to us." He swore. "If he'd told Kat, she would have told me."

"Don't be mad at him, I begged him to keep my secret."

He exhaled roughly. "Okay, okay. I'm not happy about it, but at least it's out in the open." His dark eyes settled on hers. "Your brother. Does he know you're here? What about the rest of your family? Or did you leave them to wonder what happened to you?"

She flinched. She'd meant to call her family—really, she had—but she'd had to discard her phone before she ran away, and coming clean seemed impossibly difficult. For God's sake, she came from a family of lawyers—her mum specialized in family law—and should have recognized the warning signs that Charles was abusive, but she'd still been stupid enough to fall for him. How was she supposed to admit that? Especially when she'd always been the weak link compared to career-driven Mikayla, and good-at-everything Mark. She hadn't wanted to reinforce her position as the Talbot family screw-up. Better to fix everything on her own.

But now that she thought of it, what was stopping Seeley from questioning them? And as soon as he spoke to them, they'd know something was wrong, and they'd worry. Her vision blurred. She hadn't thought this through nearly as well as she'd believed she had.

"None of them know," she whispered. "Can I use your phone to call them? Please?"

"Yeah, okay." He got up, spilling Pixie from his lap, grabbed his phone from the nightstand, and handed it over. The screen was scratched so badly she could hardly make out the time flashing across it. Despite herself, she smiled. She hadn't seen a phone like this since her parents gifted her one for her thirteenth birthday. This particular model had been old even then.

"Is this thing from the dark ages?"

He shrugged one shoulder. "It calls. It texts. Nothing else it needs to do."

Her eyes widened. "Email? Social media? Camera? Internet browsing?"

"Nope." The 'p' popped as he spoke it with relish. "Don't have email, and don't need social media. Everyone I care about lives right here in town."

"Wow." She hadn't believed it possible to exist without email anymore. Not for anyone under eighty, anyway. But it was kind of cool. He was off-grid. Living a real life. She could appreciate that. "Do you mind if I have some privacy for my call?"

He nodded. "I'll be right outside. You want me to leave Pixie with you?"

She eyed the tiny Chihuahua, who growled at her. "I don't think she likes me."

"Nah." He scooped the dog into his arms and dropped a kiss onto the top of her furry head. "She's just shy."

"If you say so."

He took the dog and left, shutting the door behind him. Megan stared at the buttons on the phone and wondered who she should call. Her mum, Rose, would worry, and her soon-to-be stepfather, Joe, wouldn't keep anything from her. Mark would insist on knowing where she was, then drive over immediately, in typical over-protective big brother fashion. That left Mikayla—her twin sister, and a force of nature.

Her fingers were clumsy as she dialed Mikayla's number and waited while it rang.

"Mikayla Talbot speaking."

"Hey, Mik." Her voice trembled, and she took a deep breath before continuing. "It's Megan."

"Meg! Whose phone are you calling from? What's going on? I haven't seen you in ages. I dropped by your place on Monday but Charles said you were sick and didn't want to see anyone."

"Huh." It hadn't occurred to her that Charles would lie about her whereabouts. In hindsight, it should have. Of course he wouldn't want anyone to know she'd gone. That would only raise questions. "Do you have a moment to talk?"

"Sounds serious." Something covered the receiver and there was muffled speech in the background, then she was back. "I need to finish a presentation for a meeting in two hours, but for you, I've got a little time."

Warmth suffused her. As well as being her twin, Mikayla was also her best friend. They were very different people, but sharing a womb—and later a bedroom—had bonded them.

"Thanks."

"Just give me two minutes to find a quiet spot."

Megan didn't bother to reply, knowing her sister wouldn't be listening. Mikayla was an executive in a big corporation. Megan didn't know exactly what she actually did, but she always seemed to be both busy and in high demand.

"All right, what's up?"

She took a deep breath, wracked by nerves. "I just wanted to let you know that I'm okay."

"Why wouldn't you be? Meg, you're worrying me."

Just say it.

“I broke up with Charles and he didn’t take it well. I’m hiding out for a while until he cools down.”

“Hiding out?” Mikayla’s voice rose. “Where? And why? You’re telling me you’re okay, but that’s really not how it sounds, sis.”

“I promise I’m okay.” She gripped the phone tighter and fought back tears. “I can’t tell you where I am because I don’t want everyone rushing over to check on me yet. I’m safe. Can you let Mum and Mark know?”

“They’ll worry.” Now Mikayla’s tone was chiding.

“I know.”

She sighed. “Fine, I’ll pass the message along.”

“You’re the best. I’ll call again as soon as I can. Bye.” With that, she hung up before Mikayla could change her mind or ask any more questions. Her head flopped back and she closed her eyes. Even that hurt, but much less than it had a few days ago. She was healing. The knowledge that her family would be concerned for her bothered her more than the physical pain of her injuries.

She summoned a burst of energy, stood, and left the cabin to find Tione. He was in the garden, tussling with a tawny brown dog with a square face and wrinkled forehead. She handed him his cell phone with a quick thanks and hurried off. She desperately needed a shower to wash away everything that had just happened.

7

Tione spent most of the afternoon trying to make sense of Megan and her predicament. He'd deduced three things:

1. She was the victim in this scenario.

2. She was running from someone, and that someone was associated with Seeley James.

3. She'd be better off looking for help elsewhere, but if she refused to turn to the authorities, then he was all she had, and he couldn't abandon her.

He *wouldn't* abandon her.

Maybe he was a terrible choice of protector, but someone had to keep her safe. She was too fragile to be alone in the world right now.

He didn't see her again until he was in the kitchen, preparing for dinner. She came in with damp blonde hair tied back, the tail curling around the nape of her neck. She'd applied makeup over what remained of the bruising on her cheek, and with the glossy sheen on her lips, she looked almost normal.

Attraction fisted in his gut. With her angelic features and graceful movements, it was difficult to tear his gaze from her, but he ruthlessly squelched his reaction. It wasn't right to feel that way about someone who'd been in the wars as much as she had.

"I'm here to help make dessert," she said, her pointed chin set stubbornly as though she expected him to argue.

"Great," he said, gesturing to the pile of apples. "Start peeling."

She helped herself to a hairnet, and he watched out the corner of his eye as she washed her hands and got to work peeling the mountain of apples as efficiently as she had the vegetables this morning. She was capable, he'd give her that, and he wondered again if she'd worked in the food industry.

"Tell me a bit about yourself."

For a long moment, she stayed silent and he thought she wouldn't answer. It wasn't as if she'd willingly shared anything with him so far. But then she surprised him.

"When you guessed earlier that I might have been a caterer, you weren't far off. I'm a qualified baker, and I used to work at a high-end French bakery in Auckland, but I've been officially unemployed for the past few months." She made a cute little huffing sound that might have been a laugh. "It's been a weird experience."

His cheeks heated, and he was grateful for his darker complexion, which masked his blush. Being a baker, she was probably accustomed to making delicate pastries and indulgent cheesecakes, while he had her peeling apples, something far beneath her skill set.

"You could probably bake an apple crumble in your sleep."

"Mm," she agreed, "but there's something about

simple desserts that I absolutely adore. I've baked for some of the most exclusive events in Auckland, and I've made thousand-dollar wedding cakes, but comfort food is my first love."

The embarrassment eased. She was a girl after his own heart.

"What's your favorite thing to make?" he asked, stirring spices into a pan of diced pumpkin and sautéed onion. He wasn't sure why he wanted to know, but it mattered. "If you could only bake one thing for the rest of your life, what would it be?"

She didn't hesitate. "Cupcakes."

"Seriously?" That wasn't what he'd expected.

"Yes, and I'll tell you why." Her voice had gained volume, and she was speaking more confidently than he'd ever heard her. The contrast only served to reinforce how *un*comfortable she'd been with him previously. "Everyone loves cupcakes. They're cute, delicious, and come in dozens of flavors. They can be sweet or savory, basic or elegant. They're like little blank canvases and you can do anything you want with them."

His lips twitched. "I can tell you're passionate about your cupcakes."

"I am." She slapped one of her hands onto the counter emphatically. "They're awesome."

She went quiet, and when he glanced over, her cheeks were pink, as though she'd just realized how passionately she'd been speaking, and was kicking herself for it.

Adorable.

"Maybe you can make breakfast muffins with me sometime," he suggested. "I've tried lots of different twists but haven't quite nailed the recipe yet."

"I'd be happy to." She resumed dicing the apples. "Although I hope you know that muffins and cupcakes are very different beasts."

"I know." He smiled. He was beginning to think she might be a snob when it came to cupcakes. "You mentioned wedding cake before. Is that something you've done much of?" Now that she was more at ease, he couldn't help taking the opportunity to gather tidbits of information about her, to hoard them like a magpie with shiny objects.

"I make—made," she corrected herself, "all the wedding cakes at our bakery. It was very rewarding at times, but high stress too. People are so focused on having everything exactly as they imagined it."

"I bet," he agreed, as if he knew anything about it. He couldn't even recall the last wedding he'd been to.

"What about you?" she asked as he started laying out sheets of filo pastry. "Have you worked here long?"

"A few years. Before that, I was out of the country." A period of his life he preferred not to think about, much less discuss.

"Whereabouts?"

"The United States." And that was as specific as he'd get. "Have you traveled much?"

"Not really." He heard her rummaging through the cupboards behind him, her voice muffled. "I apprenticed in France, but other than that, I've just been to the usual places. Australia, the Cook Islands, Fiji."

An image of Megan in a bikini sprang into his mind and he shoved it out, narrowing in on the other thing she'd said. "You trained in France? That's impressive. Which part?"

"Paris."

"Wow." So she wasn't just a qualified baker. She was classically trained in France. That made the apple crumble even more cringeworthy. In his peripheral vision, he saw Kat pass by the doorway. "Are you all right in here?" he asked. "I need to do something."

She glanced over her shoulder and smiled. "Everything is under control."

"Great." Striding out of the kitchen, he found Kat making coffee in the dining hall.

"Hey, Tee," she greeted. "I see our guest is helping you out. She's not getting under your feet?"

"Not at all. You got a moment? There's something we need to discuss."

Her brow creased. "Sure thing. Let's grab a seat."

He steered them to the corner of the room, as far from Megan as possible. "It's about the girl."

"Hope?"

He pulled a seat out and dropped into it. She sat opposite him. "Yeah, except her name isn't Hope, it's Megan."

Kat blinked. "Okay. I had a feeling she was keeping secrets. Is that all?"

"Not hardly. Someone came by earlier, looking for her. Said he was with law enforcement, but I don't buy it. She's in some kind of trouble."

Her brow creased. "The illegal kind?"

He shook his head. "I don't think so. I'd say it's more likely she's running from a man, but if that's the case, I don't understand why that guy came looking for her. She knows him, but said he wasn't the one who hurt her, and I believe her."

Kat leaned forward, resting her chin on her palm,

and studied him. "It's not like you to take up a cause. Is she getting to you, Tee?"

He scowled. "No, of course not. She's just..." What? Sweet and gentle? Someone he wanted to shield from the worst parts of the world? Or was this newfound protective urge a result of her dredging up memories from Silicon Valley? He gritted his teeth. Jesus, if he never thought about that time in his life again, it would be too soon. "She seems like she needs someone looking out for her," he finished lamely.

Kat blew on her coffee, and steam spiraled upward. "Well, this is quite a turnaround."

He tamped down his irritation. He could hardly be annoyed at her for commenting on his behavior when he'd have done the same in her place. Hell, he still didn't know what he was doing. With his track record, he'd be doing Megan a favor if he forgot he ever met her. She was probably better off without him, but he couldn't just let it go without knowing she was safe.

"Yeah, yeah. All I know is, that girl in there wouldn't hurt a fly, but she's not telling us the whole truth."

"Since when did anyone?"

His lips pursed. "You're happy for her to stay, anyway?"

Kat rubbed at the pale scar that ran down her cheek. "She's exactly the type of person I had in mind when I opened Sanctuary, so yeah, she can stay."

Relief washed over him, and until that moment, he hadn't realized how concerned he'd been that Kat would want Megan gone. He didn't know why he'd expected that, given her usual stance on people in need, but apparently he cared about the shy blonde in his kitchen, and that scared him.

MEGAN FINISHED LAYERING crumble on top of the apple and inhaled deeply, closing her eyes when the blissful scent of cinnamon and brown sugar invaded her nostrils.

"Smells good, huh?"

Leaping out of her skin, she spun around to see Kat in the doorway. Damn it, how had she not heard the woman approach? She was getting complacent, and she couldn't afford to. Especially if she'd be leaving again soon—although she hadn't decided yet one way or the other.

She laughed nervously, her hand fluttering over her chest. "Yes, it does."

Kat's hair swished like a black silk curtain across her shoulders as she approached. "Tione told me about your visitor today."

"Oh." Everything inside her deflated. Perhaps she wouldn't have to make a decision after all. Perhaps Kat would make it for her. "I'm sorry, I didn't mean to cause any trouble."

That seemed to be her mantra of late.

"You haven't." Kat touched her arm gently. "Megan, people like you are exactly the reason why Sanctuary exists. This is a place to heal, and to reconnect with yourself. Say you'll stay."

She swallowed, and her throat constricted. "He told you my name."

"He did, and I don't care that you lied. I can tell you're a good person, and that's what matters. But I'm not leaving this room until you agree to stay."

"But... but..." She trailed off helplessly, tears prickling the backs of her eyes. Why would anyone want her to stay given the circumstances? Kat was so kind, and she wasn't sure she deserved it. "Seeley will probably be back. If not, someone else will."

"Seeley is the man who came looking for you today?"

"Yes. He's not the kind of person you want hanging around."

"But the law is on our side," Kat countered. "I doubt he expected that you'd find anyone who'd stand by you. He miscalculated."

It didn't get past Megan that she'd said "our," or that she'd promised to stand by her side. "The law hasn't always stopped Seeley before."

Kat cocked her head. "I'm going to go out on a limb and guess that he won't act outside it if anyone who isn't under his thumb knows. Does that sound right?"

Yes, actually. It did. She nodded.

"Okay, then. If he comes back, we'll make it clear that we see what he's doing and we're not going to lie down and play dead." She patted Megan's shoulder. "So, you'll stay. I'm glad that's cleared up."

"Um. I—"

"If you can't afford to pay board, don't worry about it. You can work in the kitchen with Tee, and we'll call it even."

Enough was enough. Even if Kat was trying to be kind, there was a limit to the charity she'd accept.

"I can absolutely pay board." She'd squirreled away enough money from those under-the-table baking jobs to get her through a few weeks, at which point she hoped to have found employment. "But I'd love to help out in the kitchen. Baking is my passion."

"Okay, we're agreed." Kat offered a hand, and Megan shook it. Kat's grip was firm, her palm cool, and her smile wide and mischievous. Megan frowned. Had she been expertly maneuvered into doing exactly what the other woman wanted? If so, props to Kat. She hadn't even realized she'd implicitly agreed to stay until after it had happened.

"If you want to use the kitchen when Tee isn't around, go right ahead. Just clean up after yourself. He's a bear if anyone messes up his space."

"Got it." If Megan were the huggy type, she'd be all over Kat right now, but that wasn't her. Never had been. "Thank you." She chose her next words carefully. "I'm not taking your kindness for granted. I know how rare it can be."

"Oh, Megan." Kat stepped closer and kissed her cheek. "You're a sweetheart." Her gaze shifted to the door. "I can see Tee wants to come back, so I won't hold you up any longer. You know where to find me if you need me."

With one last smile, she left. A moment later, Tione entered and took up where he'd left off with the filo. Following his cue, Megan offered to help with dinner since the apple crumble was ready to go, and neither of them said anything about the conversation she'd had with Kat. They worked in sync, as easily as if they'd done it a hundred times before. When the food had been served and they'd both scarfed down their own meals, he started in on the dishes and she grabbed a towel.

"You don't need to do that," he said. "You've helped more than enough already."

She shrugged. "I helped make the mess, so I'll help clean it." That was the philosophy she'd always abided by.

"Suit yourself."

They cleaned in silence, except for the splashing of

water and clattering of dishes. When they finished, her feet and back ached, and she would have given anything for a long soak in a bubble bath, but she felt good. Really good. More like herself than she had since she'd moved in with Charles.

"I'll come to your room in a moment," he said. "I have an extra lock to install on your door." She must have looked startled because he added, "Just a precaution."

The kind of precaution that may prove invaluable.

"That would be great."

They passed through the empty dining hall together and she went to her room while he went in the other direction. She left the door ajar, but he still knocked before coming in, and she appreciated it. He held a drill in one hand and a bolt in the other.

"This will be loud. Maybe you should go to the living room and I'll get you when it's done."

"No, I'm fine here. I'd like to watch." That way she'd know with absolutely surety how well protected she was. Although she supposed putting a lock on the door couldn't stop someone from smashing a window.

"Don't say I didn't warn you." He set to work, and she took the opportunity to study him properly while his attention was focused on the task at hand. Swirling Maori designs seemed to caress his beautiful bronzed forearms and moved fluidly as his muscles flexed. They twisted from his wrists to his biceps and vanished into the sleeves of his t-shirt. Did they extend all the way to his shoulders, or perhaps even across his chest? Maybe one day she'd have the chance to see for herself—say, if she were still here when next summer rolled around. She got the impression he'd be right at home walking around in nothing but board shorts, his tawny skin gleaming in the sun. That view alone would be worth staying for.

No, don't go getting a crush. The timing couldn't be worse.

She forced herself to look away from his arms, back at the lock that his talented hands were installing. When he'd finished, a layer of dust coated the floor, and the room smelled like hot wood. He started to sweep up the debris, but she stopped him.

"I can do that."

He paused, looking up from his crouched position. "You sure?"

"Yeah, it'll give me something to do other than think." She'd done enough thinking, and stewing over her mistakes. At this point, any distraction was a good distraction.

Getting to his feet, he wiped his hands on his jeans. The action brought him closer than she'd expected, and she swallowed. Sawdust speckled his clothing and stuck to his skin, which was covered by a faint sheen of sweat. With his scruffy beard, inked body, and the way he looked like he'd spent the day doing hard manual labor, he was everything Charles wasn't, and she'd never seen a sexier man.

Don't be crazy. Your body is out of whack, that's all.

His dark eyes watched her, and she wondered what he saw. A broken woman who'd made enough bad decisions to fill a lifetime? Or someone he could one day admire? She hoped for the latter, and she intended to do her best to live up to the promise of the person she could become again.

"Thank you," she said, nodding to the lock. "I'll feel much safer tonight."

If possible, his eyes darkened. "I don't want you to ever feel unsafe again."

Well. What was she supposed to do with that?

His face scrunched up, like he regretted saying so much, and he yanked the door open, then he paused. "Would you like me to bring Trevor over? He could spend the night with you."

Yes. A million times, yes.

"If you wouldn't mind. I'd like that."

She locked the door behind him, swept up the dust, and prepared to shower. Minutes later, knuckles rapped on the wood.

"Who is it?"

"Trevor."

Opening the door, she fell back a step when the bull mastiff bounded in and nosed her thigh. Laughing, she dropped her hands to scratch him behind both ears.

"Hey there, cutie."

"I brought his bed, too."

She glanced up at Tione, who was arranging a thin foam squab with a bundle of blankets on the floor just inside the doorway. When he straightened, she stopped petting Trevor, ignoring his groan of protest, and went to his owner.

"Thank you." Tentatively, she wrapped her arms around him, maintaining a space between their chests so the hug didn't jolt her sore ribs. He smelled of wood, spiced pumpkin, and man. Even from this distance, she could feel the power of his body, but it didn't scare her. She didn't think he'd hurt her, even if she frustrated him. "Kind" wasn't a word she would have associated with him at first, but she was beginning to think it fit.

All too quickly, she released him. "This is very sweet of you."

Was it her imagination, or did his cheeks flush?

"He'll need to go out first thing in the morning," he said, voice gruff. "He'll whine loud enough to wake the whole place if you let him."

"I consider myself warned. Goodnight, Tione."

"G'night, Megan."

8

AFTER A DAY like the one he'd had, Tione should be falling into bed, but instead it felt like he'd taken a dose of intravenous caffeine. He paced the length of his cabin, Pixie on his heels, while Zee and Bella watched him with interest. His fingers drummed a rhythm on his thighs, the same way they itched to fly over a keyboard so he could learn all of Megan's secrets. What he wouldn't give to forget his morals and take the easy way out for once.

Gritting his teeth, he reminded himself that he wasn't the same person he used to be. He didn't use those skills anymore. With a curse, he snatched his t-shirt off over his head, then he turned the shower as hot as he could stand it, stripped off his jeans, and stepped in. He scrubbed the grit from his skin with brisk movements and let the water stream through his hair. Then he shut the shower off, toweled dry, and threw himself onto the bed.

What was he supposed to do? He couldn't protect Megan if he didn't know what he was protecting her from. Not that he had any right to appoint himself anyone's protector. That ship had sailed years ago.

You can't protect her. You'll only make it worse. Leave her alone.

But he couldn't. Someone needed to be looking out for her.

Kat is. She doesn't need you.

Suddenly weary, he climbed under the covers and patted the bed until Bella and Zee both jumped up and settled beside him. Pixie yapped from the floor for him to lift her up. He did, and then lay surrounded by doggy love and closed his eyes. Megan's face flashed through his mind, followed by the sensation of being hugged by her, the embrace so insubstantial it was almost nonexistent. She was so fragile, and she'd been so delicate and wonderful in his arms. How could anybody possibly want to hurt her? It was unthinkable. Hopefully having Trevor nearby would bring her a measure of peace.

His fingers tapped against his leg again, and he buried them in Bella's fur and willed them to be still. He hadn't touched a keyboard in years and he wasn't about to start now. Some promises were meant to be kept. He owed Michele's memory that much.

At the thought of her, his soul ached. He'd never met the woman, but he'd felt like he'd known her intimately, and it was his fault that her story had ended in tragedy. He couldn't make that mistake again.

As Tione approached the kitchen, the aroma of coffee drifted out to him.

"Hello?" he called as he passed through the doorway.

A smiling face appeared around the end of the pantry. Megan, looking fresh and perky, her hair in a bun atop her head. “Good morning. I made you coffee. I hope you like it strong and sweet.”

His nose crinkled. “I prefer unsweetened, but I’ll take what I can get.” Her face fell, and his stomach dropped in response. “It smells great.”

“I’ll remember that for tomorrow.” The edges of her mouth curved up, but her smile seemed forced. “Tee likes his coffee the way it comes out of a pot.” She paused. “Is it all right for me to call you ‘Tee’?”

“Of course.” He leaned against the counter. “You know I don’t expect you to be in here every morning. Especially not early enough to make me coffee.”

“I know.” She brought a mug over and handed it to him. “But I’m an early riser, and old habits are hard to break.”

Raising the mug, he sniffed. Yes, it smelled like coffee, but all he could see was a mountain of whipped cream above the rim. Who knew what concoction hid beneath?

“What is this?”

“It’s a *cafe viennois*. A shot of espresso in milk, topped with cream.”

“Wow.” He eyed the drink with distaste. It looked like something that would be served in the kind of snooty establishment he’d never been welcome in. He considered tossing it down the drain and making his own, but Megan was watching him with such eagerness that he didn’t have the heart. Cautiously, he sipped. Then he moaned. If it was possible to come from taste alone, he did that, too. The drink was heavenly. Rich coffee with a perfect silky texture that slid down his throat and warmed him from the inside. And that cream… It wasn't any old whipped cream, that was for sure. He didn't know what she'd done, but it was divine.

"It's good, right?" she said, breaking into his thoughts.

He wiped foam off his upper lip and licked his finger clean. "I take it back. You can make this coffee for me any damn time you like. Fuck, that's good."

Her expression was one of absolute glee. "I'm so glad you like it."

"Like it? I want to marry it."

"I'm pretty sure that would be illegal," she teased, drinking from her own mug. When her tongue flicked out to lick cream from the corner of her mouth, he almost moaned again. It should be illegal to think what he was thinking. "What are we making this morning?"

"Nothing fancy. We've got cereal and toast to set out, and breakfast sausages and hash browns to cook."

"Great. I'll put out the continental breakfast while you work on the cooked part," she said, and got to work. While she searched the cupboards, Tione opened the divider between the kitchen and the dining hall so they could talk while she was in the other room.

"Tell me more about your bakery," he said.

"It wasn't *my* bakery," she corrected, her back to him as she set bowls, plates and cutlery on the sidebar so he couldn't see her expression. "What do you want to know?"

Whatever details she was willing to share with him. But he didn't want to pressure her, or poke at a sore point, so he tried a different tack. "How did you get into baking?"

The frying pan sizzled as he added sausages to hot

oil. She returned to the kitchen and grabbed the orange juice from the refrigerator.

"Dad died when I was little, and Mum had her hands full putting herself through school while working and raising us. My brother and sister couldn't have cared less whether we had homemade baking in the pantry, but I did." She ducked her head, like she was embarrassed. "Home baking says someone cares, you know? And I wanted to make sure my family always knew I cared."

His heart cracked a little. If that wasn't the sweetest thing he'd ever heard. "I don't think anyone would ever accuse you of not caring."

She smiled. "Thanks."

As she carried tea and coffee equipment into the dining hall, he loaded hash browns into the oven. "Would you ever want your own bakery?"

She glanced over. "Can I tell you a secret?"

Hell, yes. "I guess so."

"That's my life goal. But I don't want a typical bakery. I want a cupcake shop with dozens of different flavors. Experimenting with new flavor combos is one of my favorite things to do."

"You can experiment here all you like," he told her. "We'd love to be your guinea pigs."

She laughed, and he relished the sound of it. "Is that a hint, Tee?"

He rolled the sausages over and checked the hash browns. "Maybe, but can you blame me?"

"Not at all." The air shifted as she stopped near his elbow, and the delicate flowery scent of her perfume carried to him. "I'd love to make you cupcakes, but I'd need to pick up some ingredients."

Satisfied everything was cooking properly, he turned

his back to the frying pan and reached for his coffee mug, which was disappointingly empty. "There's a mini-mart in town. You just follow the road until you reach Surf Street, turn left, and you'll come to the town square."

"Good to know." She tucked a loose bit of hair behind her ear and looked away. "Thanks for leaving Trevor with me last night. He was great."

"He behaved himself?"

She met his eyes again and smiled, drinking from her own coffee, which she apparently hadn't gulped down like a greedy bastard. "He was a perfect gentleman. It's so nice spending time around dogs. I always wanted one, but it's not practical when you live in the city."

Without thinking, he asked, "Do you want to come on a walk with us later?"

As soon as the words were out of his mouth, he regretted them. Her lips pursed and she looked down and twisted the hem of her shirt. He cursed his thoughtlessness. She hadn't healed yet, even if she looked okay—more than okay—from where he was standing.

"Maybe another time," she said so quietly he had to strain to hear. "I—"

"Forget I said anything." He wracked his brain, trying to come up with something that might erase the awkwardness. "Hey, you said you like experimental baking, right?"

She nodded, appearing as relieved for the topic change as he was to have thought of it.

"You should meet Faith. She's Haven Bay's resident ice cream whiz. She has a gourmet ice cream parlor down by the beach and always has a few new flavors on rotation. Some are really bizarre, but most are surprisingly delicious."

"She sounds like my kind of girl."

He nodded, stacking sausages and hash browns into a warmer. "Remind me to introduce you sometime."

"I will."

LATER IN THE DAY, Megan clutched the steering wheel of her car and stared down the driveway, over the bridge, and toward the road into town.

"Just do it," she said to herself. "Just put your foot on the accelerator and drive to the minimart."

Every cell of her body protested.

She eased her trembling right foot down. The car shot forward. For one brief, glorious moment, she thought she'd done it, but then her foot jammed on the brake and the car skidded over the gravel, the rear end spinning around. She screeched to a halt just this side of the bridge and switched off the engine. Then, with shaky hands, she wiped the sweat from her forehead.

She couldn't do it. At this rate, she'd cause an accident if she even tried. She was simply too scared to leave the lodge. Earlier, when Tione had invited her for a walk, a brick of ice had dropped into her stomach. She'd hoped she could overcome the knee-jerk reaction with logic and the power of positive thinking, but she'd been wrong.

She turned the car around, parked, then climbed out and headed in the direction of the road on foot. She reached the bridge and glanced around to make sure no one was watching. God knew she didn't need the embarrassment of having someone witness her craziness, but the coast was clear. She took one step, then another. With each step away from Sanctuary, the sensation of being exposed and vulnerable grew. The hairs on the back of her neck stood on end, and her instincts told her that she wasn't safe out here in the open. She was only safe in her room, with other guests around her and a bull mastiff watching her back. But she forced herself to keep going. If she continued for long enough, surely her confidence would kick in and she'd realize how silly it was to be afraid.

Instead, her skin crawled with discomfort. Every one of her nerves was hyper alert. Every noise seemed amplified. The scuffle of an animal in the bushes. The crash of the waves in the distance. They piled on top of each other, overwhelming her. Her pulse thundered in her ears, and she'd gone less than a hundred yards when she couldn't take it anymore.

Spinning around, she fled back to the safety of Sanctuary as quickly as her legs could carry her. She didn't stop until she slammed her bedroom door, slid the bolt home, and dropped to her knees with relief. Her vision blurred and she drew herself into a ball, dragging in long, rough breaths.

It was okay. She'd be okay. But it would take more time.

9

"Hi, can I sit?"

"Of course." Megan smiled at Brooke as she claimed the seat across from her in the busy dining hall and blew on a mug of tea. "How are you? I haven't seen you for a couple of days."

Brooke sipped her drink, then made a face. "Too hot. Yeah, I've been busy with the latest chapter of my thesis, which was due tonight. I sent it in half an hour ago."

"Congratulations. I hope you get good marks." While Megan didn't know exactly what was involved in writing a thesis because she'd never been academically inclined, she knew it wasn't easy.

"Oh, I'm not at the results stage yet. My supervisor is reading over it to give me feedback, but thanks. In some ways, this part is even more unnerving because she's completely ruthless if she doesn't think something is up to scratch."

Megan nibbled on a crust slathered in honey. "Well, in that case, I hope she thinks it's brilliant."

“Thanks, me too. Anyway,” Brooke breezed on, her sky blue eyes twinkling and her peach-colored lips tilting up, “I wanted to celebrate the milestone, so Kat and I are having a movie night in her apartment. We’d love it if you joined us.”

Hope fluttered in Megan’s belly. She hadn’t spent time with girlfriends in ages, and hadn’t realized how much she’d missed it. “Really? I don’t want to intrude.”

Brooke waved a hand, dismissing her concern. “You wouldn’t be intruding at all. The more the merrier. If you want to bring some snacks, so much the better.”

“Great, I will. Thanks for inviting me.”

“You’re so welcome.” Brooke stood, told her what time to be there, said farewell, and wandered off, teacup in hand. Megan finished her crust, watching the other guests—a couple of families and a pair of Chinese women—and hurried back to the kitchen, already skimming through possibilities for goodies to bring to the movie night.

Tione was sitting outside the kitchen’s fire escape, petting Bella, when he heard footsteps behind him. Looking over his shoulder, he saw that Megan had returned.

“Do you mind if I do some baking between meals?” She wrung her hands as she spoke, her eyes wide and excited.

“Go for it.” He stood, brushed off a shower of dog fur, and tossed a tennis ball for Bella, who rushed after it. “What’s up?”

She fidgeted with the hem of her shirt, twisting the pink cotton between her fingers. "Brooke invited me to a movie night. I want to bring brownies, and maybe something else, too. I'm still thinking about it."

"No problem. We've got brownie ingredients in the cupboards." Bella dropped the ball at his feet and he threw it again. This time, Zee gave chase, too. Stepping inside, he closed the door. The dogs could keep each other occupied for hours. Megan, on the other hand, seemed incapable of holding her hands still.

"Are you nervous?" he asked.

She giggled, and it carried on for a little too long. "Maybe. I want them to like me." She stared at her hands, like it embarrassed her to admit this. "I haven't spent time with any women who weren't family for ages."

Taking her gently by the shoulders, he looked into her gorgeous amber eyes. Immediately, her whole body stiffened, but she didn't seem afraid, just wary. She was so soft beneath his fingers that he felt like he could crush her, but instead he had to stop his hands from automatically smoothing down her arms and wrapping around her waist.

"They already like you," he said. "So quit worrying."

"Okay." Was it his imagination, or did she sound breathy? "Thanks, Tee."

He dropped his hands from her and backed away, leaning against the door frame, grateful for its support. "Do you need a hand with the brownies?"

She drew in a shaky breath. Had she been as affected by their touch as he had?

"No, I've got them under control. You go and do whatever you usually do at this time. Everything is sorted in here."

"There's nothing in particular I usually do around now." Not entirely true. He often ran the dogs along the beach, but they wouldn't be too upset if he delayed their run until the afternoon. For one thing, it was more likely they'd encounter other dogs to play with. "Tell you what. I'll be your kitchen boy if you let me steal a couple of brownies when they're done."

The smile that spread across her face was worth rescheduling a dozen running sessions. She stuck out her hand, and he shook it. "Deal."

Brushing past her, he headed to the sink and washed his hands. "What do you want me to do?"

A subtle change came over her. Her spine straightened, her expression smoothed, and her hands ceased moving. She'd assumed control.

"Get out the ingredients, a baking tray—no, make that two—and start a saucepan heating on the stove. I'm going to check out the pantry and see what else I might be able to make."

He saluted. "Yes, chef."

While she searched the pantry, he placed ingredients on the counter. Butter. Cocoa. Sugar. Eggs. Flour. Baking powder. By the time he'd finished and set the saucepan on the stove, she'd added to the assorted ingredients. He watched while she separated a portion of butter without using any measuring device and added it to the pan. Then she piled cocoa and sugar into a bowl and cracked eggs into another.

"When the butter is melted, mix in the cocoa and sugar, then remove it from the heat and slowly add the eggs."

He followed her instructions, feeling remarkably like a boy in school. While he stirred the butter, she became a flurry of activity, mixing and measuring with no tool other than instinct. He'd never seen her like this. Completely serene, in the center of a tornado of action. Her nerves seemed to have dissipated. As she worked, she explained what she was doing, like it was second nature. Perhaps it was. Perhaps she'd had apprentices working under her at the bakery. Whatever the case, he didn't say anything because he liked listening to the sound of her voice.

Despite her preoccupation, she was at his side the moment he'd removed the saucepan from the stove. She piled flour on top, sprinkled baking powder in, and gestured for him to stir. Lastly, she added a dash of vanilla, then scraped the batter into a baking tray she'd greased while he'd been keeping an eye on the butter. She eyed the uncooked brownie critically, nodded once, and slotted the tray into the oven.

"That should be ready to come out in twenty-five minutes," she told him. He set a timer. "Do you know how to make butter cream frosting?"

"About as well as anyone."

She winced, and he tried not to take offense. "Hmm. How about you take over making this pound cake, and I'll work on the butter cream?"

He shrugged. He could manage a simple pound cake. "Works for me."

He took up where she'd left off, but paid little attention to the cake batter, instead watching as she tested the firmness of a stick of butter, then diced it, added it to an electric mixer, and turned the power on. For a good few minutes, neither of them spoke, the sound of whirling beaters drowning out any other noise.

When she switched the mixer off to add icing sugar,

he took the opportunity to ask, "What part of Auckland did you live in?"

"Ponsonby."

"Go figure."

Her hands went to her hips, leaving floury handprints on her shirt. "What's that supposed to mean?"

"You've just got that look."

"And what look is that?" Her tone indicated he was treading in dangerous waters. It was the first time he'd heard her be anything other than one hundred percent sweet, and he had to admit, he liked it. Nice to know she had a little fire in her soul.

He kept his head down so she couldn't see the smile that wanted to crawl across his face. "Well-off white girl from a good family in a respectable neighborhood."

She turned away and heaped icing sugar into the butter, then switched the mixer on again. He wondered if he'd gone too far, but when she paused the machine, she took up where they'd left off, adding icing sugar as she spoke. "I don't know exactly what you mean by 'good family.' I don't come from old money. And yeah, maybe my family has a reasonable standard of living now, but there was a time when we barely scraped by." She started the mixer again before he could reply.

He waited patiently, working on the pound cake in silence, until she took another break. "I remember you telling me about that. I'm sorry for what you went through. Did your mum ever remarry?"

"Actually, she will be in a few months."

"Good for her."

"It is." She nodded. "Joe is a good guy. He'll treat her well."

He couldn't imagine what it must have been like

when she was growing up in a house silenced by grief. There had never been a quiet moment when he was young. They'd spent most of their days at the *marae*, where his *kuia* was the caretaker, and there was never any shortage of family—*whanau*—to share stories with.

The mixer whirred. He was beginning to resent that damned machine and its tendency to interrupt their conversation. He added the last ingredients to the cake batter, stirred, and split it between the two tins she'd laid out on the counter.

When it was quiet again, he asked, "Are you ready for these to go in the oven?"

"Yes, thanks."

He donned mitts and positioned the tins evenly in the oven, then leaned on the counter and crossed his ankles, watching her whip up the buttercream.

"Who are you running from?"

Her hands faltered, but she didn't acknowledge the question. "Do you have raspberry or strawberry jam?"

"Both."

"Great. Can you get the raspberry out, please? What about white chocolate?"

His lips twitched. "White chocolate jam?"

She shot him a look. "White chocolate chips."

"Not sure. We might." He checked the pantry and discovered an unopened bag near the back. The expiration date wasn't far off, but he was sure they'd be fine. He dropped them onto the counter beside her. "Here you go."

"Thanks." She added a few drops of vanilla extract into the buttercream, then combined it. Dunking a teaspoon in, she scooped out a small mound of pale frosting. "Here, try this."

His mouth closed over the spoon and sweetness exploded on his tastebuds. His eyes shut involuntarily and he hummed in the back of his throat. He swallowed, blinked, and found her staring at him with what he'd term desire if she were anybody else.

He licked his lips. "That stuff is *good*."

Her expression turned smug. "I know, right?"

A loud beep broke the moment. The timer. She hustled over to the oven and peered inside, touching the tip of one finger to the brownie. Apparently satisfied, she withdrew the tin and set it on a rack. While the brownie cooled, they discussed their favorite recipes, and he told her how he'd come to have each of his dogs.

Pixie had been first. She'd belonged to an elderly resident of the local retirement community who'd passed away. Bella had been raised on a farm, but had no skill as a sheepdog. Trevor had been turned in to a nearby shelter, an unwanted Christmas gift who no one else would adopt because of his size and breed. He'd added Zee to his pack recently, and she held a special place in his heart. Her previous owners had run a drug operation, and she'd been their affection-starved—and literally starved—guard dog. When he brought her home, her ribs were protruding through her coat, her fur was matted, and she was flea-ridden, but the worst part was how she growled when anyone tried to touch her. Only with a lot of patience and persistence had she become the gorgeous creature she was now.

"I don't understand how anyone can do that to an animal," Megan said, disgust evident in her tone. "Especially to dogs. All they want is love and attention. People who abuse them are monsters."

"I wholeheartedly agree."

She was slicing brownies and he stole one, taking a bite before she could chastise him.

"What do you think?" she asked as he licked his fingers clean.

"That is seriously amazing." The best brownie of his life, including those of the naughty variety he'd been known to consume occasionally in high school. "I want a tray all to myself."

She laughed. "Well, you can't have one. This is for the girls." He reached for another piece, and she smacked his knuckles. "Cut it out."

He pouted. "Just one more?"

"Fine," she relented. "One more."

He grabbed a brownie before she changed her mind and nibbled it, savoring the rich flavor and soft, chewy texture. "Remind me never to introduce you to my friend, Logan. He's got a serious sweet tooth, and he'd marry you on the spot."

She smiled, but something dark flickered through her gaze. "I'll consider myself warned."

AFTER SHE FINISHED HELPING Tione with the post-dinner cleanup, Megan used her foot to tap on Kat's apartment door, her nerves on edge. She held a large container of brownies and *petit fours,* and shifted her grip on it as the sharp edges dug into her tender places.

"*Haere mai,*" Kat called. "Come in."

"I can't open the door," she called back. A few moments later, it swung inward. "Thanks."

"No problem." Kat ushered her in and took the container from her. "What have you got here?"

"I brought junk food."

Brooke appeared beside her. "Of the baked variety?"

"Yes, there's brownies and miniature layer cakes with raspberry jam, vanilla butter cream, and a white chocolate ganache."

"Oh, my God." Brooke grinned. "You're my new favorite person."

Pleasure suffused Megan, and her cheeks warmed. The offhand comment shouldn't mean so much to her, but she couldn't stop the fizz of joy in her heart. She missed the confidence she used to get from baking. She should never have given it up after moving in with Charles.

"Come on," Brooke continued. "Since it's my movie night, I've chosen a film and got it all set up, ready to play."

Kat rolled her eyes. "It's a sci-fi flick. The kind with aliens and radar guns."

"I haven't seen any of those before." She preferred romantic comedies, while Charles had enjoyed action blockbusters.

"Ooh, a sci-fi virgin. Don't worry, that won't last long with me around," Brooke said.

"She's obsessed," Kat murmured. "It's kind of adorable, until you have to sit through a full-day Star Wars marathon."

To be honest, that didn't sound so bad. Spending a whole day relaxing with a friend would be pretty ideal, actually. She hadn't been able to indulge in something like that for too long. Most of her friends had faded into the background during her whirlwind courtship and she'd never noticed how isolated she'd become until after she quit her job and realized she had all day to herself but no one to spend it with.

Although if she were honest with herself, she might not have gone out even if her friends were still around. There were cameras in Charles's apartment—although fortunately not in every room—and each time she left, he asked where she'd gone. At first, she'd thought it was sweet he cared and paid attention, but after a while, it began to seem more sinister. Especially when he got it into his head that she was seeing other men or visiting friends who were trying to persuade her to break up with him.

In hindsight, she wished that were true. That someone would have warned her what she'd gotten herself into. She shivered, recalling the first time he struck her. It was the day after she hosted a dinner party for his colleagues. He'd asked her to butter up Glenn, but later he took exception to her friendliness, yelling at her that she'd been hanging all over him. She hadn't, of course. The man was a letch, and she'd tried to avoid his wandering hands from the moment he arrived. But the next day, when she went to visit Mikayla and his boss was missing from the office at the same time, Charles had flown into a rage.

She'd been so shocked when he hit her that she found herself accepting his tearful apology and the promise that it would never happen again. She'd even wondered if perhaps she had been a little too flirtatious and needed to be more careful about how her actions could be perceived. The next time she wanted to go somewhere, she decided it wasn't worth the hassle.

Everything had snowballed from there.

"Megan?"

She jerked to attention, having become so absorbed in her thoughts she hadn't noticed Kat speaking to her. "Sorry, what were you saying?"

"That we should put your delicious treats on a platter. Are you okay?"

She nodded, although her heart was still hammering. "I'm fine, and that sounds like a great plan."

She followed Kat through the apartment to the kitchen, noting that two coffee mugs sat side by side on the counter, and a photo of Kat and Sterling was taped onto the fridge.

"Where's Sterling tonight?"

"Same place Tee is," she replied. "Boys' poker night at The Den."

"What's that?"

"The local pub. The owner, Logan, hosts poker for the guys every Friday." Her lips twisted into a smirk. "Ever since he started going, Sterling has cleaned up, which hasn't gone down well with Tee. He's used to winning."

Puzzle pieces fell into place. "Logan is the one with the sweet tooth."

"That's right." Kat eyed her speculatively. "He'd like you."

"That's what Tee said."

Kat grabbed a porcelain platter from an overhead cupboard and started transferring brownies to it. "Especially if these taste as good as they smell."

"They do."

Of that, she was sure. She may not be confident of a lot of things, but she knew her brownies rocked. When the platter was full, she tried to lift it, but Kat swatted her away, so she trailed behind the other woman into the living room, where the lights were off, the only illumination coming from the TV screen.

Brooke snuggled beneath a throw on the sofa, her feet tucked under her. When Kat laid the platter on the coffee table, she reached over and popped a *petit four* into her mouth. Then she moaned in appreciation.

"Magic," she said, licking her fingers. "If rainbows were food, that's how they'd taste."

"Try the brownies," Megan urged. She loved watching people taste her baking, although she had to admit, Brooke had nothing on Tione. He'd looked so blissed-out with her brownie in his mouth that she'd had the strangest urge to curl up against him like a cat and hand feed him more.

Both women tried the brownies. Kat shuffled in beside Brooke, and Megan sat at the end of the sofa, maintaining a little distance.

"You're going to make me gain ten pounds," Kat commented good-naturedly. "Wow."

Brooke polished off another miniature cake. "If you're planning to stay around, you should consider going into business. You have serious skills and Haven Bay doesn't have a lot going for it in the baked goods department."

Megan's stomach flipped over. She'd be lying if she said the possibility hadn't occurred to her, but she hadn't allowed herself to indulge the thought. After all, who knew how long she'd be able to stay?

"Isn't there a bakery in town? I thought I saw a brochure for one in the foyer."

"Mm. Cafe Oasis," Brooke confirmed. "But their selection is mostly savory. The only place you might be in competition with would be The Shack, which is the ice cream parlor down by the beach."

"Oh yeah, Tee told me about that."

Brooke and Kat exchanged glances, then Brooke said, "Speaking of Tee, you're spending a lot of time with him."

Her cheeks flamed. "I basically foisted myself on him because I want to be in the kitchen. Don't read anything into it."

"We wouldn't," Kat said, "except that he doesn't tolerate most people in his space." When Megan made a sound of distress, she held up a hand. "Sorry, sorry, we'll stop talking. I didn't mean to make you feel uncomfortable. It's just that Tione rarely shows much interest in anyone, and we're both in new relationships, so we see romance everywhere."

Megan sat on her hands to hide their trembling. "It wouldn't bother me, except that I'm recently out of a relationship." One that had ended the moment Charles struck her across the face with his signet ring, splitting her skin. "It wasn't great, and I need a bit of time to recover."

"Oh, Megan." Kat reached over and laid a hand on her knee. "I'm so sorry. If you ever want to talk about it, we're here. But for now, how about we eat these delicious brownies and watch the movie?"

"That sounds great."

They settled in, and Brooke hit the play button, but for the first thirty minutes, Megan couldn't bring herself to relax. Not entirely. And then something strange happened. Somewhere between her new friends joking, and the sugar rush from her tiny cakes, she eased back into her old self. The one who'd never been outgoing, but who'd laughed and bantered with her friends. Who hadn't been afraid to call someone out on their bullshit, but who'd equally have dropped everything and gone to them if they were hurt. She'd liked the person she'd been, and she loved Kat and Brooke for bringing that woman to the surface again, even for a night.

10

"Did you clean up at poker last night?" Megan asked, studying Tione as she handed him an unsweetened black coffee. She thought he might prefer it to anything fancier if he'd had a few beers before he went to sleep. He took the mug and gulped it down, and she had to admit, he didn't look any worse for wear. His eyes were clear, skin tone normal, and he appeared to have trimmed his beard. The tension coiled in her shoulders eased away. Charles had always been mean when he was hung over.

"I did okay," he replied. "Sterling did better, though." He swallowed more coffee and grimaced. "You've ruined me. This isn't nearly as good as that creamy stuff you made."

She tried not to smile. "If you remember, you told me you preferred your coffee to be boring and black."

"A man is allowed to change his mind." His eyes crinkled at the corners, and the twinkle in them sent a pulse of attraction through her. He was such a magnetic guy. Not in an obvious way, but he wasn't easy to impress or amuse, so the slightest change in his expression seemed to put her hormones into overdrive.

She reminded herself of what she'd told Brooke and Kat last night. She wasn't in a position to be interested in anyone. Her life was a mess. She didn't know where she'd be in a week, let alone a few months, and she'd been living with another man until very recently.

No, she couldn't get involved with him, but that didn't make her like him any less.

They worked in sync to prepare breakfast, and when the guests had come and gone, they shared a meal in the dining hall. She opted for fruit salad and yoghurt, while he wolfed down a breakfast muffin.

"You know, the muffin won't get up and run away if you take your time," she teased.

"How do you know?" he asked, around a mouthful of food. "It might."

"We can be reasonably sure."

They finished eating and cleared away their dishes. On impulse, she asked him what his plans were for the next couple of hours.

"I'm taking the dogs for a run," he said. "You're welcome to join me, if you'd like."

Her heart sank. "Oh, no. I couldn't. But thanks for the invite."

If she went, she'd run the risk of someone seeing her. She also hadn't run more than the length of a city block in over a year. Tione, on the other hand, took his dogs out every day. His calves were muscular, his thighs strong, and she had no doubt he'd leave her in his dust. She wasn't equipped to deal with the embarrassment of that.

"Shit." He face-palmed. "Stupid of me to ask. I forgot about your ribs."

She let his assumption stand, too much of a wuss to own up to the truth—that her ribs hadn't even been a consideration. They reached the foyer, and she started to turn toward the hall to return to her room, but his hand on her arm stopped her. She flinched, and he retracted it immediately.

"Sorry," she said. "You surprised me."

"No, I'm sorry. I should have known better." His expression became pinched. "I'm heading into the bush for a short hike after lunch. I need to check whether the waterfall trail is still safe for people to use. Do you want to come along?"

She turned the question over in her mind and examined it from all angles. The bush. Chances of anyone seeing her there were slim. She also wouldn't be expected to run. But she'd be further from the safety of Sanctuary, and alone with Tione. Did she trust him enough for that?

Yes, she decided, she did.

"If you don't mind, that would be great. The only thing is..." She nibbled her lip, wondering if he'd think less of her for what she was about to admit. "I'm a bit of a city girl. I've actually never been out in the bush before."

His lips twitched in that way they had, as though he was laughing on the inside. "We'll be twenty minutes from the lodge at most. I'll be right with you all the time." His gaze raked from her head to her toes, and his pupils expanded. "If anything were to go wrong, I'm confident I could toss you over my shoulder and carry you down."

She gasped, her hand flying to her face. "You wouldn't!"

His mouth softened into a smile. "Relax, Megan. Unless you're worried about being alone with me—and I'd understand if you were—you've got nothing to be scared of. What do you say?"

"Okay." Why was it that she felt like she was agreeing to far more than a walk in the bush? "Count me in. After lunch?"

He nodded. "Wear shoes with a decent sole."

"You got it, boss."

WHEN THE SUN was high in the sky, Tione knocked on Megan's door. He hadn't been inside her room for a while and was curious to see how she'd settled in. His nosiness was not satisfied, unfortunately, because she opened the door and slipped out before he could catch a glimpse beyond. Reminding himself it was none of his business, he greeted her with a nod.

"All set?"

"I think so." She looked down at herself. "Will this do?"

He scanned her. She'd opted to wear faded shorts and a long-sleeved shirt with sneakers. Once again, her outfit could have been plucked from a Salvation Army bin. "You'll be fine. The walk to the waterfall isn't hard."

That was one of the reasons he'd invited her. It couldn't be good for her to be stuck inside twenty-four seven, even if she was still healing. A slow-paced hike up the hill would do her good.

"If it's not hard, then why do you need to check whether it's safe?" she asked.

"Sometimes at this time of year the path gets slippery. If you stick with me and take it slow, you'll be perfectly fine. It's only an issue when inexperienced people barrel up there without looking where they put their feet." He caught her expression. "Trust me, it happens more than you'd think."

He strode back down the hall, and she followed, catching up to him in the foyer, where he held the door open for her. The thud of dog paws heralded Trevor's arrival. The mastiff flew at Megan, who'd squatted to his level, and licked her with a long pink tongue, then collapsed to the ground, tail wagging, as she rubbed his belly.

"Oh, you're such a good boy," she crooned. "Such a pretty boy."

So much for his manly tough-guy dog. Trevor looked at Megan with more devotion than he'd ever shown Tione. Not that he could blame him. She was easier on the eyes, and he'd bet her touch was gentler, too.

"You're going to turn him soft," he said, as if he didn't already spoil his dogs like crazy.

Her golden brown eyes met his. "Can he come with us?"

"Not today, sorry." Her visible disappointment created a lead-like lump in his stomach. "The rangers have been laying possum bait on some of the trails, and this big old doofus would probably snaffle it up."

"Sorry, boy." She patted Trevor and stood, putting her hands on her hips. "Which way are we going?"

He led her across the lawn, then past his cabin and

onto the earthen trail, where he paused and waited for her to stop, too.

"How long did you say this was?" she asked, staring dubiously up into the trees.

"Twenty minutes or so. Don't worry, I wouldn't have asked you to come if I didn't think you could handle it."

She huffed and her breath stirred her hair. "I think you overestimate my fitness. Being slim doesn't mean I'm fit. There is zero muscle in these legs."

Hiding a grin, he started up the hill. "You'll manage."

He heard her huff again before coming after him. He'd known she wouldn't be able to resist. They hiked in silence except for her labored breathing, and a few times he stopped under the guise of pointing out a bird or a particular type of plant to allow her to catch her breath.

When they reached their destination, she gasped. "It's beautiful."

The natural pool was set in a clearing in the trees, with emerald-colored moss fringing the water. A waterfall thundered down from far above their heads, spilling over a cliff and splashing into the pool. The scene was like something from a postcard. He never tired of it.

"I thought you might like it."

"Like it?" She stepped forward, her lips parted while she took it in. "I love it. I've never seen anything so inspiring in my life."

"Inspiring?" An odd choice of phrase.

"Absolutely." She crossed the clearing and knelt on the moss, sitting back on her heels. "It's like a faerie glen. And the ground is so soft I could sleep on it."

He resisted pointing out that she'd end up sick from the damp if she did. "Well, now you know it's here, you can visit any time."

She didn't reply, just gazed out over the water like she'd found her own personal paradise. An insect flitted onto her shoulder, and she didn't seem to notice. He joined her and swatted it away. Immediately, she flinched, her entire body shrinking from him.

His chest tightened, and it broke his heart that she'd react in such a way to something so simple. His fists clenched, and he itched to rip the head off the guy who'd hurt her, and then, once he'd finished that, he'd stand between her and anything else the world wanted to throw at her.

His jaw firmed. Her eyes had already skittered away, masking her thoughts from him. Her shoulders hunched, and he got the feeling that she wanted him to ignore her slip and pretend it never happened. Well, he couldn't do that. He may not know the full story, but he could read between the lines.

Lowering himself to the ground, he sat cross-legged beside her. She didn't look at him.

"I'm sorry for frightening you," he said, in a voice so gentle he barely recognized it as his own. "There was a bug on your shoulder. I hope you know I'd never hurt you. At least, not intentionally." She still didn't say anything, so he continued. "Men who hurt women are scum. I'm sorry for what you've experienced, but I want you to know that most men aren't like that." His chest rose and fell heavily. "*I'm* not like that."

MEGAN LOOKED DOWN at her hands, searching for something to say. "I-I—"

"Shh, it's okay," he soothed, like she was one of his rescue pets.

She picked at her cuticle, unsure how to respond. She wasn't used to people being so direct with her. Not about this. She'd hidden her secrets well, and if anyone had ever guessed, they'd stayed quiet.

"I just want you to know I'm not like that," he repeated. "I'd never hurt you."

The aching sweetness of his words, no matter how gruffly delivered, combined with the beauty of the place, brought tears to her eyes, and tangled her insides in a knot. She swallowed past the lump in her throat.

"I know," she whispered. "I know most people are basically good, and I try to remember that, but it's still my gut reaction to flinch." She forced herself to inhale and exhale before her voice became strangled into nothingness. "I wish I could turn it off, but I can't. It's going to take a while before I react like a normal person again."

If she ever did.

Don't be a pessimist. You'll get there one day.

"How can I help?" His tone made her turn toward him. His stoic expression had creased, harsh lines bracketing his mouth. He was upset on her behalf. Warmth crept into the corners of her heart.

"I'm not sure you can."

The lines around his mouth deepened. "How about if I help you acclimate to touch?"

She frowned. That sounded an awful lot like he was coming onto her, and if he was about to put a move on her, she wasn't in the mood. "How did you intend to do that?"

He held out his hand, palm up. "Give me your hand, Megan."

"What are you going to do with it?"

"Just hold it. Nothing else."

She couldn't see anything wrong with that, and she'd never have been out here with him in the first place if she didn't trust him. She laid her palm over his. It was rough and warm. He intertwined their fingers and clasped her hand.

"Relax," he said, and she realized her entire arm had stiffened. She tried to do as he asked, but she'd never been particularly comfortable being touched, even before her relationship with Charles. "You're wound so tight."

His thumb rubbed tiny circles on the back of her hand, and a soft sound escaped her. Her limbs melted and she closed her eyes. All she could feel was the exquisite friction of his thumb pad on her skin. No one had touched her like this in... well, ever. Like touching her was the point, and it wasn't a lead-up to something more. Like she was precious, and her pleasure was all he had on his mind. She blushed. Okay, so maybe "pleasure" was the wrong word.

"Is this okay?" he asked.

"It's good," she murmured, absorbed by the sensation of their hands touching, and his thumb moving against her. She'd never known that holding someone's hand could make her feel so much she might burst. She gave herself over to his ministrations. Their eyes locked. His were dark, and watched her with a fierce tenderness that had her heart flip-flopping in her chest.

He raised her hand to his mouth and kissed the back of it. Then he let her go. Electricity danced over her skin where his lips had been, and she could still feel them there even as they got to their feet.

He cleared his throat. “We should head back.”

“You’re probably right.” She wasn’t in a good headspace to be getting close to anyone. But that didn’t stop her disappointment as he stepped away and started back down the track.

11

FROM HIS VANTAGE point just outside the foyer, Tione watched Megan stand motionless in the parking lot. At any moment a car could hurtle down the drive and smack straight into her. What the hell was she doing?

She glanced over her shoulder and he ducked out of sight. It seemed like she was having some kind of breakdown—or breakthrough—and he didn't want to end it prematurely. He counted to ten and peeked back around the corner. Perhaps it was his imagination, but he thought she'd moved closer to the driveway. She took a step forward, then another.

Finally, it clicked. She was trying to work up the courage to leave Sanctuary. It hadn't escaped his notice that she hadn't done so yet, except during their hike to the waterfall. She was acting like a fugitive, too afraid to venture from her hideout. She kept walking, all the way to the bridge that demarcated the edge of the property, then stopped. She seemed to be debating something internally, and he found himself holding his breath.

Come on, wahine. *You can do this.* Kia kaha, *be strong.*

But she turned away, stuffed her hands in her pockets, and headed back toward the lodge. Stepping out of the shadows, he gestured for her to stop, thinking quickly. If he let on that he'd been spying, there was no telling how she'd react.

"Hey, Megan."

Her eyes met his, then slid to the side. "Hi, Tee. Have you been there long?"

He shook his head. "Nah. I'm about to head into town. Need to pick up some things from the minimart. Want to join me?"

She looked wistful. "I'd better not. I have other things to do."

"Like what?"

She seemed taken aback by the question. Her spine stiffened and her arms folded protectively over her chest. "Just stuff. Nothing important."

He leapt on that. "If it's nothing important, then you won't mind delaying for an hour."

"But..." She trailed off, her cheeks pale.

Guilt squelched in his gut, but he kept pushing her. It was for her own good. "What are you afraid of?"

He didn't think she'd answer, but she surprised him. "I'm scared he might be in the area. Or that Seeley will have shown everyone a picture and told them to call if they see me." Her eyes glittered, and her voice rose. "I haven't done anything wrong, but that bastard will have spun a good story, you can count on it."

Who was the "he" she was talking about? The way she'd mentioned "him" first, and then Seeley James by name made him think they weren't one and the same.

"It's okay," he said, gentling his tone. "I promise you that no one will give you up. Our people are loyal, and if they see you with me, they'll have your back. The locals always trust each other over outsiders." He offered her his hand, and she eyed it for a long moment before taking it. He pulled her closer, but not close enough to make her nervous. "They'll protect you, and so will I, okay? If you leave Sanctuary with me, I swear that no one will lay a finger on you."

"I don't know..." She worried her lower lip. "It would be safer just to stay here."

With his free hand, he tilted her chin up. "But that's not what you want, is it? If it was, I wouldn't have caught you trying to build up the courage to leave."

Pink blossomed on her cheeks. "You saw that?"

He fudged the truth. "Only the tail end of it." He could see he hadn't swayed her, so he played his trump card. "We could bring Trevor."

She softened, a smile flickering over her features. "That would be pretty great. You'd walk him though, right? I couldn't keep him under control with my ribs the way they are."

"Of course. I have a harness for him." The dog was too strong for a regular leash. "Does this mean you'll come?"

She took a deep breath and nodded, a determined slant to her mouth. "Yes. Let's do this."

MEGAN STAYED CLOSE by Tione's side as they crossed the parking lot. Trevor was attached to a harness that encircled his chest, and was enthusiastically sniffing the ground. When they reached the bridge, she paused, and Tione did the same, even though Trevor was trying to pull him over the water.

"You're ready for this," he said.

"I am." Gritting her teeth, she forced herself to take a step. Her footfalls seemed to echo, alerting everyone in the area that she was journeying beyond her safety net. She counted to twenty, and then she was on the other side. Every part of her wanted to turn around, run back to her room and lock the door, but she envisioned her legs as chunks of lead and stood firm.

"Keep it up," Tione urged.

She did. Forget lead. Her legs were magnets, drawing her toward the township, and she let them carry her forward. Her vision blurred and she was aware of nothing other than the rush of blood in her ears. After what seemed an eternity, the rushing ceased, and she heard ringing. An arm closed around her back, supporting her. Her vision cleared, and she looked around, noting Sanctuary in the distance.

"I did it," she said, leaning into the solid planes of Tione's body. "Thank you."

"Don't thank me. That was all you."

She knew it wasn't. If not for him, she'd be locked in her bedroom by now, a prisoner of her own fear. But she didn't argue, instead taking in the scenery. The bush was on one side, with patches of native vegetation interspersed with bell-shaped tents on the other.

"Are those the glamping pods?" she asked, recalling reading about them during her research.

"They are. Did you want to have a look?"

"Not now. Trevor would probably rip them up by mistake. I'll come back later and explore them properly."

He raised a brow. "By yourself?"

"I'll ask Brooke to go with me." She was feeling more confident in her budding friendships every day, and she was ninety percent sure Brooke would agree. Besides, surely if she'd managed to leave once, she could do it again.

"Good for you."

They kept walking, and after a while the strip of land between the ocean and the road narrowed until she could see waves washing up on the shore. A few surfers spotted the horizon between the sea and sky, but otherwise the beach was empty. Autumn had arrived and the water was too cold for swimming.

"It's beautiful," she said. "Do you surf?"

"Yeah," he replied. "But I'm not a die-hard. I just catch some waves every now and then. You?"

"No. I'm not very athletic." Something that had bothered Charles, because his co-workers and friends played tennis during summer and squash in winter. He'd wanted her to join them, but she hadn't been interested. She'd rather go for a walk or attend a yoga session. Still, she had no doubt that if she'd stayed, he'd have eventually gotten his way—probably by playing a guilt card over how much his boss and colleagues enjoyed her company. She could almost hear his voice in her head: *today's the day I get that promotion, I can sense it, as long as you play your part perfectly.*

She shook her head. As far as he was concerned, she'd never gotten it right, and his criticism had piled on until she wondered if there actually was something wrong with her. But those days were over, and she was done with playing a role. They passed a sports field and a school. When she squinted, she could make out a cluster of buildings up the road, centered around a wooden pavilion.

"Have I mentioned Faith to you?" he asked.

"You said she owns the ice cream parlor, and that she'd like me." She'd filed away every piece of information anyone had mentioned about the locals in case she needed it.

"See the little place on the far side of the pavilion?" He pointed. "That's hers. Want to get an ice cream?"

"Definitely." They crossed the wooden pavilion, passing by a seafood restaurant, and entered the ice cream parlor, which had a sign reading "The Shack" in large scripted letters above the door. It was brightly lit, with dozens of ice cream flavors arranged in square tubs behind a glass screen, each identified by a small, golden nameplate. The walls were tiled white and green, and the flooring was pale pink. Funky and retro. A woman with deep red hair and lips beamed at them as she came around the counter, a fifties-style floral dress swishing around her knees.

"Tee!" she cried, loudly enough that Megan flinched and drew closer to his side. The woman's eyes tracked her movement from behind rectangular spectacles. "I don't see enough of you these days. You're far too healthy for your own good. And who's this lovely person?" She held up a hand. "Don't tell me you have a girlfriend." She winked at Megan. "You've got yourself a good one. Never dates around. In fact, I can't remember the last—"

"Not my girlfriend," Tione interrupted, and Megan wondered why his sharp tone hurt. "This is Megan. She's a guest at Sanctuary, and a professional baker. Megan, this crazy cat is Faith."

"Nice to meet you," Megan said.

Faith eyed her, a line forming between her brows, her lips pursed. A moment later, she declared, "Emma Watson."

Megan glanced at Tione, searching for a clue as to what she meant.

"Faith remembers people by the celebrity they most resemble," he explained.

"Oh." She smiled at Faith. "Thank you, that's a very flattering comparison."

Faith waved a hand. Megan was getting the impression she liked to express herself with them. "Oh, please. Girl, you're gorgeous as all get out, and you must know it."

Her cheeks burned. Charles hadn't thought the way she looked was good enough. She'd had potential, he'd told her, if only she would try a little harder. Perhaps not eat quite so many cakes, and attend regular appointments at the beauty salon.

She lifted her chin and said, "Well if I'm Emma Watson, you must be a fifties Alexandra Breckenridge."

Faith stared at her for so long that she wondered whether she'd said the wrong thing. But then she pointed a finger. "Tee, I like this one. You need to keep her." To Megan, she said, "How do you feel about experimental flavors?"

"I love them."

"Do you have any allergies? Anything you hate?"

"Nope. I'm game to try whatever you've got."

"Fantastic." She spun around, her skirt flaring, and strode to the chiller. The heels of her pumps clacked on the floor. The shoes were as quirky as the rest of her outfit, pale green with a white trim and straps criss-crossing the tops of her feet. She grabbed a waffle cone and rolled ice cream from two different tubs. Megan withdrew her purse from her pocket, preparing to part with some of her cash, but Faith stopped her with a shake of her head.

"First one is on the house, as long as you promise you'll come back before you leave."

"Really?" No one in Auckland would ever have just given their product away. "Are you sure?"

"Absolutely. I want your opinion. The top scoop is hot chili and the bottom is buttermilk."

Tentatively, she licked the pink scoop. At first, nothing much happened. Then, after a few seconds, her tongue started to tingle. She tasted more, and warmth spread through her, the same way it might if she'd eaten a hot curry, but the heat was pleasant rather than burning, and the cream soothed the inside of her mouth. The combination was strange. Perhaps not something she'd want to eat on a midsummer day, but she liked it.

"It's good," she told Faith, who was awaiting the verdict. "The heat is well balanced, and the texture is smooth. I don't think it'll be something that everyone loves, but some people will."

Faith's white teeth flashed. "You don't think it's too much?"

"Not at all." She moved to the bottom, already expecting to like it. Buttermilk was something many people were wary of, but as someone who spent a lot of time experimenting in the kitchen, she knew it could be delicious if used properly. The ice cream didn't disappoint. "Okay, that's amazing."

"You like?"

"I love."

Faith clapped her hands, her manicure glittering beneath the overhead lights. "And I love you." Her attention didn't leave Megan as she scooped hazelnut and chocolate ice cream into a cone and handed it to Tione. "Seriously, how long are you staying?"

Megan shrugged, then wiped her upper lip. "I'm not sure yet. Maybe a day, maybe forever."

"You're thinking of moving here?" The question came from Tione.

"I am. It seems like a nice place." As good a place as any, and she didn't want to return to Auckland, where everything reminded her of Charles, or of her own weakness.

"You should do it," Faith told her. "I need a foodie friend."

Suddenly, she felt shy. She didn't know how to initiate a friendship. It had been a long time since she'd had to, because she'd known most of her friends forever, or met them through her sister. What would it feel like to start a friendship with nothing but her own merit to recommend her? And how terrifying would it be to let someone that close to her again?

She ducked her head. "I'm not in a hurry to make a decision."

"Well, if you're still in the area a couple weeks from now, you should come with me to the food festival. I dragged Bex along to the last one, but her heart wasn't in it."

She nodded, despite having no idea who Bex was. "If I'm still around, I'd like that."

It was the best she could do. Faith's expression

dropped, and Megan could tell she'd been hoping for a more definite answer, but she wasn't in a position to be giving those to anyone.

The other woman picked herself up. "What kind of baking do you do?"

Megan smiled. This, she could talk about.

12

"SHE'S GREAT," Megan said after they'd left The Shack, heading for the minimart.

Tione's arm brushed hers as they walked. "Told you you'd have a lot in common."

They crossed Marine Parade, the street running parallel to the beach, and she could already see the town square a couple of blocks away. Would it look the same in person as it had in her photographs?

"You should take her up on her invitation to the festival," he continued.

"I will, if I'm still around." She didn't want to get ahead of herself. Anything could happen between now and then. They cut over another road and the street opened out into a cobblestone square. In its center, within a fountain, stood a life-size statue of a guy with a surfboard, just as she'd seen online.

She grinned. "I love this place."

Tione grunted. "Just wait. It gets its teeth in you really good after a while."

Scanning the buildings, she noted a jewelry shop to

her left, and beside that, a blown glass studio. To her right was a building labeled “The Hideaway” with a sign proclaiming it to be both a gym and art studio. There was a minimart, a cafe, a library, and on the opposite side of the courtyard, two historical buildings. One looked to be a local pub—perhaps the one that hosted the men’s poker night—and the other was the town hall.

“So cool,” she breathed. “Exactly like I imagined it, but better.”

Better because she was out of Charles’s shadow. Free of her beautiful prison. If she wanted to sip coffee and people-watch out the window of Cafe Oasis for hours, she could. If she wanted to buy blown glass vases in every color of the rainbow, no one would stop her. Trevor nudged her leg, and she stroked his head.

“Dogs are allowed here?” she asked.

“Dogs are allowed anywhere in Haven Bay,” he replied, lips twisting wryly. “This isn’t the city. No one stands on ceremony.”

“I want to look at everything,” she declared. “But not right now. I don’t want to make you wait outside with Trevor while I browse. Shall we go to the minimart?”

They passed The Hideaway and she tried to peek through the window to see what a combination gym and art studio looked like, but was disappointed when the only thing visible was a staircase.

“The gym is upstairs,” Tione said. “Bex, who owns it, lives on the ground floor.”

“Is this the same Bex whom Faith mentioned?”

“Sure is.”

“So she’s a personal trainer?”

“And a painter.”

“Multi-talented.”

"She's also mother to a monster."

Megan stopped walking. "I beg your pardon?"

He grinned. "She has a five-year-old daughter, Izzy, who's the cutest thing you'll ever see but has an evil streak to rival a Disney super-villain."

"Oh." For some reason, that made Megan feel better. She'd screwed up her own life spectacularly, and it was comforting to know that other women had their struggles. Did that make her a bad person?

"I'll wait out here," he said, sinking onto a bench outside the shop. "Do you mind grabbing my things as well?" He handed her a list and a wallet. "You'll be all right in there by yourself?"

Taking a breath, she mentally fortified herself. "I will."

She stepped away from him, feeling like she was climbing out onto an exposed ledge, away from the safety rope she'd been clinging to. Ridiculous to feel that way when he wouldn't be more than a hundred meters from her, and no one would be entering or leaving the minimart without going past him and Trevor, but if she'd learned one thing from her bad relationship, it was that emotions rarely made sense.

As she entered the minimart, cool air rushed down on her from an overhead fan and she paused to retrieve her personal shopping list from her pocket. She wanted to make cupcakes, and for that, she needed ingredients and equipment they didn't have at Sanctuary. She wasn't certain this little grocery store would have what she needed either, but she could improvise.

She slung a basket over her arm and gathered the first items on her list. She was investigating the contents of the chillers when a hand landed on her arm and she spun around so violently, she nearly fell over. It was fortunate she didn't, because she would have knocked down the two little old ladies staring at her with wide eyes.

The one who'd touched her snatched her hand back and her wrinkled mouth formed a moue of disapproval. "Well, I never."

"Now, now, Mavis. Don't go getting overwrought," the other woman said, giving Megan a cheery smile. She was short, with plump cheeks stained by blush, and mischievous eyes. "Hi dearie, I'm Betty. And yes, I know I look just like Betty White."

Megan's mouth dropped open. "I didn't say—"

"Of course you didn't," Mavis muttered. "But everyone thinks it, and it's plain to see why. What's your name, girl?"

She blinked, startled by the difference between the two women, and wary of their motivation. What interest could they possibly have in her? Her mind whirled with possibilities, and she backed up, her breath coming in short pants.

This had been a bad idea. She never should have let Tione talk her into coming. She should have stayed at Sanctuary where she knew she was safe.

"W-Why do you ask?"

"Because we're interested," the one called Mavis said. "Is that a crime?"

"Mavis," Betty chided, scowling at her friend. "You have the tact of a seagull." She turned back to Megan. "You don't have to tell us your name, dear, although we *will* find out. What we really want to know," she lowered her voice, "is whether you're a new transplant, or just passing through."

"Oh, I'm not..." She trailed off, glancing from one woman to the other, her heart battering against her ribcage as she realized they'd cornered her against the chiller. Other customers were eyeing them with interest, which was the last thing she needed. She just wanted to buy her ingredients and get out. Was that too much to ask?

"I don't know if I'm staying," she finished. "Excuse me, I have shopping to do."

She started to move, but Mavis blocked her, spindly arms crossed over her chest. She was taller than Megan had initially thought.

"Are you dating Tione Kingi?" she demanded. "We saw you together, and you seemed close. It's about time someone scooped that boy up."

"I'm not dating Tione." She tried to step around them again.

"Where are you from?" Mavis asked, following her into another aisle.

Megan gritted her teeth. Did the old ladies never give up? "Around." She packed several bags of icing sugar and one of fondant into her basket. "It's sweet that you care about Tione, but I really have nothing to do with him other than the fact I'm staying at Sanctuary."

"He doesn't usually bother getting to know the guests," Betty said, puffing as she tried to keep up.

"We share a love of cooking." She grabbed a couple of tubes of food dye and vanilla paste.

"There's something else going on here." This statement came from Mavis. "And who is that man who's been showing your picture around town?"

Megan stopped dead in her tracks. "What?"

Rounding on her, Mavis poked a finger into her

chest. “You’re up to something, and we want to know what.”

Her throat closed over, and she struggled to draw a decent breath. The room seemed to spin around her. “Someone has been asking about me?”

“A sweaty fellow in a suit,” Betty said as she caught up. “Mid-fifties. Balding.”

The floor seemed to tilt, and the aisle closed in around her. “Seeley.”

They frowned, and Betty reached out a hand to steady her. “Are you okay, sweetheart?”

Her knees weakened. She could hear a rasping sound and realized it was her.

“I need to… sit down.” Grabbing a shelf, she lowered herself to the ground and dropped the basket beside her.

“Now you’ve done it,” Betty muttered.

“Me?” Mavis’s voice was muffled, like she was speaking through a layer of fabric. “This was all you.”

Then their voices faded away and all she could hear was her own pulse thundering in her ears. Boxes of cocoa swam before her eyes, their edges blurring. She drew her knees to her chest and hugged them, unsure how long she stayed that way. The next thing she knew, Tione’s dark eyes were looking into hers, his warm hand on her shoulder.

“Megan.” Her name echoed around her, like she was in an empty underground cavern. “Just breathe.” He was rubbing her back, and she could hear his concern. “It’s all right. Mavis and Betty got carried away, but you’re fine. They’re gossips, that’s all.” He shot a glare over his shoulder. “You’re safe, I promise.”

She tried to nod.

“Good girl,” he crooned, the same way he might

speak to one of his dogs. She blinked a few times, and he came into focus. "I've got you. Do you think you can stand up?"

She reached for the basket, but he stopped her.

"Don't worry about the groceries. You're all I care about." He offered a hand, and she took it. His palm closed around hers, strong and sure, and he yanked her upright.

She wobbled. "I'm gonna be sick."

"No, you're not." He kept a hold of her hand, but otherwise maintained his distance, and she appreciated that. She couldn't handle a man in her space at the moment. "We're going to walk outside and sit down," he continued. "Give Mavis the shopping lists, and she'll finish for us."

She didn't want to entrust anything to the old witch. "But—"

"No buts. Everything will be fine. Come on."

"But they said that Seeley..." She sucked in a breath, fighting off panic. "He's been showing my photo around."

He froze, a flash of raw rage passing over his features before they settled into a neutral mask. "It's okay. I won't leave your side. He can wave your picture from the fucking rooftops for all I care. He's not getting you." He gestured for her to give Mavis the list, and she did. Then he lowered his voice and addressed her. "A guy has been asking questions?"

Mavis nodded. "Is she in trouble?"

"If he comes back, steer him around in circles. Don't let him near her."

"We won't."

He squeezed Megan's hand and she tried to take reassurance from it. "Like I said, we take care of our own."

She bit her tongue to keep from reminding him that she wasn't one of them. When he started to move, she let him lead her away. Outside, she dropped onto the bench where Betty was waiting with Trevor and leaned back against the building, feeling shaky and unable to support her own weight.

"I'm sorry for making a scene," she said, her eyes closed so she didn't have to look at him.

Tione settled beside her, hand still in hers. He started drawing circles on her palm and the sensation centered her.

"Take a deep breath for me."

She did.

"Now look at me."

Reluctantly, she opened one eye, then the other, and turned to face him. When he had her full attention, he raised her hand and pressed his lips to the back of it. If she hadn't been sitting, her knees would have given out. His lips were soft, his beard rough against her skin. Dimly, she was aware that Betty had gasped, and was fanning herself with one hand.

"Everything is okay," he said. "You're safe. We won't let him get you."

She exhaled, and the breath rattled as she released it. "Thanks."

Pulling her hand from his, she busied herself petting Trevor, ignoring the weight of his gaze. Trevor rested his head on her knee, and she scratched behind his ear, secure in the knowledge that anyone who meant her harm would have to get through him first.

When Mavis exited the minimart, she handed Tione a cardboard box, and looked down at Megan. "I didn't mean to distress you," she said. "I'm sorry."

"I know," Megan replied, feeling more than a little embarrassed at how she'd reacted. The women were nosy, not dangerous.

"Ladies." Tione stood and crossed his arms. He was at least a head taller than Betty. "I'm disappointed in both of you." Their eyes fell to their shoes. "If you wanted to know my business, all you had to do was ask. Don't go making a nuisance of yourself and upsetting people who've already endured more than their fair share of crap from others."

"Sorry," Betty said, then aimed a cautious smile at Megan. "Truly, dear. We hope you're all right."

"I'm fine."

"No thanks to you," he grumbled.

"So, are you stepping out with each other?" Mavis asked. When he scowled at her, she raised her chin. "You said to ask directly."

"We're not dating," Megan said. "I already told you that."

The women looked to Tione for confirmation.

"We're not," he agreed.

The corners of Betty's mouth lifted. "You will be soon," she said. "I'd bet my favorite scarf on it."

"What did you see?" Mavis demanded.

"He kissed her."

"On the hand." Tione sounded exasperated. "Can you two busybodies find someone else to pester? I need to get Megan home."

"Ooh, did you hear that?" Betty asked Mavis. "He said 'home.'"

"I heard it," she said. "How long, do you think?"

Betty eyed them. "I give it two weeks."

Megan wanted to sink into the ground and disappear.

If she looked anything like she felt, she'd be beet red with green undertones. When Tione told the women to zip it and helped her up, she gladly bid them farewell and tried to take the dog leash.

"Not in your state," he told her.

"But you can't take the groceries *and* the dog."

"Can and will."

The stubborn man did, too.

THOSE MEDDLING OLD BATS. Tione glanced at Megan, relieved to see that some of the color had returned to her cheeks. She was so damn pale when he found her on the shop floor. If he hadn't been taught to respect his elders...

He gritted his teeth. What mattered was that she was okay, and at least now they knew that Seeley had been asking around. Better to know than not. Hot protectiveness flared within him. He'd assured her that she'd be safe with him, then this awful episode had happened *because* she'd been seen with him. He wouldn't blame her if she never wanted to leave Sanctuary again, or if she didn't want anything more to do with him. It seemed half the population of Haven Bay had bets on his love life. The goddamn Bridge Club and their love sweepstakes. It had amused him when they were betting on Sterling's future happiness, but it wasn't funny now.

"Your expression is scaring people," she murmured.

Huh. He hadn't realized that his brows were knitted together and his jaw clenched until she pointed it out. He made an effort to relax. She didn't need him on edge; it would only add to her nerves. He forced himself to smile at Doug, who owned the seafood restaurant down by the pavilion. Doug raised a quizzical brow, and Tione sighed. Was it so shocking that he might smile at someone?

They rounded a corner and someone called his name. On the opposite side of the street, Kyle Pride waved at him.

"Hey there," he called.

Kyle motioned them over, but Tione shook his head. Kyle studied Megan with a little too much interest. Tione's eyes narrowed, and he picked up his pace.

"Who was that?" she asked.

"Kyle. Friend of mine. Works at the library."

"*He's* a librarian?"

He could hear her incredulity, and it grated on his nerves. Kyle had the clean-cut good looks many women seemed to favor, and library patrons had been known to swoon at the sight of him with his nose in a book. Tione read books, too. They covered every available surface of his cabin. But did women fall at his feet? Not bloody likely.

"What's so surprising about that?"

They were heading down Marine Parade now, back toward Sanctuary. The sky was overcast, but the air was warm. He slowed again. No need to exhaust her.

"Nothing," she replied. "He's just not what I pictured when Brooke told me about him."

He was confused. "Brooke told you about Kyle?"

"Yeah." She stepped closer to him to dodge a pothole. "They're friends. She offered to introduce us, but I got the feeling she wanted to set us up and I'm nowhere near ready for that, so I put her off."

Satisfaction ripped through him. She'd rejected Kyle. Even if she hadn't known who she was turning down, the thought pleased him. And what was Brooke thinking, trying to get her together with a man? It was clear she needed time to recover from the last one. She shouldn't be spending time with any men other than him and Sterling, because she'd be safe with them.

Doubt filtered through the haze of his possessive thoughts, dousing them.

No, she'd be safe with Sterling, *not* him. If he was actually a good guy, he'd stop finding excuses to spend time with her when he wasn't capable of protecting anyone.

"Who's that?" she asked, bringing his attention back to the present. She pointed to where a man stood outside the school gates, a little boy by his side, smiling at them.

"That's Shane, another of my friends. He's a teacher at the school. Would you like to meet him?" Unlike Kyle, he had no qualms about her meeting Shane, who was a little older and rendered nonthreatening by his two sons.

Megan smiled, appearing to have pulled herself together again. "That would be nice."

"*Morena*," Tione said as they approached.

"*Morena*, Mr. Tee," the little boy replied.

Tione nodded to Shane and reached down to ruffle the boy's hair. "Hunter, this is my friend Megan. Can you say *kia ora* to Megan?"

"*Kia ora*, Megan," Hunter repeated dutifully, keeping one arm around his dad's leg.

"It's lovely to meet you," Megan said, bending to his level and extending her hand. Hunter stared at it with wide eyes, then pulled his slobbery thumb out of his mouth and held it out to her. To her credit, she shook the kid's hand without missing a beat, and straightened to smile at Shane. "Hi, there."

"Hi." Shane glanced from Tione to Megan with a

brow raised. "Nice to meet you. Are you a guest at Sanctuary?"

"Yes, I've been staying there for a little over a week now, but I haven't been very well, so today is the first time I've left the lodge. You have such a gorgeous town."

Tione hid a grin. A week ago, she'd never have shared so much information with someone she'd just met. He was proud of her progress.

"It's not so bad," Shane agreed. "Great place to raise the boys."

"You have another son?"

He nodded. "Dylan is older. He goes to an intermediate school out of town." A car passed them and Trevor yanked on his leash, nearly pulling Tione off balance. He cursed, and Hunter moved behind Shane, using him as a shield. "Will you be staying in the bay for long?"

"I'm not sure yet. I've got a few things to figure out."

Tione winced. That question seemed to be the first thing anyone asked her, and he guessed the answer was far more complicated than she made it out to be.

"We'd better make tracks," he said to Shane. "Lots to do back at the lodge. It was good to see you, man."

"You, too. A pleasure to meet you, Megan."

Megan nodded, a little shyly, and his heart squeezed. She was the cutest damn thing. "Likewise. Bye, Shane."

13

MEGAN DUG her toes into the soft sand and rested her chin on her knees, gazing out over the endless expanse of the ocean. A breeze stirred her hair, tickling the back of her neck, and she rubbed it as she watched gulls swoop low over the water. There were no surfers on this stretch of the water, and her only company was an elderly lady a hundred yards away with a book, and Trevor, who was frolicking in the waves. She'd been keeping him around her as much as possible since their trip to the minimart. The quiet was exactly what she needed after an exhausting day.

She shifted, crossing her legs, and picked up the notebook and pen she'd dropped earlier. Rolling the pen between her fingers, she pondered what cupcakes to make to show how much she appreciated everyone here. She wanted to try something new. Something adventurous. Something she hadn't had before. Trying the chili ice cream had inspired her.

Peanut butter and chocolate, she jotted down. *Lemon and lime. Strawberry lemonade._Berry with a cheesecake topping. Pineapple and coconut.* Mm, she liked that option. Tropical flavors weren't ones she often used. But she could do better. She crossed out *pineapple and coconut* and replaced it with *pina colada*. She smiled. Yeah, that was more like it. Below that, she added *passion fruit mojito.*

Tropical cocktails. That was a theme she could really get behind. She tapped the pen against her lip as she thought it over. They could have a cocktail night, and pair actual cocktails with cocktail-flavored cupcakes. But would that be a little much?

No, she decided. There was no such thing as too much when it came to cocktails and cupcakes. Rolling with the idea, she noted a few more options. The sound of a door slamming niggled at the edge of her consciousness. When a square of light zipped across her notebook, she looked over her shoulder just as the sun glinted off Charles's designer watch, and her heart stopped. She froze like a possum in the headlights of an oncoming truck, so terrified her feet became rooted to the ground. Her lungs seized and ice trailed down her spine.

Charles.

He was immaculate as ever in a stylish navy suit, and the breeze didn't dare ruffle his sleek brown hair. His eyes met hers, and if not for the slight flaring of his nostrils, she'd think he hadn't seen her at all. He could be very controlled when he wanted to be. Nevertheless, cold fury lit his eyes, along with the promise of retribution.

She glanced around, searching desperately for some sign of Trevor, but he seemed to have run off while she'd been engrossed. Her chest pounded, pressure building up in it so tightly she felt like it might explode, and she gasped, realizing she'd forgotten to breathe. The small sound filled the air between them, and seemed to jerk them both into motion. Dropping her notebook, she clambered to her feet and stumbled away—there was no way she'd turn her back on him, not even to run. At the same time, he shot forward and grabbed her arm, his fingers closing around her so firmly that she cried out. She wrenched away from him, but overbalanced and fell, landing on her knees. Before she had a chance to move, two hands slid beneath her armpits and yanked her to her feet.

"I found you, Megan," he spat, his face so close to hers that she could smell his minty breath. Her stomach rolled, and threatened to empty itself all over him. She tried to break free, but he gripped her tightly and lifted her until her toes barely touched the ground. "Did you really think you could leave me?"

She didn't reply. She couldn't. The sight of his cruel eyes and sneering mouth had paralyzed her. Her worst nightmare in the flesh.

"You've had your fun," he growled, his voice far too loud considering how close he was. "You made a fool of me. Threatened my promotion. Was that what you wanted?"

"No," she whispered. In truth, she didn't want anything when it came to Charles, except for him to be out of her life.

"Of course it fucking was," he said, and she knew he honestly believed it. In Charles's eyes, everything she did was intended to have an effect on him. He couldn't comprehend that she might ever do anything for a reason other than impressing, hurting, or humiliating him. He was the most self-centered person she'd ever known. "And now it's time to come home and fix the mess you made." He let her go, and when her legs gave out, he turned away in disgust.

She got to her feet and threw her shoulders back. "I'm not coming with you."

He raised a hand, and she flinched instinctively. His lip curled. "You will, Meggie. You'll do exactly as I say."

"I won't." She hid her trembling hands behind her back and tried to act like someone stronger than herself. Someone like her sister, Mikayla, or any of the women she'd met here. "You can't hit me. We're in public."

He glanced around. "Who's going to stop me? That granny over there who's pretending not to watch you make a scene? Give me a break."

Megan didn't look where he'd gestured. She wasn't stupid enough to take her attention off him. Raising her chin, she repeated, "I'm not coming with you."

He advanced, and her head spun so dizzyingly she feared she'd faint. He didn't stop until they stood chest to chest. He wasn't a bulky guy, but he was larger than her, and they both knew it.

"Don't be ridiculous. Get in the car. We're going home. You have a fuck ton of damage to repair."

"No." Her heart was a butterfly fluttering against the inside of her ribcage. She'd never been so frightened in her life, but it was time to make a stand. She wouldn't let this bastard control her anymore. "Go away, Charles. I'm not coming back with you. Leave me the hell alone."

When his cell phone rang, Tione set down the vegetable peeler, dried his hands, and answered. "*Kia ora*."

"Tione," a voice hissed down the line. "It's Nell."

He frowned. He hadn't even known Nell—another of the local retirees—had his number. "What do you need?"

"Come down to the beach immediately." Her tone was urgent, and he responded without thinking, covering the vegetables with a napkin and striding to the exit. "There's an angry guy in a suit talking to your lady friend," she continued. "I think he's threatening her. Trying to get her to go with him."

Motherfucker.

Shoving his phone into his pocket, he broke into a run. In a matter of seconds, the beach came into sight, and so did the tall asshole who was dragging Megan over the sand while she flailed, trying to break free. Her face was twisted in pain, and deathly pale, which highlighted the fading bruises left by the monster who had her in his grip.

Tione's vision tunneled until all he could see was the man's crushing hold on Megan's forearm. He wanted to smash the fucker's face. To beat him until he apologized for every ounce of pain he'd ever caused her. But he checked himself. She was frightened enough. She didn't need him adding fuel to the fire. She needed him to stay calm. She needed a hero, even if he was undeserving of the title.

The man caught sight of him, and his lips curled into a smirk. Tione knew his type. Expensive suit, expensive watch, probably had a car worth six figures to overcompensate for his tiny dick and shitty personality.

He halted, blocking the man's way. "Get your hands off her, and back the fuck away."

The man's eyes narrowed, and Tione didn't like the coldness in them. "Mind your own business, buddy. My girlfriend and I have private matters to discuss."

Megan shot him a look full of desperation and fear. He wished he could tear the man to shreds so she never had to worry about him again. "Doesn't look like she wants to talk, *buddy*, and if you're the bastard who hurt her, you'd better leave before I call for reinforcements." His hands fisted at his sides. "My friends don't like men who hit women."

The man jerked Megan's arm, and she yelped. He reeled her into his side and put an arm around her shoulders. She immediately shrugged out of his embrace, but he didn't release her.

"You've been busy, Meggie. You screwing him so he'll protect you? I'll bet he's not the only one. How many others are there?"

She wrenched away from him, although it clearly hurt. Tione expected her to deny the accusation, and was surprised when she didn't.

"Who I screw or don't screw is none of your business anymore, Charles. We're not together."

Charles shook his head, his eyes flat. "You're nothing more than a whore. I should have known it when you wore those short dresses and flirted with every man at our dinner parties."

"You asked me to be nice to them!"

"Not like that," he snapped. "I just wanted you to hand out a few compliments. You took it too far. You always do."

"Then let me go." Walking in an arc around Charles,

out of his reach, she circled to Tione's side. Instinctively, he stepped closer and their arms brushed. A zing of relief passed through him at the physical contact, as if that was what he'd needed to assure himself she was okay.

"Please leave." She angled her face up to look at Tione, but he didn't take his eyes off the douchebag opposite them in case he tried to grab her again. "Tee, I don't want to see him. We have nothing to talk about, and if he doesn't leave, I have no problem with Trevor gnawing his leg off."

Tione's chest expanded, and he felt a hundred feet tall. His girl had spunk, and she trusted him to keep her safe. Winding an arm around her waist, he rested his hand lightly on her hip, the gesture intended to convey to Charles that he was fighting a losing battle. When Megan sighed and leaned into him, the other man's lips firmed into a thin line and his eyes flicked from Megan to Tione and back again.

"Get in your car and drive away," Tione said, burning inside with a complicated tangle of emotions he didn't understand. He focused on the rage. That, he was familiar with. That, he knew how to handle. "Get the fuck out of Haven Bay, and don't come back. Megan doesn't want you, and as far as I'm concerned, that's all you need to know. If you want to touch her, you'll have to go through me."

Charles scanned him, no doubt noting the fact that Tione was shorter than him, but also broader. "I'll go," he said, "but it won't be the last you see of me." He turned to Megan. "When you ran off, you screwed me over. You know I need you for the partnership. You're supposed to be my ace. If I lose out because of you, I won't let you get away with it."

Tione rolled his eyes. He was sick of this guy already. "Don't threaten her, and don't show your face in my town again."

Charles's expression became petulant, rivaling a sulky child, then he strode past them, jolting Tione's shoulder.

"Yeah, you better keep walking," Tione called at his back. He didn't turn.

14

"OH, THANK GOD," Megan said when Charles was out of earshot. She buried her face in her hands. "How did he find me?"

"I take it that's the guy you're running from." Tione moved his arm from her back, and all of a sudden, she felt exposed. She wanted to snuggle back into the shelter of his strong, stocky body, but she didn't. She needed to stand on her own two legs. Being dependent on a man was what had gotten her into this god-awful mess.

"Yes." She straightened and tried to meet his eyes, but couldn't. She was so embarrassed. What must he think of her, now that he'd seen exactly the sort of person she was, and the kind of man she'd been with? All she could say in her defense was that she'd been fooled by Charles's charm—which he had in spades, when he wanted to—and by his pretty face.

"My ex-boyfriend." Almost her ex-fiancé. She'd found a ring in his sock drawer when she'd been doing the laundry once. Proposing had been the last piece of his plan to secure a partner position in his old-school law firm. Afraid of what she might see if she looked at Tione, she kept her eyes trained on her feet.

"I'm so sorry you had to intervene like that. I don't know how he tracked me down. I thought I'd gotten rid of anything he might use to find me." She'd tossed her phone in a trash can between their apartment and the building where she'd stored her ancient car. All of her clothes had been abandoned, and she'd cut up the credit card he'd given her. She'd even left her treasured kitchenware behind, deciding it was a small sacrifice for freedom.

She saw Tione's hand move, and then he was cupping her chin and tilting it up. "Hey, look at me. You're not responsible for what that asshole does, okay?"

She nodded, although she didn't truly believe it, and he let her go.

"Good, now that we've got that cleared up, there's plenty of ways he could have found you if he has resources, and he looks like the kind of guy who does."

She scoffed. "You mean money? Yeah, he's got that. His family are one of the oldest, wealthiest, and most respected in New Zealand, or so he's always told me. Doesn't mean they're not horrible."

He made a sound of agreement. "Money brings out the worst in people." He reached for her hand, but stopped short, letting her decide whether or not to close the distance. She did, slipping her fingers between his. "Come back to the cabin. We need to talk."

"Wait, I need to get my notepad. I dropped it when he..." She let the sentence hang in the air, unfinished. She didn't want to think about what might have happened if Tione hadn't arrived when he did. Although she liked to think she'd have screamed bloody murder and drawn someone out of the lodge to help her.

Releasing him, she retrieved her notebook and pen, and then returned to his side so they could head for his cabin. As they crossed the parking lot, she checked to make sure Charles's car had gone.

"You're okay," Tione murmured. "He won't get to you while I'm here."

"I'm not one of your rescue dogs," she muttered, but regretted the words as soon as she'd spoken them. She was being snarky when he'd just saved her ass. It wasn't that she was ungrateful—quite the contrary—but she didn't want to be just another stray he took under his wing.

He stopped and looked down at her, brow furrowed. "I know that. But you've had a rough day, and there's nothing wrong with letting someone else carry the load for a while."

She nodded as if she agreed, and they continued up to his place, where Zee was sprawled in a patch of sun on the deck. Zee raised her head to give them a doggy grin as they came up the stairs, and Megan bent to pat her. Zee leaned into it, then stretched, and followed them inside.

Megan lowered herself into the armchair beside the unlit fire, and Pixie leapt from the bed, landed with a thud, and trotted over to Tione's feet. He scooped her up and deposited her on Megan's lap. The Chihuahua looked less than impressed at being unceremoniously passed off, but curled into a ball all the same.

"They can sense when you're upset," Tione told her. "They want to comfort you. Dogs are good like that."

She tried to smile. "They're sweethearts."

Closing her eyes, she drew a few steady breaths and tried to take comfort from the warmth and closeness of the dogs' bodies. It didn't help. She felt frozen on the inside. Like she should be crying, but all of her tears had turned to ice and she couldn't squeeze them out.

Tione dragged a stool over to sit directly in front of her. "Were you hurt?"

"No. All he did was grab my arm."

"Let me see."

She held up her limb for him to inspect, and he gently turned it over. She knew the moment he saw the faint finger-shaped bruises because his jaw clenched, his nostrils flared, and his expression became downright fierce.

"That fucker."

Her breath caught. She knew she ought to be scared by his temper, but she wasn't. Not when his anger was on her behalf. She took her arm back and angled it so the bruises were hidden.

"I'm okay," she said, meaning it. "They'll be gone in a couple of days."

"I hate that you know that." He reached over and rubbed Pixie between her ears. "You're welcome to sit on the bed—that way Zee could join you, too."

"Really? You don't think that's too..." *Intimate* was the word that came to mind, but she didn't want to say it. "Intrusive?"

One corner of his mouth lifted. "Not hardly. Intrusive is having Trevor try to spoon me at two a.m."

Grinning at the image, she stood and carried a squirming Pixie to the bed, where she positioned herself carefully on the bedspread and rested on a pillow. Tione stayed where he was, but she patted the spot beside her.

"Come on, there's plenty of room for both of us."

He didn't move. "You sure? Because I'm fine over here."

"Don't be silly."

Hesitantly, he rose and approached, with Zee close behind. The dog leapt easily onto the bed, while Tione sat stiffly as far from Megan as he could. She appreciated his thoughtfulness, but considering the day they'd had, he was being a bit ridiculous. Besides, she liked being close to him. It made her feel safer, as if the solidness of his body was a physical barrier between her and all the world's evils.

"There's no point in you balancing on the edge of the bed," she told him. "You can come closer." When he eyed her dubiously, she added, "I know you, Tee. At least, I know you enough to believe you won't hurt me." A horrible thought occurred to her. Maybe he didn't *want* to be any closer to her. Maybe he didn't feel the same connection between them that she did. God knew she'd brought nothing into his life but trouble and drama. "If you aren't comfortable being near me, that's fine though. I won't push you."

He snorted a laugh. "That's not the problem here, Megan. I don't want to do anything to stress you out after you've had to deal with that asshole. I feel bad enough for pressuring you to walk into town with me this morning, considering how that turned out."

She scooted over. "I'm glad you did, because now I've done it once and I know I can do it again." Finally, he closed the distance between them, and Pixie jumped from Megan's lap onto his. She smiled. "I guess we know where her loyalties lie."

She turned her attention to Zee, rubbing the dog's belly. When she stopped, Zee looked at her plaintively.

"Later," she said, then summoned her courage. While she was facing her demons today, it was time to deal with another. "Can you put an arm around me?" she asked. "I don't want to be scared of people touching me anymore."

"All right," he agreed tentatively. "But the second you've had enough, just say so."

"I will."

With painstaking carefulness, he wrapped an arm around her. She wriggled closer, snuggling into his body, and rested her cheek on his chest. She could hear his heart beating, the rhythm strong and regular. It was nice, and she tried to relax, but softening her body into his was difficult. For months, she hadn't allowed herself to just exist with another person, without second-guessing their every movement and breath, and wondering when the other shoe would drop. She still couldn't manage to give herself up to the moment completely.

"You'll need to tell me everything," he said, after a few minutes passed. "The police, too. We can't protect you if we don't know the full story."

"No." She'd answered before he even finished talking. "No, no, no. The police can't be trusted. Charles has connections, and many of them are in law enforcement. Being cops doesn't make them the good guys."

He took her hand and squeezed it. "The local police can be trusted, I promise. I know most of them, and they're moral guys. They'll take you seriously, and they won't let him off because of his connections."

"Mmph." She didn't know what he wanted her to say.

Almost anyone could be bought or manipulated for the right price. "I'd really rather not."

"What?" he demanded, lifting his arm from her, taking away her source of comfort. "Are you just going to hide out forever?"

Put that way, she supposed not. "I figure he'll get sick of looking for me and give up."

Surely she wasn't so indispensable to his career that it was worth endangering his freedom by doing something illegal.

"And then?" he demanded. "Did you think about the next girl who'd fall into his web?"

Shame welled within her, hot and unwelcome. "I didn't think."

"You were in a tough spot." His voice gentled. "But you know what he's like. You need to tell someone, so some other girl doesn't end up in the same situation as you."

She drew her knees to her chest and hugged them, wishing with all she had that she could simply end the chapter of her life that involved Charles Wentworth. It seemed that was not to be. But then, after how epically stupid she'd been, she didn't deserve to take the easy way out.

She sighed. "I have to, don't I?"

He shifted, rubbing a palm in circles on her back. "You never have to do anything, but yeah, I'd recommend it."

"Okay. You can call them." She sighed. "Make sure you get everyone here who needs to know the story. Kat, too. I only want to tell it once."

"You're being very brave."

She wanted to grump at him, to say that his tone was

patronizing, but she knew he was doing his best to soothe her.

"I'll be with you every step of the way."

She nodded, but inside she wondered if he'd change his mind. Promises like that were so easy to break.

15

TIONE HAD NEVER SOUGHT to be anyone's hero, but damned if he didn't want to do everything in his power to help Megan. He wasn't the kind of guy who enjoyed being wrapped up in drama, but the universe had handed him an opportunity to atone—at least in part—for past mistakes, and he was determined to do things right this time around. That meant getting the police involved and stepping back before he could endanger her with any well-meaning interference.

Grabbing his phone, he dialed the local policeman's number and spoke without waiting for a greeting.

"*Kia ora*, Elliot. Can you come over to Sanctuary? I've got a woman here who'd like to talk to you."

"You want to tell me what this is about?" Elliot asked, gruff as ever.

"Not right now. It's not my story to tell. But suffice it to say, something has happened to her."

A heavy sigh came down the line. "Okay. I'll be there in five."

"Thanks, man." He hung up and dialed Betty. "I've got a favor to ask."

"Anything you need," she replied, probably because she still felt guilty about their run-in earlier—a fact he'd been counting on.

"Can you come over and prepare dinner for the guests? Something has come up."

There was a brief silence, during which he had no doubt her gossip-seeking radar had gone off. "What kind of something?"

He rolled his eyes. "Can't tell you right now. Can you help, or not?"

"Of course I can," she said, as though it had never been in doubt. "I'll head over right now. Shall I meet you at your cabin?"

He suppressed a smile. She wanted to know what was going on, and she wasn't about to give up. "No need for that. You know where the kitchen is." She made a sound of disappointment. "Thanks Betty," he continued, not giving her a chance to protest. "All my *aroha*. Bye, now."

His last phone call was to Kat. Two minutes later, she appeared in the doorway, and raised her eyebrows at the sight of the two of them snuggled on the bed with Pixie and Zee.

"You might want to make yourselves less comfortable if Elliot is on his way over," she said. "You know how he is."

Anything that could be termed "physical affection" made the policeman immensely uncomfortable, and if he was uncomfortable, he might fail to notice important details.

"Good point." Tione slipped off the bed, displacing Pixie, and returned to the chair by the fire.

Kat perched on the edge of the bed beside Megan. “Hey, sweetie. You want to tell me what’s going on?”

Megan’s eyes darted to Tione before returning to Kat, and she wet her lips. “Can I tell you when the policeman arrives? I don’t want to say it twice.”

Kat scratched Zee’s haunches. “Sure thing. He shouldn’t take long.”

He didn’t. As per usual, he knocked on the door three times and waited for someone to open it. Elliot wasn’t the type to let himself in, even when he was off duty. He didn’t want to see something illegal and then be accused of entering unlawfully. Tione thought the guy was a bit too concerned about abiding by the rules, but he was in his fifties and there was no changing his habits at this point.

“Afternoon.” Elliot nodded respectfully when Tione opened the door. “Came as fast as I could. What seems to be the problem?”

“Hello, officer,” a soft voice said behind Tione.

He jerked around. To his surprise, Megan had crossed the room and was offering a hand to the policeman, whose cheeks pinkened.

He shook her hand. “Well hello, little lady.”

“Megan,” she told him. “My name is Megan Talbot.”

“Nice to make your acquaintance, Megan Talbot.”

Tione turned away so they wouldn’t see him smile. Instantly, he could tell that Megan had acquired a new admirer. Elliot’s shoulders went back and his expression softened when he looked at her. She seemed to have that effect on people, with her gentleness and delicate frame. Elliot wasn’t the most progressive of men, and he’d want to protect her, exactly as Tione had hoped.

He cleared his throat. “Let’s sit down, and Megan can tell us whatever she needs to.”

She paled, and he brushed his hand against hers as they moved around the small table, hoping she’d take comfort from the touch. Her gaze flew to his, and he gave her an encouraging smile. She sat and wrung her hands. Elliot withdrew a notepad from his pocket and jotted the date, location, and time at the top, followed by her name.

“Megan,” he said. “Why don’t you tell me what happened?”

She studied a coffee ring on the table, refusing to make eye contact with any of them. Tione’s heart went out to her. He had a pretty good idea of what she was about to say, but it couldn’t be easy to verbalize.

“Where do you want me to start?” she asked.

“At the beginning.” There was no trace of irony in Elliot’s tone. He wasn’t like that.

“Okay.” She closed her eyes, her mouth set in a determined line. “Okay,” she repeated. “I met Charles—that’s Charles Wentworth Junior,” she added, for Elliot’s benefit, “around eight months ago, and we started dating. It was at a wedding. He was in the bridal party, and I was there to put the finishing touches on the cake. He was handsome, charming, likable. We flirted.” A puff of laughter escaped her. “I couldn’t understand why he’d be interested in me, but I drank it up like a little fool.”

“What next?” Elliot prompted, taking notes.

Tione’s fingernails dug into his palms hard enough to draw red lines on them. Intellectually, he’d known that Megan had dated the bozo from the beach, but hearing her speak about him this way made him want to drag the man back here and rend him limb from limb. Why wouldn’t any man be interested in her? She was a sweet, pretty woman with a heart of gold. Charles had been a lucky sonofabitch to be allowed to touch her, so why the fuck had he abused that privilege?

"We started dating," she said, her eyes still squeezed shut, like she couldn't bear to look at them. "As I said, he was charming. He swept me off my feet. Bought me flowers and jewelry, took me to expensive restaurants, invited me to work events and bragged to his colleagues about how perfect I was. Told everyone who'd listen that he'd known it was love the moment he saw me and that he intended to marry me one day soon." She lifted her shoulders in a shrug. Tione couldn't take his eyes from her, and based on the stillness in the room, he suspected Kat and Elliot were spellbound, too.

"Three months after we met, I moved in with him. I knew it was fast, but I didn't care because I was crazy about him and I was certain he felt the same way." She broke off, hauled in a deep breath, and pursed her lips, as though she was pulling herself together. Dread curdled Tione's stomach. He had a feeling he didn't want to hear what came next.

"Go on," Elliot prompted.

"I'd always known he wasn't perfect. He could be jealous, but he kept his temper in check. He'd just grumble if another man paid me attention, and to be honest, I was flattered. I didn't see it as a red flag, but when I moved in, he changed."

"How so?"

"He started criticizing me. Not in overt ways, and any time I called him on it, he made me feel like I was overreacting. He suggested I was tired because of the hours I worked, and he convinced me to quit my job and let him take care of me. I think he liked me being dependent on him."

"That's certainly something I've seen before," Elliot said. "Keep going, sweetheart."

"Once I was at home all the time, I got lonely, so I started visiting friends and family to fill my time, but he got paranoid and asked me if I was seeing other men. I realized he had cameras in the apartment and the security system was rigged to notify him any time I left and then again when I returned. When I asked him about it, he said he just wanted to make sure I was safe, and when I mentioned going back to work because I was bored, he started planning weekly dinner parties, inviting his boss and colleagues over, to keep me busy. It was during those dinner parties that I started to wonder if he'd had an ulterior motive for dating me."

She opened her eyes and looked directly at Tione. He was so caught off guard that he stared right back. It was like she was talking to him, and only him. He wished he could reach out and take her hand, but he didn't want to disrupt the flow of her story. "Charles is a lawyer, and he's intent on making partner. His father is a judge, and they have this whole career planned out for him."

"His dad is a judge?" Kat asked, echoing Tione's disbelief.

Megan nodded. "Of the variety you can have in your pocket if you're rich or powerful enough."

Elliot clucked his tongue. "It's not right, people in positions like that thinking they're above the law."

"I know," she agreed. "Anyway, it soon became apparent that I was part of their plan." She snorted derisively. "The firm he works for has old values. They prefer their partners to be in settled relationships. I suited nicely because I didn't say anything I shouldn't, and because my mother and brother are both respected lawyers in their own fields. On top of that, I overheard his boss telling Charles not to let me go. He said that the ability to hold onto a good woman was an indication of a man's potential." She shook her head. "I think it was a bunch of bullshit. The old creep hit on me every chance he got, and he knew that Charles would never call him on it. Charles had no problem lashing out at me because of it though."

Tione's gut clenched. Regardless of the audience, he reached over and patted her hand. She intertwined her fingers with his.

"After one party, he got upset because he believed I'd been flirting with his boss. In reality, I was just being nice, because he asked me to, but Glenn is one of those men who can't keep his hands to himself, so it looked like there was more going on. The next day, Charles actually thought I'd set up an assignation with the guy because I went to visit my sister and Glenn happened to be out of the office at the same time." Her throat worked as she swallowed. "He hit me, and I was so shocked I didn't know what to do, but he seemed so sorry about it afterward. I slept in the spare bedroom and figured we'd talk about it later, but we never did. It was like he'd completely forgotten."

"What was the date when he first hit you?" Elliot asked, pen moving furiously.

She cocked her head, considering. "I couldn't say for sure. A little after new years, I think."

"Would you be able to find out the exact date?"

"Yes, I suppose so."

"Good." He stopped writing and looked up. "Please, continue. How many more times did he hit you?"

"I don't know," she said, and damned if that didn't make Tione want to break the dickhead's face. She'd *lost count* of how many times he'd hurt her?

"After the first time, he didn't hit me again for a couple of weeks, but then I wore a dress to a dinner party that he'd picked out for me but later decided was too revealing. From then on, it seemed like I did something to set off his temper most weeks, although he didn't always hit me. I was walking on eggshells. I never knew what would upset him. One night I ran out of wine when he had guests over, and he pitched a fit. He... uh..." Her voice cracked, and she lowered her gaze to the table.

"When they'd all left, he grabbed me and shoved me into the wall. I bashed my head and I think I must have been knocked out. I don't think he meant to go that far because when I woke up in the morning there were flowers on the pillow beside me, and pastries from my favorite cafe in the kitchen. He'd left a note for me to treat myself at the spa. Despite all that, I realized that his apology was an empty gesture. He wasn't truly sorry, and by staying with him, I was putting myself in danger." She shook her head. "The trouble was, I didn't have money to leave him and I didn't know how to ask for help and admit that I'd been so fucking stupid."

They all flinched at the curse word coming out in her soft, sweet voice.

"Sorry," she muttered, looking contrite.

"You're entitled to a swear word or two," Kat replied.

"Damn straight," Elliot agreed. "And you can't blame yourself."

She shrugged, looking so helpless and ashamed that Tione ached to gather her in his arms and shelter her.

"Why can't I?" she demanded. "My mum is an attorney and she's worked with women in abusive relationships. I should have seen the signs and known better, but I was so caught up in the fairy tale I'd woven for myself that I missed it all. But that wasn't the only thing that stopped me leaving. Charles's dad could cause a lot of professional problems for Mum, and she worked really hard to get where she is. I couldn't bear to ruin it for her just because I'm an idiot when it comes to men."

"So when did you decide to go, regardless of your financial situation?" Elliot asked. "Did something in particular happen to push you over the edge?"

Squeezing her hand, Tione did his best to silently remind her that he was there for her. He wished there was more he could do.

"I'd started taking on baking jobs behind his back to make money. It was difficult because the apartment was wired with cameras, but not impossible with a bit of planning. Then, around two and a half weeks ago, at another of his work events, the senior partner groped my thigh beneath the dinner table. I'd had enough and I made a show of pretending to think it was Charles, and being confused when it wasn't. I wanted him to realize that it wasn't okay, but then later on, Charles was furious because I'd embarrassed him. I asked if he expected me to sit there and take it, and he said yes, if that was what it took for him to get his promotion. He said I should support him in every possible way."

Tione thumped the table. "That bastard!"

She raised her eyes to his, and it pleased him to see

the spark of anger glowing in them. Her ex hadn't taken away her fighting spirit.

"Yeah, so." She held his gaze, as if pretending it was only the two of them in the room. "That was the final straw. I used the money I had to buy a car, and decided to stay long enough for one more job so I had a little more padding in my wallet."

"Couldn't you have gone to your family?" Elliot asked, more gently than Tione had heard him speak in his life.

Megan glanced away, and pulled her hand free, her shoulders hunching. "Yes, but I wasn't exactly in a good headspace, and like I said, I didn't want to be responsible for Mum's career ending. I was also embarrassed. My family never liked Charles and they told me I was moving too quickly, but I ignored them because I thought I knew best." She sighed. "He hadn't injured me too badly up until that point and I figured I could fix the whole thing without them finding out. My sister, Mikayla, is so strong. She'd never have let herself get into a situation like this. And Mark, my brother, is the golden boy. I didn't want to give anyone another reason to think of me as the weak link, so I gathered my things and had a bag ready to go. Unfortunately, a partner position came up during that last week, and one of Charles's colleagues got promoted over him. He took out his anger on me. I don't think he broke anything, but he cut my forehead and bruised me all over. I knew I needed to get out of there immediately, so I ran."

16

Tione's jaw worked. He knew what came next. She'd fled to Sanctuary, where he'd attacked her. God, he hated that he'd had any part of hurting her when she'd already survived hell.

"Did you tell anyone you were leaving?" Elliot asked. "Who knew what was happening in your relationship?"

Megan's gaze was steady as she met the lawman's eyes. "No one, as far as I know. I didn't tell anyone what was going on because I was too embarrassed, and I didn't share my plans to leave in case it got back to him." She paused, then added, "I just wanted to get on with my life and not have to face up to my mistakes."

His heart ached for her. How lonely she must have been. He knew how it felt to be in trouble, with no one to talk to. A time machine would come in handy right now. He'd go back and beat the ever-loving hell out of her ex before he laid a finger on her.

"Why Haven Bay?" Elliot prodded.

Megan's shoulders slumped, and she looked weary as she answered, "My brother is friends with Sterling, who raved about what a nice place it is for starting over."

Kat's brows shot up. "You knew Sterling before you came here?"

She shrugged. "We met once or twice."

Kat's eyes sparked. "He didn't say a word. I'm going to kill him."

"Please don't," Megan said, turning to her. "He was only trying to help me by staying quiet, and it's not that I didn't trust you, I just wanted a fresh start. I didn't want you to judge me based on my past."

"Oh, honey." Kat's expression softened, and she reached over and patted Megan's shoulder.

"Okay, folks, back to the matter at hand," Elliot broke in, steering the conversation into safer territory. "You saw Mr. Wentworth today, is that right? And is it the first time you've seen him since you left?"

"Yes, although one of his associates was here last week. Seeley James." She glanced at Tione, then Kat, and added apologetically, "He's a private investigator who works for the Wentworth family. He's licensed, but I don't think his operation is strictly legal."

"Seeley James," Elliot muttered, making a note of the name. "What happened when Mr. Wentworth approached you today?"

Tione awaited her answer with interest. He'd only arrived in time to catch the tail end of their confrontation. She nibbled on her lip, and closed her eyes, like she very much didn't want to relive it.

"He told me to come home with him. I said no. He threatened to hit me, and I reminded him he couldn't do that in public. I told him to leave me alone. He called me names—"

"What kind of names?" Elliot interrupted.

If possible, her shoulders hunched further. "Is it important?"

"Yes."

She inhaled deeply. "Bitch. Slut. Useless skank."

Air hissed between Kat's teeth. "Jeez."

"He's not a nice guy," Megan said, in the understatement of the year. "After that, he tried to drag me to his car. Tione arrived, and told him to let me go. Between the two of us, we convinced him to leave, but he said it wouldn't be the last I saw of him."

"He threatened you?"

"Not directly," she said, at the same time Tione interjected with a "Yes."

Elliot looked from one of them to the other and grunted. "Okay." Then he set his pen down and gave Megan his full attention. "I appreciate you stepping me through that, Megan. The big question now is: do you want to press charges?"

You can do it, Tione silently encouraged her. *Be brave.*

She straightened her back and set her jaw. "Yes."

He tried to communicate with his eyes that he'd make sure she wouldn't regret her decision. When she didn't respond, he took her hand, raised it, and kissed the back of it, heedless of the others in the room. She needed to know he was here for her.

"Good," Elliot said with satisfaction. "Now, let's talk through your options."

As Elliot ran through the options for going forward, Megan's mind swam with too much information, and she struggled to retain any of it.

"Wait, wait, slow down," she said. "Can you repeat that please?"

"I asked if you'd be interested in filing for a restraining order," Elliot told her. "I know it won't physically keep Mr. Wentworth away from you, but if he violates it, we'll have more to use against him if the case goes to court."

"What would I need to do?" she asked, thinking this all sounded like she'd be keeping Charles in her life for much longer than she'd planned. If only she could pretend he didn't exist, but that was no longer an option, and she'd been selfish to ever consider it.

"Write and sign an affidavit, then your lawyer can handle the rest." Elliot raised a bushy gray brow. "Do you have a lawyer?"

She fought the urge to crawl under Tione's bed and hide with Pixie until everyone left. It seemed she'd have to come clean with her mother after all. She could never afford a lawyer, other than the ones she was related to.

"My mother is in criminal law. I'll ask her to help."

She noticed Kat and Tione exchange glances, and ducked her head because she didn't want to know whatever they were silently communicating with each other.

"Good. Glad to hear you've got that under control." Elliot seemed oblivious to the undercurrent rippling through the room. "Here's what will happen next. I'll photograph those bruises on your arms and the cut on your face—I assume that is also Mr. Wentworth's work?"

She nodded to confirm.

"Do you have any evidence that he has previously assaulted you?"

"We have photos," Kat broke in, looking apologetic. "Remember those ones I took when you first arrived?" To Elliot, she said, "They show the damage to her face and body, including a lot of bruising around her ribs. We think a couple of them may have been fractured, but she wouldn't go to the hospital."

"Would've been no point," Megan muttered. "Nothing they can do for them anyway."

"No, but it would have been more evidence to use against your ex," Tione said.

She felt her face flame. "Can you not gang up on me right now please?"

They fell silent.

Elliot shifted awkwardly in place and continued. "I'll want copies of those photographs, and if you have any threatening texts, messages, or emails, that would help, too."

Megan closed her eyes. "I threw out my phone."

Couldn't she do anything right?

"If he sent you emails or messages on an online app, someone will still be able to access them," Tione said, a flush crawling up his cheeks when they all turned to look at him. "I watch a few true crime shows."

Huh. She frowned. There was no television in the cabin. Perhaps he watched them in the lodge, but that was hardly relevant, so she let the thought go.

"I don't think he ever explicitly threatened me in writing," she said, disappointed not to be of more use. "He implied it, but he was subtle."

Elliot made a sound in the back of his throat, like he was thinking. "Every little bit helps in a case like this.

Once we've got all the evidence we can, including a written statement from you, we'll issue an arrest warrant. Keep in mind that we won't be able to prosecute him here. The case will be heard in court in the location where the offending occurred, which for you, is Auckland."

Her shoulders slumped. Seriously? She'd gone through all of this only for one of Charles Senior's buddies to hear the case and dismiss it, or somehow make it vanish before she even reached the courtroom?

"Hey now, what's all this about?" Elliot asked when her face fell.

"He's never going to get what he deserves, is he?" she said, feeling defeated.

"Of course he will." The gruff policeman patted her back awkwardly. "He's not the only ones with friends in Auckland, missy. I don't look like much, but there was a time when this old dog was one of the best officers in the city. I have friends aplenty in the legal system, and I'll drop a word in the right ear to make sure no funny business goes on behind closed doors."

Tears welled in her eyes. "You will?" She sniffed, and tried to get herself under control. "Thank you, that's so sweet."

"There, there, none of that," he muttered, turning dangerously red. "Let's push through. When the case goes to court, it might be heard by a judge, or it may go to a jury, depending on what the defendant prefers. It's not compulsory for you to speak at the hearing, but it would be best if you did."

She swallowed. "I can manage that."

"Okay." He continued. "The restraining order will be handled separately, and you can get that underway as soon as your lawyer is available." He cleared his throat. "Considering she's your mother, I should imagine that's very soon. Once she's completed the paperwork, Mr. Wentworth will be advised and will have a chance to respond. After that, a court date will be set for a judge to determine whether to grant the order. You'll need to attend that session in person."

The mere thought of heading back to Auckland again made her spirits sink. Now that she'd gotten some distance from the city, she realized how little she actually cared for it. She'd much rather be in a place like Haven Bay, which had character, and where everyone was a potential friend.

"I can do that." It would be a small price to pay for having Charles out of her life, especially if it helped put him far away from other women.

Elliot rummaged in his pockets and drew out a camera. "Can you show me your arms?"

She held them out, turning the pale insides of her forearms—where the bruises were more visible—upward. He took several pictures, then also snapped one of her face, and several of the smudges ringing her neck.

"Do you mind if I capture one of your ribs?" he asked. "To show how long the healing process takes."

Standing, she glanced at Tione, hoping he'd volunteer to look the other way because she didn't want him to see the mess of her torso, even if it was much better than this time last week. Unfortunately, he seemed riveted to her. With trepidation, she lifted the hem of her shirt and turned to show Elliot her left side, which was the most battered. She didn't need to look at her skin to know it was a mottled patchwork of yellow and brown. The quick intakes of breath told her the men were shocked. Megan looked to Kat, who'd already seen the bruising, and who watched her with sympathy but not horror.

Elliot cleared his throat. "That sonofabitch."

The camera clicked as he photographed her, but she kept her attention on Kat and ignored Tione, even though she could feel him trying to catch her gaze. She couldn't stand to see the pity in his eyes.

"Done."

She dropped her shirt and sat. "Thanks."

"Kat, you'll email me the other photos?" he asked.

"As soon as I'm back in my room," she agreed.

"Good. Megan?"

She blinked a few times to refocus, and looked at Elliot. "Yes?"

"If you see him again, I want you to call me immediately. Here's my number." He handed her a card, and she tucked it into her pocket. "In the meantime, I'll get things moving on my end, and you call your mum to get the restraining order underway." He stood, but gestured at the others to remain seated. "I'd better head back to the station, but you'll be hearing from me soon."

"Thank you," she said, meaning it one hundred percent.

He dismissed her gratitude. "Just doing my job."

"I'll head back over to the lodge, too." Kat bent to kiss Megan's cheek. Her dark eyes were filled with concern. "You'll let me know if you need me?"

She nodded, and Kat followed Elliot out, leaving her and Tione alone. Strangely, the room seemed more crowded when they were gone, rather than emptier. She moved to the armchair to put some space between them, and eyed him cautiously. His hands were clenched at his side, the cords of his forearms threatening to burst out through his skin.

"I can't believe he did that to you," he growled. "I can't believe anyone would hurt you like that." His voice became so gravelly she could hardly understand him. His chest heaved as he breathed, visibly trying to calm himself. "Why would anyone want to?" He dropped to a whisper. "You're so sweet. So gentle. I can't get my head around what a sick fuck he must be to have beat you like that." He yanked a hand through his hair. "How did he do it? Did he kick you while you were down?" Going to her, he fell to his knees, his hands resting on each arm of her chair. "Tell me. I need to know."

Megan felt his anger like a weight on her chest. "Knowing won't help," she told him. "And that's not the image I want you to have of me."

He took her hands, and his were cold and clammy. She rubbed them between her own, amazed that she was the one comforting him.

"I need to know," he repeated, his dark eyes burning into hers. "I don't think any less of you for what happened. That's on him. You're strong and smart. You were planning a way out. None of this is your fault."

She blinked back tears. "You really mean that?"

"Hell, yeah. So tell me."

She coughed to clear the thickness in the back of her throat. "He kicked me when I was on the ground. I was near to passing out so I couldn't get away. I just curled up and took it."

His throat worked when he swallowed, his Adam's apple bobbing. "I want to rip his head off."

She laughed, surprised by how much his fury pleased her. "It's okay. I'm away from him, and we're going to make sure it stays like that." Her words didn't ease his expression at all, so she cupped his face. His soft beard tickled her palms. "I'm all right, Tee. Nothing has changed."

He turned his cheek into her caress, his breath warm as it skated across her skin. His lips pressed into her palm and his shoulder shuddered as he exhaled.

"Are you sure you don't want me to track him down and do to him what he did to you?"

She rolled her eyes. "No, Tee. I want to think about him as little as possible. I'd prefer not to let him taint my fresh start any more than he already has, so let's not go there."

"I could," he said, as if he needed her to know that. "I'd make him pay."

A cold shiver ran up her spine. "No. Stay here with me. Violence isn't the answer to violence."

Tione seemed to disagree, but he didn't say so. Instead, he disconnected from her, collected Pixie and deposited her in Megan's lap. The dog huffed, but Megan petted her until she calmed and settled into a ball.

"I'm surprised Officer Elliot is taking me seriously."

"It's just 'Elliot,'" he corrected her. "His last name is Tanner. Of course he's taking it seriously. The asshole beat the crap out of you, and that's a serious crime."

She gnawed on her lip, torn between relief and worry. "I'm afraid nothing will come of it," she confessed. "What if Elliot's boss tells him to back off? Charles Senior has his fingers in a lot of pies."

He waved a hand dismissively. "Elliot is like a bulldog when he gets something between his teeth. Trust me, he won't let it go."

She wasn't sure she had as much faith in the man as

Tione did, but arguing the point wouldn't get her anywhere, so she turned her mind to another concern she'd been pondering. "I know I need to call my mum, but I don't want to."

"Why is that?"

"I feel terrible about everything. Her wedding is soon and she's in planning mode. She's so excited, and I don't want to put a damper on that."

Tione sat cross-legged on the floor and Zee sprawled over his lap. "Answer me something. Your mum, brother, and sister are all in Auckland, yeah?"

"Yes, that's right."

"How is it that none of them noticed what was happening with you?"

"It's not their fault," she snapped, quick to defend them. "I hid it well, and none of them ever saw anything to hint about what was going on. Besides, I've hardly seen them lately. Charles always found something to get in the way of our visits."

"There must have been signs." He leapt to his feet, displacing Zee, who fled to the corner and moped. "For God's sake, you must have had bruises or something else to clue them in. They should have been looking out for you."

Hugging Pixie close to her chest, she ignored the little dog's growl. She knew he was trying to help, but this felt like yet another attack. "Quit it, okay? All your pacing is putting me on edge."

He stopped instantly, as she'd known he would. "*Arohamai.* Sorry." He glanced down at his hands, like he didn't know what to do with them, and settled for cramming them into his pockets. "You should tell your mum, and I'm not just saying that because you need her help."

"Okaaay." She drew the word out. "Why, then? Other than the obvious."

"Because she'll be more upset if she finds out down the road and thinks you hid it from her."

She frowned. He had a point. Her mother would be hurt if she thought one of her daughters had needed help and not come to her.

"Fine." She combed her fingers through Pixie's fur. "I'll call her tomorrow. I think I've reached my limit for today."

17

When Megan woke on her second Monday at Sanctuary, she felt lighter. The sun streamed weakly through a gap in her curtains, and she smiled. She'd told people about Charles, and she'd survived. They hadn't turned away from her. In fact, thanks to them, she was proactively reclaiming her life. Surely that was worth celebrating.

She showered, changed into a pair of jeans and a navy blouse, dabbed pink lip gloss over her split lip, which had nearly healed, and walked through the dining hall—where a young couple were flirting over coffee—to the kitchen. Tione had beaten her there and was standing over the stove, scrambling eggs. When he turned to greet her, she bounced onto the balls of her feet and kissed him on the cheek. His eyes widened, but before he could say anything, she wrapped her arms around his waist and rested her face on his chest.

"Thank you for yesterday," she said.

He tentatively hugged her back, his hands pressing into the curve of her lower spine. "You're welcome."

A moment passed, and gradually, she became aware of the way she was plastered to him. She wouldn't dare to hug another man this way, but she couldn't bring herself to let him go, and he seemed to feel the same, lowering his chin to the top of her head and breathing her in. His chest was firm beneath her cheek and she wondered if he worked out. She was seized by the urge to trace the outline of his muscles and discover whether they were as defined as she suspected.

She drew back, but couldn't move away completely because his arms were locked around her and he didn't seem to want to let her go. She allowed herself to drink in the wonder of that. Could a man like him be interested in someone with as much baggage as her? It seemed too much to hope for.

Cut it out, she scolded herself. *You've been single for all of a week. You need time to get your head on straight.*

Nevertheless, she couldn't help thinking that her heart had been detached from Charles for much longer. She had absolutely no lingering feelings for him. That didn't mean she was ready to move on, either. It would be a good while before she recovered from the trauma of her last relationship.

"Do you mind if I make cupcakes while you prepare breakfast?" she asked to break the fraught silence.

"That's fine," he replied, releasing her and turning away to continue scrambling the eggs. "Just don't take up all the counter space."

She watched the lines of his back as he moved, and wanted so badly to kiss the spot between his shoulder blades. "I won't."

She collected the ingredients she'd purchased yesterday and started making a base mix, to which she'd add several different flavorings. She'd decided on four types of cupcake based on the basics she'd purchased and what else she'd found already in the cupboards and freezer—pina colada, passion fruit mojito, tropical mai tai, and strawberry daiquiri. Alcoholic cupcakes was something she'd always wanted to try, but Charles had said they were too unrefined.

Screw Charles and his refined taste buds. She was sure someone else would appreciate her efforts. She separated the mixture into four portions and added the flavorings. Real fruit, a number of essences, and assorted other goodies such as desiccated coconut and miniature alcohol samplers. As she worked, she hummed to herself. She was in her happy place, so preoccupied she didn't notice when Tione left, only twigging that she was alone when she finished scooping batter into cupcake cases and loaded them into the oven.

He'd washed the dishes so the sink was empty. She loaded her mixing bowls and utensils into it and left them to soak, then she hunted down Kat and asked to borrow her phone. It was time to make a long overdue phone call to her mother.

Leaning on the counter in the kitchen, she dialed the familiar number. It rang twice before her mum picked up.

"Rose Talbot speaking. How can I help you?"

"Hi, Mum. It's Megan."

"Megan!" she shrieked. "Where are you? Are you okay? What's going on?" The questions all strung together on a single breath, as happened when her mother was frantic.

"Don't panic. I'm okay." She debated whether to say where she was, but considering Charles had already found her, she had no reason to keep it secret. "I'm in a little town called Haven Bay. The place Mark's friend Sterling moved to. I'm sorry I haven't called. I left my phone behind in Auckland."

"Why?" Rose demanded. "Please explain to me what's happening, darling, because I can't piece it together."

"I... uh..."

Why was this so goddamn hard? Lowering herself to the floor, she squeezed her eyes shut to combat the wooziness. She'd kept her own counsel for so long that now she didn't know how to share. Rose stayed quiet, giving her time to collect herself.

"The thing is..." She wished she didn't have to do this. She didn't want to admit what she'd let happen to her. Not to the strongest woman she'd ever known. She tried again. "The thing is that Charles hit me." She heard a sharp intake of breath but didn't stop. If she didn't get all of this out now, she might never. "More than once. It started a little while ago. On the Friday before last, I left him and came here. I didn't tell any of you because I was so ashamed that I let it happen. God, I should know better, but I didn't see the warning signs, and you all told me I was moving too quickly and I ignored you." She swallowed. "I need your help, Mum."

"Oh, my God," Rose said. "Oh. My. God. He hit you?"

Picking at her cuticles, she said, "Yes."

A wail came through the line. She held the phone away from her ear.

"My poor baby," Rose cried. "You know you can tell me anything, darling. Anything at all. But oh, how did I not see it? You stopped visiting so much, and when you did, he was always there. I just thought he was being attentive. And yes, I was concerned when you decided to move in with him, but I never dreamed he was violent."

"Please don't blame yourself." She held the phone closer to her ear, guilt swamping her. She and her pride were responsible for making Rose feel this way. "He was sneaky, and I hid it well. I'd hoped I could get away from him without anyone ever knowing."

Rose made a tearful sound. "I should have noticed something was wrong. You're my daughter. It's my job to know these things."

Shame washed over her anew. She hated to hear the self-recrimination in her mother's voice.

"Shh, Mum. It's okay. I'm all right. Please don't feel bad. It's not as if it's been going on forever. I just... well, I never thought I'd be the kind of person who was weak enough to let an abuser into my life, and I didn't want you to think worse of me for it. Especially when Mark and Mikayla would never make a mistake like that."

"Oh, baby, I could never think poorly of you. In my line of work, I see all kinds of women who end up where you've been, through no fault of their own. Some of them are strong career women with dozens of staff reporting to them, and they're just as vulnerable to a man like Charles as anyone else."

She wished that made her feel better. But deep down, she couldn't believe it. Rose had been an awesome role model, and yet, Megan had still strayed down this path. Surely that meant something was wrong with her. Some part of her was broken.

"Thank you for saying that."

"I mean it, Meg." Her tone was firm, and Megan felt like a child being scolded. "I can hear the self-pity in your voice, but that's not going to do anyone any good.

Now, you said you needed my help. Do you want me to come and get you? Arrange to have charges filed against that nasty piece of work? Whatever you need, just ask."

She balled her fists until her nails pricked her palms. The tiny jabs of pain kept her from traveling down a road of 'what ifs.' Rose was right. Dwelling on her poor decisions wouldn't help anyone.

"Can you witness my affidavit and help me apply for a restraining order against him?"

"Yes, darling. I can absolutely do that."

TIONE JOGGED ALONG THE BEACH, three of his dogs harnessed to his waist and the salt spray stinging his nostrils. He nodded in greeting as he passed Sterling, who was unlocking the shed where Kat kept the surfboards. The dogs tugged him toward the path back to Sanctuary. Trevor's ears flapped in the wind, Zee grinned widely, and Bella's legs worked overtime to keep up. The combined effect of this was that his pace had increased significantly since he'd adopted them. There was no going slow when he was being pulled along by a two hundred and twenty pounds of dog.

As they crossed the parking lot, he unclipped them from the harness one by one. Trevor bounded around the side of the lodge, disappearing from view. He set Zee free, then Bella, and gratefully slowed to a walk. Trevor came trotting back into the parking lot.

He whistled. "Here, boy."

To his surprise, Trevor didn't race over, instead circling around and heading away. A moment later, he understood why. Trevor had been leading Megan to him.

She rounded the corner and raised a hand to shield her eyes from the sun. For the first time since he'd met her, she was wearing a skirt, her legs on display. They were pale, as though she didn't spend much time outdoors, and slender.

Tione's mouth went dry. God, she was beautiful.

She smiled, and he noticed the scab on her lip had healed. The only signs she'd been injured were the pinkness of new skin, and the cut at her temple. His heart pumped double time, and he hoped that if she noticed, she'd attribute it to the run he'd just returned from.

"You've finished your cupcakes?"

She stopped a few feet from him and bent to scratch behind Trevor's ear. "I finished the cupcakes themselves. Haven't iced them yet." She blew kisses at his dog and didn't look up. "I also talked to my mum."

Pride surged through him. "What did she say?"

Straightening, she looked somewhere over his shoulder. He could tell she wasn't comfortable discussing this, but she was making an effort, and he appreciated that.

"Naturally, she was upset, but it went well, considering." She licked her lips and brought her eyes to his. They glowed amber brown in the sunlight. "The restraining order is under control."

"Good." He reached out and squeezed her shoulder. "We're all so proud of what you're doing."

She nibbled on her lip, and he wanted to tell her to stop and let it heal properly. "I don't understand why you and Kat are going to these lengths for me," she said. "You hardly know me."

"We know enough," he replied. "You're a good person, and we care about you." He swallowed, his throat suddenly scratchy. "*I* care about you."

"I care about you, too, Tee." She gave him the sweetest damn smile he'd ever seen. "Because of you, I have a chance to start over."

"Yeah, well." He shrugged, uncomfortable with the praise and not certain he deserved it. If she knew what had happened in his past, she might not be so willing to entrust herself to his care. In fact, if she knew what he'd done, she'd probably run from him just as eagerly as she was running from her ex. She'd be right to, too.

"Don't be like that," she said. "It's true. I'm not just saying that to butter you up, but I am hoping you'll do me a favor."

He heaved the biggest sigh he could muster. "All right, what do you want from me?"

Her grin widened, and she stopped pestering her lip. "Will you take me into town? I, uh," she shuffled from one foot to the other, a flush creeping up her cheeks, "I want to invite Faith and Brooke over to have cocktails and cupcakes for supper with Kat and I—if Kat has time." She peeked up at him from beneath her lashes. "Is that super lame?"

His heart felt like it was expanding in his chest. Super adorable was more like it. He longed to drop a kiss on her nose, and tell her so, but settled for saying, "Having tasted your baking, I don't think anyone would call it lame." She still looked uncertain, so he continued, "They'll love it."

"You think so?"

"I know so."

"Thanks."

"No problem. I'll whiz through the shower, then we can head out."

They started toward the lodge.

"What about the lunch service?" she asked.

"All ready to go," he said. "You were completely zoned out this morning. I did it all with you right there in the room. The only thing Kat needs to do is lay it out, and I'm sure that won't be a problem."

He glanced over in time to see her lips twist. "Kat's your boss, right?"

"Yeah." Where was this going?

"You must have known her for a long time."

"Three years, give or take. Ever since I moved back from the States. She'd been here for a year or so already. Long enough to have a couple of rooms in the lodge ready for guests."

"Ah. That explains why she lets you get away with so much."

He laughed. "Excuse me?"

Her shoulders hunched, as though she regretted what she'd said. "I just meant that your job seems to be very flexible. I'm a little jealous, to be honest. My bosses have always been demanding and impatient."

He took the stairs to his cabin two at a time, unwilling to admit that his job was simply a means to keep boredom at bay, and that he had enough money in the bank to live several lifetimes without needing to work.

"I didn't mean that as an insult," she said, sounding worried.

Finally, he turned to her. "I know, and I didn't take it that way." Much. "Wait out here. I'll be ready in a few minutes."

Shucking his shirt, he tossed it on the floor and stepped out of his shorts. He turned the shower on and stepped under the blasting water. The high pressure shower head had been one of his few indulgences when he built the cabin. He allowed the sweat to rinse from his body, then soaped, toweled himself dry, and dressed in jeans and a black t-shirt.

On the way out, he caught sight of his liquor cabinet beneath the counter and recalled the dozen or so bottles of spirits stored from when he'd first moved to town. He'd never opened them, taking it as a personal challenge to ignore them for as long as possible, but he'd passed whatever test he'd set himself, and they should be used. There was no point in them sitting in his cabinet for another three years.

"Hey," he said as he closed the door and joined Megan on the deck. She was leaning on the railing, looking out over the garden. The sun touched her blonde hair, turning it golden. She could have been an angel. "I've got some alcohol you can use for those cocktails tonight, if you'd like."

"Really?"

He went to her side. "Yeah. From memory there's vodka, rum, whiskey, tequila, and a few other things."

She glanced over at him. "It's very kind of you to offer, but I don't want to use up your stash."

He chuckled. "I haven't touched the stuff since I moved here. You may as well take advantage of it. No one else is going to."

She squinted, and pursed her lips, assessing him in a way that made him squirm. "Okay, if you're sure. That would be lovely, thank you."

"No problem." He straightened and jangled his keys in his pocket. "Shall we go?"

She nodded. "Let's."

18

As they passed over the bridge, Tione sensed Megan's tension ratchet up a notch, but she didn't say anything. He switched the radio on to Tahu FM for the short drive to The Shack. When he couldn't find a park, he pulled over a couple of blocks away and they walked side by side along Marine Parade to the ice cream parlor. There were only two customers browsing the options, so they headed straight for the counter.

Faith beamed, her hazel eyes sparkling behind black-framed glasses. "Emma Watson, delightful to see you again."

"Alexandra," Megan replied with a smile. "Do you have a minute?"

"For you, I have ten."

"Excellent." Megan looked down at her hands, and fidgeted with the hem of her shirt. She was nervous, he realized, and totally enchanting. Didn't she know that nobody could refuse her anything? Especially not when she resembled a little girl about to ask her crush to the Sadie Hawkins dance.

"I, um, made some cupcakes earlier," she said. "They're cocktail themed, and I have frosting and fondant to decorate them with. I was wondering if you'd like to come around this evening and do that with me? We could have actual cocktails at the same time. Tee has volunteered to share his stash."

Faith's gaze flitted to him, and she raised a brow. He winced. She knew that he was hardly an altruistic guy, and now she was onto him. He crossed his fingers behind his back and hoped she wouldn't call him on his obvious attraction to Megan.

"I would love to," she replied. "That honestly sounds amazing. Thanks for thinking of me." She winked. "I can't wait to try your baking."

Joy stole over Megan's expression, and Tione's heart beat a little faster. His fingers curled into his palms, and his gut twisted with how much he wanted her. But he kept his hands to himself and studied the floor. He'd already given away too much in front of Faith.

"Hopefully they came out okay," Megan said. "It's my first time trying them, but it's something I've wanted to do for a while." Her chin took on a stubborn set, and he suspected Charles Wentworth was to blame for why she hadn't made them sooner. The guy had a lot to answer for.

"I'm sure they'll be divine," Faith said. "Say, you should come over and help me brainstorm new ice cream flavors some time. It's so hard to find anyone who knows as much about what makes a winning combination as I do."

"I'd be happy to help." This time, she didn't make any disclaimers about how soon she might be leaving, and something warmed inside him. Had she decided to stay? God, he hoped so.

"Brilliant."

"So I'll see you tonight? Around eight?"

"You're on." The customers approached the counter, and Faith smiled at them. "I'll see you then, cutie pie."

As they exited The Shack, Megan was vibrating with barely suppressed energy.

"Did you really think she'd say no?" he asked.

"Yes." She shrugged. "No. I don't know. It's been so long since I hosted anything for my own friends, it feels strange. I got used to only hosting dinners for Charles's colleagues, and they were fairly tense."

He understood why, and if he was ever alone with that jackass, he was going to rip his kidneys out through his throat.

"Where to next?" he asked.

"Brooke's place." Their arms bumped against each other, and he wished she were wearing short sleeves so he could have felt her skin on his. The few hugs they'd shared weren't enough. He longed for more contact. "Kat said she lives with her boyfriend, Jack. I don't know where that is, but maybe you do?"

He rolled his eyes at her. "This is Haven Bay. Of course I know. Jack has a place at the west end of town." He unlocked his car, and they hopped in. He circuited around the town center, in no mood to drive ten miles an hour while tourists wandered over the road willy-nilly. When he parked outside, Megan sat there for a moment studying the house.

"It's nice," she said.

"Probably nothing like you see in Auckland."

She grinned. "Exactly."

An old model of car was in the driveway and they passed it on their way to the porch. Megan strode to the door and knocked. When it opened, Brooke filled the doorway, balancing her laptop in the crook of her arm, her hair piled haphazardly atop her head.

"Hi, Hope—uh, I mean, Megan." Her nose wrinkled. "Sorry."

"No need to be," Megan said. "It's not your fault I gave the wrong name."

Brooke nodded. "Well, it's nice to meet you properly. Hey, Tee."

He jerked his chin at her, the equivalent of a greeting.

Brooke glanced down at her computer, then asked, "Would you like to come in?"

"No, no, that's all right," Megan said. "I can see you're busy. I just came by to ask if you'd like to come to a cupcakes and cocktails night at Sanctuary this evening. Perhaps around eight?"

Brooke laughed. "As if you even have to ask. If there are cupcakes, I'm there."

Megan's grin spread wider, threatening to re-open the split in her lip. She bounced on her toes, and he got the impression she barely restrained herself from squealing.

"That's great! I've invited Faith as well, and I'll stop by and see if Kat can come when we head back. Is it pathetic to say I'm really looking forward to it?"

"Not even a little." Brooke laid her laptop down and hugged Megan. "You've got to be the sweetest person I've ever met. I can't believe how totally cute you are." She shot a look at Tione, as if daring him to contradict. "Isn't she the cutest?"

"Without a doubt."

Cocking her head, Brooke frowned at him, as if she

wanted to know whether he was taking the piss. He didn't explain himself. She didn't need to know how completely Megan had him wrapped around her little finger.

"Glad you agree."

"Quit it," Megan muttered, clearly embarrassed. "We'll let you get back to studying. I'll see you later, okay?"

"Okeydokey. Bye for now." Brooke waved them off.

They returned to Sanctuary and Tione went to the kitchen to make a start on dinner while Megan searched for Kat. He'd never say it out loud, but she had such a positive energy about her and it gave him warm fuzzies to see her feeling more confident in her own skin. He could see her slotting so easily into his life that he had to remind himself she may only be around temporarily. Even if she stayed, it would be best for her if he kept his distance.

If only it were that easy.

AFTER DINNER, Megan helped Tione clean up, then waited while he brought his bottles of liquor up from the cabin. Once she had them, she ushered him out, grabbed a slab of fondant from the cupboard, assembled the tools of the trade—a rolling pin, a couple of tiny brushes, a number of knives, a miniature pizza cutter, food dye, edible glitter, sugar paste, and a few other bits and pieces—and set to work preparing a batch of royal icing. Lastly, she made a start on the buttercream, beating butter and confectioner's sugar together until it had the right texture and the color had paled. She gathered a number of flavorings and dithered over whether to add them herself, or wait and see what the girls wanted to do. She opted for the latter.

While she washed her hands, she debated whether to play background music, and if so, what type. At one of Charles's events, it would have been a no-brainer. Some variety of upmarket classical music so he could pretend to be sophisticated. But this wasn't a supper to hobnob with the elite, and she was determined to have fun. In a gesture of defiance, she selected a girl power playlist and connected it to the speakers. If her new friends didn't approve, they could tell her so. Checking her reflection in the shiny surface of the refrigerator, she was pleased by how much her bruises had faded.

"Not too shabby," Kat said from the doorway.

Megan flinched, her hand going to her heart. "God, you frightened me."

The smile dropped off Kat's face. "Sorry. I thought you heard me coming."

"I was a little preoccupied," she admitted, embarrassed at having been caught checking herself out.

But Kat didn't comment. She came into the kitchen and leaned against the counter. "Do you need a hand with anything?"

"Nope." She wiped her sweaty palms on her jeans. "Everything is good to go. Would you like a drink?" The question came easily. She was accustomed to plying people with alcohol and food to keep them happy.

"Sure." Kat looked over the selection. "What have we got?"

"A whole lot of booze, by the looks of it." They both turned as Brooke entered, wearing a t-shirt that had "talk nerdy to me" written across the chest.

Faith followed, carrying a cardboard box. "Mm." She stopped and inhaled deeply. "It smells amazing in here. What is that, coconut?" She sniffed again. "Pineapple?"

"Yes, and yes." Megan crossed to her as she set the box on the counter. "What have you got there?"

Faith grinned, her teeth flashing between crimson lips. "In honor of your cocktail theme, I brought Irish cream and chocolate stout ice creams."

"Together?" Megan asked, both intrigued and horrified by the prospect.

Laughing, Faith waved a hand in the air. "Lord, no. Separately. Where can I put them?"

Kat opened the freezer, and shifted items around until the box would fit. "Over here."

They lifted it in, then gathered around the liquor bottles, eyeing them appreciatively.

"Nice collection," Faith said. "Are these yours, Megan?"

"No, they're Tione's. He said he's had them for years and not drunk them, so we may as well."

"Really?" The gleam in Brooke's eyes became speculative. "He hasn't let anyone else touch his stash. He hardly even lets people through his front door."

Megan shrugged, unsettled by the observation. She'd certainly spent her fair share of time in the cozy cabin, and hadn't realized that was out of the ordinary.

"So, what's the plan?" Kat asked.

"First, cocktails. Mix and match however you like. Then I thought we'd decorate the cupcakes I made earlier. I have a bunch of different things we can use." She gestured to the frosting, fondant, and other tools on the counter. "We can be creative."

"It's like arts and crafts, with food," Brooke said, grinning. "I love it."

Relief filtered through Megan, and her shoulders relaxed. She hadn't realized how much tension she'd been holding in them. "Exactly, and if anyone needs help working out how to use something, or coming up with ideas, I'm here to help."

"Awesome." Kat selected four tall glasses from the cabinet and poured a generous portion of cranberry juice into one, then added a splash of pineapple juice, and a healthy dash of coconut rum. She took a sip and smiled, which stretched the scar down the left side of her face. Megan wanted to know how she'd gotten it, but hadn't asked because she didn't want to be intrusive. "That's good."

Faith shimmied Kat to the side and took her place, expertly mixing liquids together in two of the glasses, offering one to Megan when she'd finished. "Do you trust me?"

In response, Megan drank the amber liquid, sweetness exploding in her mouth. As she swallowed, the alcohol burned down the back of her throat.

"You like it?" Faith asked.

She nodded. "I do. What is it?"

"My own variation on an amaretto sour with bourbon."

Brooke wrinkled her nose. "Bourbon. Not my favorite thing." She poured herself a simple vodka with orange juice and checked out the labels on the other bottles.

Meanwhile, Megan took the cupcakes from the pantry and pointed out the different flavors. "There's pina colada, passion fruit mojito, tropical mai tai, and strawberry daiquiri. The frosting over there," she motioned toward it, "is a basic buttercream, but there are a bunch of ingredients you can add to flavor it. Liquor, coconut, vanilla, fruit sauce. If you'd like to try using fondant, there's plenty of that, and also cookie cutters to make shapes." She'd lost all of her specialized fondant cutters when she ran away, and cookie cutters was the best she could get from the local minimart.

"Yum," Kat said, placing one of each flavor on a plate and scooping a dollop of frosting into a bowl. "This was a great idea, by the way."

Her cheeks warmed. "Thanks."

"You don't mind if we eat them, right?" Brooke asked.

She laughed. "Of course not. That's the whole point. Go right ahead. Anything you don't eat, you can take home with you. I don't want two dozen cupcakes left behind. Do you know what that number of calories would do to me?"

Brooke and Kat exchanged glances, and Faith rolled her eyes. "As if. Girl, I get the impression you could eat an entire batch of brownies and not gain an ounce. Have some sympathy for us mere mortals. The sugar goes straight to my hips."

Megan scanned the outline of Faith's body. The other woman had opted to wear high-waisted three-quarter-length pants and a striped tank top that was knotted at the waist. On Megan the outfit would have looked ridiculous, but Faith wouldn't have been out of place in a fifties pinup calendar.

"There's nothing wrong with your hips," she said. "You're gorgeous, and you rock that retro vibe."

"Aw, thanks sweetie!"

"Agreed," Brooke added. "If cupcakes give you curves like that, I say eat as many as you like."

Faith piled cupcakes on a plate, shaking her head. "You two are going to be bad for my waistline."

Brooke grinned. "But good for your ego."

Megan chose a strawberry daiquiri cupcake, whisked a smidgen of strawberry sauce into buttercream, and spooned it into a piping bag. With deft movements, she covered the cupcake in a series of buttercream rosettes, and then sprinkled edible glitter over the top. She drank more of her cocktail and wandered around to see what the other girls were doing. Brooke had smoothed frosting over one of her cupcakes, rolled out a portion of fondant, and was cutting a shape from it, her lip between her teeth as she concentrated.

"Is that the Starfleet insignia?"

Brooke finished a precise cut and dropped the knife. "Guilty."

"Impressive." The design was reasonably intricate. "If you have trouble moving it, try using a spatula, but be gentle."

She moved on and paused by Kat, who'd taken a break to drink her cocktail. She seemed to have completely ignored the frosting and dug around in the refrigerator for fresh fruit, which she'd sliced and set atop her cupcakes.

"Sweet isn't really my thing," she explained.

"Fair enough. They look great."

Faith had gone the opposite of Kat. The lone cupcake she'd started on was extravagantly decorated, with coconut in the frosting, piled high, edible glitter scattered over it, along with sugar pearls that she must have brought herself. She was working on a complex fondant butterfly, coloring it pink and purple with food dye.

"Wow."

Faith bent low, her glasses perched on the end of her nose, moving a tiny paintbrush with confidence. “Let’s hope it tastes as good as it looks. By the way,” she nodded toward a pile of crumbs that had once been a cupcake, “your baking is amazing. They’re fluffy and moist. The best I’ve had in ages.”

Pleasure suffused her, and Megan hoped her blush wasn’t as obvious as it felt. “Thanks. They’re nothing fancy, but I adore cupcakes.”

“Nothing fancy?” Faith put the finishing touches on her butterfly and straightened. “Do you have any idea how much people would pay for cupcakes like that?”

Megan shrugged. She’d never tried to sell them. The bakery she’d worked at hadn’t been the right place, and she’d had nowhere else to trial them.

“I’m serious,” Faith continued, her hazel gaze direct. “These babies are *good*. Have you decided whether you’re staying in the bay?”

“Please stay,” Brooke chimed in. “We’d love to have you here.”

Megan wet her lips. “I’d like to,” she began cautiously, “but I’m not sure how things will play out yet.”

“You’re welcome here for as long as you need,” Kat told her, and excitement fizzed through her insides. It had been a long time since she’d experienced this level of kindness from anyone outside her family.

Faith placed the butterfly atop the frosting. “If you do stay, you should consider joining me at The Shack. I’ve been looking for a business partner to help me expand for ages, but I haven’t found the right fit. I think you and I would be dynamite together, and your cupcakes are just the thing to pair with my ice creams.”

Wait. Hold up. Was Faith asking what she thought she was?

The pulse in the base of Megan's neck thrummed wildly, and all of her senses heightened. She could smell the sweetness of the fondant, the tartness of strawberries, the sharp aroma of alcohol. Tilting her head to the side, she watched the woman's lips move.

"Are..." Her voice came out high and squeaky. She was so thrilled she couldn't speak properly. Taking a breath, she tried again. "Are you asking me to be your business partner?"

Faith bit into an unfrosted cupcake, her eyes closing as she savored the taste. When she swallowed, she replied, "Yes, I suppose I am."

Megan grabbed the counter for support. The invitation was everything she'd never been brave enough to admit to herself that she wanted, but as soon as she embraced the possibility, she heard Charles in her head, reminding her—as he always had—that her cupcakes were nothing special and she should aim higher. Or not aim for anything at all, and be content to play second fiddle to him for all her life.

Screw him.

"Thank you, that sounds like a wonderful opportunity. I'll think about it."

"Tee would like it if you stayed," Brooke added slyly.

Embarrassment churned in her gut when she realized how badly she wanted Brooke's words to be true.

"Butt out," Kat admonished. "It's not our place to interfere with anyone else's love life."

"Now that you mention it, he did seem quite taken with her," Faith said, and Megan wished the floor would swallow her up. Despite that, a secret corner of her heart wanted them to continue. Could she dare to believe that Tione was interested in her romantically?

Don't get ahead of yourself.

"I don't think there's anything to it," she said, even as disappointment soured her stomach. "He's just being nice to me out of pity, and because I help him cook."

Brooke rolled her eyes. "Tee has never been nice to a person out of pity. That man does and says exactly what he likes." She paused for a moment, then added, "And he likes you."

"Come on, Brooke. Stuff a cupcake in your face and leave the poor girl alone," Kat ordered. She turned to Megan. "Can you show us how you piped the frosting into roses like that?"

Resisting the urge to wipe her sweaty upper lip, Megan latched onto the distraction with gratitude. "It's super easy. If you all gather round, I'll demonstrate."

19

When the lights in the kitchen flickered off, Tione put the dogs to bed—with the exception of Pixie, who he tucked under his arm—and left the cabin. He'd been keeping an eye on the women, because for some reason, he was nervous on Megan's behalf. He wanted the evening to go well for her.

He entered the lodge through the back entrance and traipsed down the hall to her door, where he knocked softly. He heard shuffling in the bedroom, then the door opened and she blinked up at him, a big smile on her face.

"Hey," she said, her eyes dropping to Pixie. She petted the dog's head while Pixie squirmed and tried to hide her face in Tione's t-shirt. "She'll warm up to me eventually."

"Don't hold your breath. She's a territorial little devil."

"I don't blame her. Hey, would it be okay if Trevor stays with me again tonight? It makes me feel safer when he's nearby, and I like his company."

Considering what she'd been through, this didn't surprise him. "He's yours any time you want. I can bring him over shortly." The big baby wouldn't mind being roused from bed if it meant he got to cuddle with Megan.

"Yes, please."

He shifted on the spot, wondering if it would be rude to invite himself in. Hovering in the hallway made him uncomfortable. If Kat found him here, she'd be onto him in a flash.

"How was your cupcakes and cocktails thing?"

She beamed. "It was great. Everyone seemed to enjoy themselves, and guess what?" She didn't give him the chance to speak. "Faith asked me to be her business partner and sell cupcakes at her store. Can you believe that?"

What he couldn't believe was how breathtakingly beautiful she was when her cheeks were flushed with excitement. She was the most exquisite thing he'd ever seen. Better than any expensive piece of artwork on display in the homes of the Silicon Valley millionaires he'd been friends with.

"I'm not surprised at all," he told her. "You shouldn't be either. People like to be around you, and your baking is some of the best I've ever tasted."

She dipped her head, a veil of dark blonde hair falling over her face. "You don't have to flatter me."

His brows drew together. The woman had no concept of how appealing she was to others. "I'm just being honest."

She tilted her head, bringing her hot cocoa eyes into the light. "Really?"

He sighed. Reassuring others wasn't his style. "Would I say it if it wasn't true?"

She stared at him for a moment as though trying to read his expression, then she stretched onto her toes and kissed him right on the mouth. Her lips were soft and lingered on his, and she smelled of sugar and pineapple. His mind reeled. He hadn't expected this. What should he do?

Kiss her back?

Disengage?

He wanted to slip his tongue inside her mouth and taste her, but it might not be that kind of kiss. Maybe it was just a kiss of gratitude.

In the end, he was saved from making a decision when Pixie yelped and Megan drew back, averting her eyes. "I'm sorry. I don't know what I was thinking. I shouldn't have done that; it was totally inappropriate." She refused to look up. "I—just—you're such a great guy, and I..." She trailed off miserably.

Tione was spinning out. He wasn't equipped to deal with a situation like this, but it was clear she felt embarrassed and she had no reason to. If he was some other guy, and they were in a different situation, he'd be jumping for joy.

"Hey, it's okay." He swallowed and searched for something soothing to say. He thought of Shane. Shane was a sensitive guy. What would he say in this position? "It's perfectly reasonable that you'd feel something for me after everything you've been through," he said, wondering if he sounded like as much of a douche as he felt. "But you're in a vulnerable place, and I don't want to take advantage of that."

"Oh, my God." She buried her face in her hands and groaned. "This is so humiliating. I can't believe I kissed you."

"It's okay," he repeated, wishing he could take back this entire conversation and start over. "I didn't mind."

Didn't mind? He'd happily have devoured her if he thought he could live with himself afterward. If he thought he deserved her, and that he wouldn't fail her. But he would. If she let him close to her, he would fail her.

She dropped her hands and her eyes were bright with tears, effectively sucker punching him in the gut. He wanted to take her in his arms and comfort her, but considering he'd been the one responsible for her pain, he doubted she'd want that.

"You wouldn't have been taking advantage of me if you'd kissed me back," she said, her tone firm. "I made the first move, and I'm sorry if it made you uncomfortable." She pressed her lips together and he opened his mouth to talk, but she shushed him. "I really am sorry. I would never have done it, except that I thought you might feel the same way, even if the timing sucks." She shrugged. "I like you, Tee."

With his free hand, he grabbed hers and held it tightly so she couldn't escape into her room. His brain had finally stopped glitching, and words spilled from his mouth so fast he didn't have time to mull them over or moderate them.

"I like you, too."

So damn trite. Such a poor representation of how the mere sight of her made his heart do an extra beat.

"You didn't read me wrong. God, you're the sweetest person I've ever met, and you're so fucking beautiful, but you've just come out of a traumatic relationship, and I'm not the kind of guy you need right now, and even if I was,

I don't want to rush you into anything you're not ready for."

By the time he finished, he was panting, and her eyes were wide, her lips parted. Breath eased between them. One of the tears that had been gathering in her eyes trailed down her cheek.

"Don't cry," he begged.

"They're not sad tears," she said, sniffling. "Why do you have to be so nice?"

He chuckled, relieved beyond reason. It wasn't often that people accused him of being overly nice. "It's customary to smile when people say nice things."

Her lips curved up, and now that he knew the sensation of them against his own, he longed to drop a kiss onto them.

"By the way," she added. "If you're worried about being a rebound, you don't need to be. I haven't felt anything for Charles for a while." The smile fell away. "But you're right that I should get my life sorted out before I try to move on."

He'd been right about something? Hallelujah.

"Would you like to have a cupcake and snuggle up to watch a baking show?" she asked, stepping to the side so he could come into her room. "I won't make any moves on you, I swear. Just snuggling." She sent him a cheeky grin. "Or are you too manly for that?"

"Hell no, I'm not too manly for that." He crossed the threshold before she changed her mind, and that single step felt momentous. As if he was stepping over a precipice that signaled a change in their relationship from friends to something more, and even though a whispered voice in the back of his mind told him he shouldn't, he sat on the bed, setting Pixie down. She skittered over to a pillow, circled several times, and settled in the center of it.

"Little diva," he muttered.

Megan closed the door and turned on the television, which she must have borrowed because guest rooms didn't usually have them. She switched through the channels until she found *The Great British Bake Off*. The episode had started ten minutes ago, but the contestants hadn't gotten very far yet.

"Where do you want me?" he asked.

"Well, I plan to climb under the covers and get comfortable," she said. "You can sit wherever you like."

Once she'd wriggled into place, propping a pillow between the wall and her back, Tione slipped in beside her. Reaching over, he switched off the light, then put his arm around her waist. She rested her head on his shoulder, and proceeded to narrate the show to him, explaining who each of the contestants were, and what they were doing right and wrong. It was the most confident he'd heard her, and he allowed himself to relax and enjoy the sensation of her soft, slender body beside his. He turned to nuzzle the top of her head. Even her hair smelled of sugar paste. Smiling, he brushed a kiss over her temple so gently she didn't notice.

He wished the moment could last forever. There, in the dark, they were closer than they'd ever been, and it felt like they belonged together. As though he could be someone who deserved her. It was a pipe dream, but he clung to it as he listened to her quiet words and pretended it was an accident when he scooched closer, until she was nearly on his lap.

What he wouldn't give to end every night like this. It was perfect. *She* was perfect. But much as she might be under the impression he was her knight in shining armor, he wasn't, and he couldn't ever be. Instead, if she wasn't careful, he'd be the devil who dragged her under.

After a while, her arm flopped across his stomach and her breathing deepened, indicating that she'd fallen asleep. He extricated himself, switched off the television, and left Pixie in the bed while he trekked out to the cabin to bring Trevor back. When the mastiff was curled on the floor, he locked the bedroom door and returned to his cabin with Pixie, where he lay sleeplessly in his own bed, staring at the ceiling and wondering how the pint-sized city girl had come to mean too much to him.

MEGAN PRESSED her face into the pillow and groaned. Oh God, had she actually thrown herself at Tione last night? Yeah, she had, and he'd let her down ever so gently. She groaned again. Man, she'd messed up. Big time.

Rolling over, she reached for the light switch and blinked as her eyes adjusted. She was about to get up when she noticed something that didn't belong. In the center of a small plate on her bedside cabinet was an apricot Danish, with a hastily scrawled note beside it. Tione must have brought it in for her. Her insides turned gooey as caramel sauce. The Danish had to be a good sign, right?

She leaned over and read the note.

Megan

Eat this and come find me.

T

The words were simple and to the point. So very him. They shouldn't have caused a flurry of excitement in her belly, but they did. He wanted to see her. Maybe he'd been telling the truth when he said he was interested but didn't think the timing was right.

She bit into the Danish, savoring the explosion of sweet yet tart apricot onto her tongue. It oozed out the corner of her mouth and she wiped it up with a finger and licked it off. Mm. This was what it tasted like to have a man in her life who cared about her. Charles had never brought her pastries for breakfast. Heck, if she'd served herself a pastry, he'd have clucked his tongue and taken it away with a remark about how she needed to watch her figure.

Bastard.

In a burst of defiance, she crammed the rest of the Danish into her mouth and chewed while she hunted for clothes. Trevor stirred on the floor, and she experienced another wave of happiness. Tione must have brought him over after he'd left, and why would he do that if he didn't care?

Trevor stretched, releasing a doggy sigh, then shook, his floppy ears slapping the sides of his head. She snorted, covering her mouth so she didn't spill crumbs everywhere. The dog sidled over and leaned against her leg. She dropped to her knees and wrapped her arms around him, rubbing her cheek on the fur of his shoulder and petting wherever her hands landed.

"You're such a good boy," she crooned, and he gave a giant yawn of agreement. "Such a brave boy, watching out for me all night." He slumped onto his back, his feet in the air. Laughing, she rubbed his belly. "Is that what you want?"

His hind leg kicked as she found a particularly good spot, as if to say "yeah, just like that." She scratched his stomach for a few moments more, then dressed in fresh clothes, combed her hair, and brushed her teeth. When she emerged from the bathroom, he was sitting by the window, looking longingly outside, so she set him free. He beelined out into the garden while she went in the other direction, to find Tione in the kitchen. He was standing at the sink, elbow deep in dishwater, his tattooed arms glistening wet, muscles bunching as he worked. She swallowed. Holy hell, he was hot. Nothing like the men she'd dated before, but perhaps that was part of the appeal. There was a rawness about him, and she loved it.

"Gonna stand there and ogle me all morning?"

She jumped, blushing furiously. Caught in the act.

He turned, a funny little smile on his face, and dried his hands on a towel. She just stood there, not sure how to react, and he sauntered over, took her hands, and pulled her into a loose hug. Suddenly her face was buried in man-chest, and she tried not to sniff him like a freak, but he must have showered recently because he smelled amazing. His forearms rested low on her back, a gesture intimate enough to ease her fears, and she wanted to stay there, in the warm cocoon of his embrace, forever.

Angling her head up, she smiled. "Hi. Thank you for the Danish."

His dark eyes searched hers, and his lips twitched up. Unable to resist, she ran a hand over his bearded jaw. He tucked her hair behind her ears, and his gaze fell to her mouth only a moment before his lips did. The kiss was chaste and over before she could react, but it left no doubt in her mind that whatever was between them had become more than a friendship.

"You're welcome," he said, his breath whispering over her. "And good morning."

"Good morning," she repeated, all capacity for rational thought gone. His whiskers brushed her skin as he pulled her into another half-hug. He buried his face in the crook of her neck but left enough space between them that she didn't feel overwhelmed. In fact, if he kept this up, she'd be a puddle on the floor. Then he cleared his throat and stepped back, his expression returning to its typical neutral setting.

"You should make one of those foamy coffees and get ready to go. I have plans for us."

Flutters of anticipation filled her. "You do?"

"Yeah, I do."

She could tell from his smirk that she wouldn't find out any more details. Her heart lifted, and she buzzed with excitement. He'd made *plans* for them. He'd been thinking about her, and he wanted to spend time with her. No games, no manipulations. He'd said yesterday that he was interested in her, and his actions so far supported his words. What a pleasant change.

"Okay." Grinning, she fixed herself a coffee and also made one for him, sprinkling extra chocolate powder on top. Then she headed back through the dining hall, with the intention of getting her shoes and a jersey. Before she made it out the other side, Kat waved her over, and gestured for her to sit.

Leaning close, she whispered, "What have you done with Tee?"

Megan frowned, sipping her coffee to buy herself time. "What do you mean?"

"That man is usually as affectionate as a brick wall."

"I—uh—he is?" she stammered. That wasn't the sense she'd gotten from him at all.

"Yeah. He means well, but he can come off as a little cold."

"Oh, no." Her jaw dropped. "He's not cold at all. He might be the loveliest, most supportive guy I've ever met, with the exception of my brother." But the love she felt for Mark was a world away from what she felt for Tione. It was like her heart had grown wings, and they were unfurling, ready to fly.

Kat smiled in satisfaction. "Good. I'd hate to think his attraction to you is one-sided."

Megan's eyes darted to the kitchen. Seeing that he was still occupied with the dishes, she turned back to Kat and murmured, "It's definitely not one-sided. But he wants to take things slow. He's worried about my mental state, I think."

She nodded. "As he should be." She spread cream cheese on her bagel and topped it with jam. "That said, I hope you don't let fear hold you back. Tee is a great guy. He'd never hurt you. Not in any way."

Megan swallowed, and focused on her coffee, which was safer than trying to keep an even expression. "I know he wouldn't. Don't worry, I'm not about to miss out on something wonderful because I'm scared, or because the timing sucks." She licked cream off her upper lip. "It might surprise you to learn this, but I actually know what I want from a relationship. My brother fell in love last year. His girlfriend lived at the other end of the country and the relationship wasn't convenient for either of them, but they love each other so much they made it work. That's the kind of love I dream of having for myself."

Kat's hand landed on hers. "You'll get it." She squeezed, and returned Megan's smile. "I know you will."

20

TIONE'S MOUTH remained dry no matter how much water he drank, and his stomach quivered in a way it hadn't since he first moved to Silicon Valley, back when everyone he met had intimidated him. On top of that, his palms were sweating, and he badly needed to get his beard trimmed. He'd glanced in the mirror this morning and been taken aback by his reflection. But he'd get to that soon. For now, he needed to get through his outing with Megan.

Please let her like this surprise.

He knew she loved his dogs, but plenty of people liked dogs without being as dog-mad as he was. If this backfired, she might think of him as the crazy dog man forevermore. Damn, but he was out of practice with this man–woman thing. He swept the kitchen floor and tried to recall the last time he'd taken a girl out.

It must have been years ago. He'd had a wild time in Silicon Valley, partying and sleeping with more than his fair share of women, but it had gotten old. Indiscriminate affairs had long since lost their shine, and he'd never been one of those guys who needed sex, as much as he certainly enjoyed it. At the very least, he hadn't been on a date since he'd been hired to dig into Michele Franklin and inadvertently wound up with feelings for her. After things went terribly wrong, he hadn't thought he deserved to be romantically involved with anyone. He still wasn't sure he did, but he'd woken up with a brilliant idea and hadn't been able to ignore it because he was so sure it would make Megan smile.

He was a sucker for her smile.

He finished sweeping, wiped down the counter, and glanced through into the dining hall, noticing that Megan had joined Kat, and was deep in conversation with her. A sense of rightness settled in his gut. From what he could tell, she was slotting seamlessly into his group of friends. Kat liked her, as did Brooke, and Faith was prepared to take her on as a business partner. She fit here, and he hoped she could see that as clearly as he did. The last thing he wanted was for her to up and go back to Auckland.

Slipping out the fire exit, he grabbed the harness from his cabin and corralled the mutts, then knocked on her window to see if she'd returned yet, not wanting to stampede through the house with Trevor, Bella and Zee tied to his waist. When she appeared behind the glass, he gestured for her to come outside and join him.

"What are we doing?" she asked as she closed the foyer door.

"It's a surprise."

"But the dogs are coming?"

"Yeah."

She grinned. "Well, okay then."

He handed her the leash attached to Pixie's rhinestone collar. "Do you mind taking Pix? We've got a short walk to get where we're going."

"Sure thing."

He kept an eye on her as she carefully wrapped the leash around her wrist, as if to make sure the Chihuahua wouldn't suddenly bolt and rip it from her grasp. He concealed a smile. She'd obviously spent enough time around dogs to know the correct way to walk them, but not enough to be able to judge when caution was or wasn't warranted. Pixie could pull so hard she strained a muscle and Megan would still be able to remain in control of her with nothing more than a couple of fingers.

They made their way around the end of the building, crossed the bridge, and started down the road. The dogs battled to go faster, but he maintained his pace, although he'd be sore around the middle later.

"Are we going far?" Megan asked, breezing alongside him, apparently oblivious to his struggle for control.

"Not too far," he replied, noncommittal. She narrowed her eyes, but he pretended not to see. He wanted to surprise her, so sue him. She'd find out what they were doing soon enough.

A crisp breeze stirred his hair, and in the distance, the sun was rising to reveal a cloudless blue sky. It was a perfect autumn morning. They passed by the glamping ground, which was largely empty because the temperature had dropped too low for people to camp, regardless of how nice the tents were. Beyond the glamping ground, they reached the school, where buildings were silhouetted against the ocean, and he turned into the adjoining sports field.

Megan gasped, and clapped a hand to her mouth.

"Oh, my God." She jumped with delight, then winced, her hand flying to her ribs. "Ugh. Keep forgetting about that." Straightening, she grinned at him. "Are we doing what I think we're doing?"

Out on the open field he'd set up an agility course with a ramp, several jumps, posts to run between, a crawl tunnel, a seesaw, and an elevated ring.

"Wait and see." He unclipped the dogs and set them free, knowing that they wouldn't leave the field. Then he called Bella to heel and, as Megan watched, he led her through the course. He'd never done this with an audience. Bella wasn't a competitive agility dog, and he'd only purchased this equipment to keep her from getting bored, but she'd taken to it well. Now she performed like a champ, climbing over the ramp, leaping the hurdles, crawling through the tunnel, and winding between the posts. When she jumped through the ring to finish, he came to a stop, puffing, and Megan clapped.

"Bravo!" she cried. "That was incredible. I've never seen anything like it."

Bella sat, and he rewarded her with a treat. She snaffled it from his palm, wolfed it down, and padded over to Megan, who patted her head and fussed over her.

"What a clever girl! You're so pretty, and so well-behaved." Bella drank up the praise, and Tione rolled his eyes. There wasn't much she enjoyed more than attention. "Does she do shows?"

"Not unless you count showing off for the kids. They love to put her through her paces during afternoon break."

"I bet they do." She unhooked Pixie from her leash and the little dog trotted off to join the others. "Can

Trevor…" She trailed off, laughing. "Of course not. He's too big for the tunnel."

"Bella is the only one who does the course. I'd like to teach Zee, but so far, I haven't been able to get her interested." He strode to Megan's side and dropped a kiss on her cheek, unable to resist. She smelled of coffee and vanilla, and he wanted to bury his face in the crook of her neck and breathe her in, but instead he offered her a dog treat to give Bella. "Would you like to have a go?"

A smile split her face. "Really? Yes, I'd love to. What do I do?"

"Come with me." Placing a hand on her elbow, he steered her to the beginning of the course. Bella ran ahead of them, eager for a repeat.

"I can't believe you organized this for me," she said, and when he glanced down, her cheeks were flushed a delicate pink and her eyes sparkled. "This is the best surprise ever."

That smile hit him like a shot put to the gut, and he had to clear his throat before he could respond. "Glad you like it."

"Like it?" she asked. "I love it. I can't believe people really do this. I always thought it was one of those things you saw on TV, but no one actually did in real life."

His lips twitched. Her joy from something so simple was endearing as hell. "It's a real thing, all right, and you're about to do it." He released her. "There are a few hand signals you need to use. This," he demonstrated for her, "means 'jump.' This," he changed his gesture, "means 'down' or 'crawl,' and this means 'up.' Repeat them for me."

She did, and when she made a mistake, he took her hand and guided her fingers into the right position, relishing the opportunity to touch her and feel the sizzle of attraction between them. Each brush of skin on skin drew the tension tighter.

He dropped her hand and backed away. "Your turn."

"Now?" She nibbled her lip, and looked nervously at the course. "What if she doesn't do what I say?"

He shrugged. "Then there's no harm done, and we start again."

"Okay." She sounded dubious, but she bent and called Bella over. Bella's fluffy black and white tail swished as she sat on her haunches at Megan's feet. "Good girl." She stepped hesitantly toward the ramp, and Bella watched as she made the signal for "up."

"You have to run with her," Tione said. "She won't do it by herself."

"Oh." She laughed. "Of course. Why would she?" She jogged to the ramp, and made the signal when she reached it. Bella scrabbled up one side and down the other. Megan giggled. "I did it!"

"Good start. Keep it up."

He watched as she trotted to the first jump and gestured for Bella to leap over it. She did easily, and Megan's goofy grin widened. He loved that grin. The sight of it made coming out here at the ass crack of dawn worth it. Bella cleared another two jumps, and with only a little coaxing, dropped her belly to the ground to wiggle through the tunnel.

He crossed his fingers behind his back, hoping she'd make the jump through the ring without him there to guide her. The ring was a recent addition, and they'd only successfully completed it a few times. Perhaps he should have left it at home.

No, he needed to have faith in his girls. They could do this.

Bella ran up the seesaw, waited for the other end to thud to the ground, and dashed off it. Megan was on a roll now, more confident in herself, and he held his breath as they approached the elevated ring. Five meters... two meters... and they were through it.

Megan whooped. "We did it!"

Bella flung herself into the air like a dolphin, excited by the commotion. Megan raced to Tione, and he opened his arms wide, catching her as she threw herself into them. He hugged her, but not tight enough to hurt her ribs, and when he drew back, his breath caught in his chest. Her eyes glittered golden in the light, her happiness a potent aphrodisiac.

God, she was so beautiful he ached just looking at her.

Her tongue flicked out over her upper lip and his heart puttered like a car backfiring. He knew the fantasies running through his mind were wrong, considering how vulnerable she was, but he didn't think he could survive another second without knowing how she tasted, or what it felt like to truly kiss her. He'd never wanted a woman the way he did her. He'd never had the desire to take one in his arms and protect her from the world until now. In this moment, Megan was everything. Everything he'd ever wanted, everything he could never have.

Before he'd made the conscious decision to move, he was kissing her. Her lips were satin-soft beneath his, and they parted on an intake of breath. Then she was kissing him back, twining her arms around his neck, pressing herself into him. His heart sang with triumph and he became hyper aware of the heated friction at every place their bodies connected.

His fingers dug into her hips and he kissed down the length of her neck, loving the way she sighed and tilted her head to give him better access. As his mouth worshiped her skin, his nostrils filled with the scent of her, at once sugary sweet and alluring. His tongue darted out to touch a pulse point, and she clutched his shoulders tighter.

She was decadent. Like the richest dessert he'd ever tasted, and he wanted to savor her forever. But he couldn't. Reluctantly, he released her and put distance between them.

Her eyes had closed, but now they fluttered open, slowly focusing on him. "Wow."

MEGAN HAD NEVER BEEN SO THOROUGHLY KISSED in her life. Her mind whirred, struggling to process anything, too glazed by the effects of Tione's expert lips and potent pheromones. She didn't know what it was, but man did he smell good. And the way he kissed... her knees weakened, but she managed not to swoon.

"Wow," she repeated, like an idiot. "You really know what you're doing."

Shut up, Meg. Stop making it worse.

He turned to scan the field, checking on the dogs. She followed his gaze, pleased for the distraction.

"We should get back," he said. "I need to make a start on lunch."

She stared at him. Really? Were they not going to talk about the mind-boggling kiss they'd just shared?

He called the dogs in. Her jaw set, and her lips firmed. They weren't going to ignore this. Not on her watch. She'd spent too many months staying quiet when she should have said something. She wouldn't make that mistake again.

"I enjoyed that," she announced. "We should do it again some time." If she sounded moronic, she didn't care. Better that than let the moment slip through their fingers.

Tione scowled, and rubbed his chin. Her core heated in response. She knew how soft that beard felt against her face, and she had intimate knowledge of how wonderful his stubborn mouth could be when he stopped being so determined to keep his distance.

"It was nice," he agreed.

It had been a darn sight better than nice, but she let the comment pass. "What are we making for lunch?"

He raised a brow, but answered, and she kept up a steady stream of small talk while they collected the dogs and walked back to the lodge, where she followed him to the kitchen and washed her hands. Together, they prepared ingredients for BLTs, and oddly, she couldn't remember the last time she'd felt so in control. They worked like a well-greased wheel, as though they'd been a team for much longer than a couple of weeks.

"Tell me more about yourself," she said. "You know a lot about me, but I don't know your story."

"I disagree." He washed lettuce leaves and handed them to her to shred. "One bad relationship isn't your whole story."

Awwww. She melted a little. So many people would make generalizations based on what they knew, but she liked that he didn't.

"How about we take turns answering questions?" she suggested. If their outing earlier had been a date—and she hoped it was—she wanted to know everything she could about him before going further. She liked him, and she thought she could trust him, but the problem was, she didn't trust her own judgment. That's what had gotten her into this mess.

"Okay. You first."

She worked through the list of information she'd compiled about him in her head. "You said you lived in the U.S. for a while. Which part were you in?"

"California."

"Ooh." Images of golden sand and beaches flashed through her mind. "That sounds lovely."

He gave a noncommittal grunt. "It was all right."

She shook her head, wondering how he could be so blasé about travel. When she lived in France, every day had been an adventure, although there'd been back-breaking hard work, too.

As if he'd overheard her thoughts, he asked, "Do you speak French?"

"I do." She finished piling lettuce into a bowl and dropped bacon strips onto a sizzling pan.

"Will you say something for me?"

She turned to him, curious. "Why? Do you speak French too?"

"No." He grinned toothily, and her heart gave an extra thump in response. "But it's hot when women speak foreign languages."

She'd speak French to him all day, if that was what got him going. "*Je crois que je suis en train de tomber amoureux de toi.*"

He shivered, and his grin widened. "Say it again."

She did, translating for herself in her head. *I think I'm falling for you*. She wouldn't let him know what the words meant. At least, not yet.

"My turn."

"Nah-uh. You asked if I speak French, too."

She gaped. "That doesn't count!"

"Sure it does. You asked a question, I answered it."

She huffed. "Cheater. Fine, what's your question?" As she waited, she began to assemble the lunch options to carry them to the side table in the dining hall.

"Your dad." He paused. "Do you remember him?"

Sadness flooded her, and she kept her face turned away so he wouldn't see her eyes mist over.

"Not much." Her voice was thick. Even though she'd never had the chance to know him properly, her father's loss weighed on her heavily. "Just flashes. Short bits of memory."

"Oh. *Arohamai*. I'm sorry."

She forced herself to meet his eyes. "It's no big deal. It was a long time ago. How about you? Are your parents around?"

"No. My *whaea* died when I was a baby. I don't remember her at all."

"And your dad?"

He shrugged. "I have no idea who he was."

The pressure on her chest quadrupled. "So you never knew either of your parents?"

"Nope."

"That's so sad." She thought she might cry, and blinked rapidly to dispel the oncoming tears.

He shrugged again. "Don't feel sorry for me. You can't miss what you never had."

He gathered dishes and carried them to the sideboard. She followed behind, and together they laid out lunch. She fixed herself a BLT and waited while he did the same, and then they retreated to one of the tables in the corner that had been left free by the other guests.

"Who raised you?" She'd asked more questions than she had a right to, according to the rules of their game, but he didn't seem to mind.

"My *koro*. Mum's father." He bit into his sandwich, and when mayonnaise oozed out the side, she reached over and dabbed it away with a napkin. "He has a cottage in Paihia, right on the beach." He was smiling now, and gazing over her shoulder, but she knew he was seeing something else. "He spends most of his time teaching the children at the *marae* to fish and speak *Te Reo*. I visit a couple of times a year. He's really got it made."

"He sounds wonderful." From the way he spoke of his *koro*, Megan could tell the old man was the most important person in his life. She couldn't help but wonder if he'd approve of her, and whether she'd ever get the chance to meet him. She hoped so. She wanted to thank him for taking Tione in and raising him to be the man he was.

"Enough about me," he said. "I must have three or four questions up my sleeve by now. Tell me about the most extravagant cake you ever baked."

21

WHEN THE LUNCH dishes had been cleared away, Tione drove into town and parked outside the police depot. He greeted the receptionist, a kid just out of high school, and asked to see Elliot.

"Officer Tanner is on patrol," the kid informed him. "But Officer Wilson is available."

"I'll see him, then."

Dennis Wilson had been on the job for even longer than Elliot, and Tione suspected he was just waiting to reach retirement age. The kid went to find Dennis, and Tione gave the officer a tight smile when he lumbered into the foyer and offered his hand.

"S'pose it's too much to ask for this to be a personal visit," Dennis said gruffly.

"Yeah." Tione hooked his thumbs into his pockets. "Did Elliot fill you in on Megan Talbot and her dickhead ex?"

Dennis glanced at the kid and jerked his head toward the door that led into the warren of tiny rooms making up the better part of the depot. "Come on back. Let's talk in private."

Tione followed him to an ugly yellow door with "Wilson" printed across it in neat letters. The department was too cheap to spring for a proper label, even though the man had worked there for most of his adult life.

"Sorry," he said as he closed the door behind them. "Young Jimmy out there is the biggest gossip I ever had the pleasure to meet. That boy never met a rumor he didn't care to share. If he heard about your girl, the story'd reach as far as Gray before nightfall."

Tione barked a laugh. "Let's not get carried away. Anderson Gray wouldn't be told if his own house were burning to the ground."

Dennis tipped his head, acknowledging the truth. When Gray, a former Hollywood star, first moved to Haven Bay, the residents had been delighted. One by one, he'd alienated them all until they left him alone in his mansion on the fringe of town to drown in his misery. As far as Tione could tell, the guy had gotten exactly what he'd wanted.

"Has anyone seen Charles Wentworth in the area?"

"Don't believe so." Dennis adjusted his belt buckle. "No reports of a man fitting his description, but we haven't got the manpower to have patrols looking for him. If you're concerned, you'd do better to pass his photo around town yourself."

Tione nodded. "I'll do that." He'd already planned to stop at the library and print a couple of dozen pictures of the guy to hand out at The Refuge—the local retirement home, which was a thriving hub of local news. "Thanks for your time, Dennis." He shook the man's hand again and left without any fanfare.

Next, he drove to the library, where he used one of the public computers to do a Google search for the name "Charles Wentworth," and was surprised when many of the results showed a well-dressed elderly man. Then he recalled that the Charles Wentworth he'd met had been the second Charles Wentworth, so he tried a variation with "Junior" on the end and hit pay dirt.

There were a number of photographs of Wentworth the Second wearing expensive suits, his dark hair styled and expression disdainful. They'd been taken at soirees, galas, and even a couple at the theater. In more than one photo, he had his arm around a petite honey blonde with exquisitely delicate features and downcast eyes. *Megan*.

His fists clenched and he forced them to loosen, an audible breath easing out. Hell, he could tell something was wrong from these photographs. How had her family and friends not known? He wished he could drag the motherfucker back here and plant his fist in the guy's face.

Instead, he kept dragging in slow breaths until he'd calmed, then he selected three of the clearest images and printed a dozen of each, writing a short explanatory note beneath them. At the counter, he paid the librarian—one of his poker buddies—and rotated the pages to face him.

"You seen this guy?" he asked, stabbing Charles with his finger.

Kyle leaned closer, peering through his glasses. "Not that I can recall. What's going on, Tee? Why do you want all these photos of him?"

Tione considered how to phrase his response. He'd have to repeat it many more times over the next hour. "That woman he's with." He pointed to Megan. "She was his girlfriend, and he beat her. She's hiding out at Sanctuary, but he's been sniffing around, trying to get her back." He took the stack of photos from the desk and lowered his hands to his side, hoping Kyle wouldn't see how they were shaking.

"You think he wants to hurt her?" Kyle asked, reading the subtext.

"Yeah, I'm afraid so."

He made a sound of contempt in the back of his throat. "Asshole. If I see him around, you'll be the first person I call."

"Thanks." Tione leaned over to bump fists with him. "Let Elliot know, too."

"Will do." Kyle taped the photo to the pillar beside the counter. "No one around here is going to let him get his hands on her."

From the library, Tione walked to the minimart, the pub, the cafe, and a number of boutiques, passing around photos and answering questions. By the time the Bridge Club had finished interrogating him at The Refuge, he'd worked up a sweat and was well and truly ready for a shower and a beer, but the interrogation had been worthwhile because Betty promised to photocopy the pictures and coordinate distribution to every power pole and bulletin board in town. With her onside, maybe they'd get somewhere. Much as he hated to admit it, the old biddy wielded a fair bit of power with her generation.

Rinsing off the troubles of the day, he told himself he'd done all he could, at least for now. He cracked the lid off a Heineken and brought it to the kitchen, where the first thing he did was kiss Megan. He didn't mention how he'd spent the afternoon. There was no need to worry her more than she already was. That said, he'd do whatever he could to make sure that people more trustworthy than him were out there, keeping her safe. She deserved that, and so much more.

THE NEXT FEW days were the most blissful of Megan's recent memory. They passed in a blur of kisses, murmured conversations, and cooking. There was no sign of Charles, and with her mother's guidance, she wrote an affidavit. As she lay in bed at night, stroking Trevor's head, she considered Faith's invitation to partner with her. The offer was tempting. *Very* tempting. And she decided to discuss her options with Sterling, who was an expert at that type of thing.

On Saturday morning, she and Tione were returning from a walk on the beach, the dogs bustling around their heels, when she recognized a black van parked outside the lodge. It belonged to Joe, her soon-to-be stepfather. Alarm bells blared in her head. Had her mother come here? Her hand went to the cut on her face. It had almost healed, but she'd hoped it would be nothing more than a white line before she saw Rose again. Thank God the bruises ringing her neck had vanished.

"I think Mum is here," she warned Tione as they approached the entrance. "That's her fiancé's car." She watched his face, waiting to see how he'd react. His expression didn't flicker.

He nodded. "Good. It took her long enough."

"Hey, she had court this week. She couldn't leave Auckland."

He just grunted. She was beginning to understand his nonverbal communication, and this grunt sounded disapproving. Opening the door, she stepped into the foyer. As one, a crowd of people turned in her direction. She stopped short, jaw dropping. Her mother hadn't come alone. She'd brought Joe, Mikayla, Mark, and Mark's girlfriend, Clarissa. Rose had been deep in discussion with Kat at the front desk, but now the crowd moved toward Megan.

"Meg!" Mikayla cried.

Rose shoved Mark aside to get to her. "Darling!"

A chorus of other greetings sounded, but Megan was still trying to process the fact that her entire family was at Sanctuary. They mob-hugged her, and she struggled not to be suffocated. Glancing at Tione, she saw his eyes widen in shock as they drew her away. She breathed in their familiar scents, waiting for them to calm down enough to let her speak.

"I can't believe you're all here," she said, when they finally quietened.

"Where else would we be?" Mark asked, grinning. "We ran out of cake without you around."

She laughed, and appreciated him lightening the mood. Mark could always be counted on to have a light-hearted quip up his sleeve.

"It's so good to see you." She turned to Tione, and they seemed to notice him for the first time. "This is Tione." She smiled up at him, and he held her gaze, whether because he was as drawn to her as she was to him, or because her family scared him, she didn't know. "He's a good man. He's the one who helped me be brave enough to tell you the truth and file charges against Charles. Tee, meet my family." She gestured to each person in turn. "Rose, Mikayla, Mark, Clarissa, and Joe."

Rose took his hand. "Bless you. I can't thank you

enough." Warmth and sincerity infused her voice. "We're so grateful to you for taking care of our Meg."

Was it her imagination, or did his swarthy cheeks stain crimson?

"And thank you," Rose continued, gesturing to Kat, "for taking in my baby girl and keeping her safe."

"*Mum*," Megan muttered.

"No." Rose squared her shoulders. "We let you down, but these people were here for you, and I'm going to make sure they know how much I appreciate it."

"It's been our pleasure having her here," Kat said, smiling first at Rose, then Megan. "Like I've always said, you're welcome to stay for as long as you like. Especially if you do more baking."

Megan returned her smile. "Thank you."

Mark came forward and shook Tione's hand, staring him down. If she didn't know her brother so well, she'd think he looked downright hostile. A far cry from his usual good-natured self.

"Thanks," he said, sounding anything but thankful.

Megan was about to ask what his problem was when she realized it was obvious. Tione was a stranger to them —one who was rough around the edges. Mark was already kicking himself for not seeing what was going on with Charles, so he was treading carefully around other men in her life. She couldn't blame him, since Tione wore tattoos and a scowl so well. Joe followed Mark's lead, shaking Tione's hand but assessing him carefully.

Tione locked eyes with her. "I need to make a start on lunch. See you later?"

She nodded. "Bye, Tee."

The instant he'd exited the foyer, Mikayla waggled her eyebrows. Megan ignored her.

"Here you go." Kat handed two sets of keys to Rose. "You're all booked in. Lunch is served from twelve until one, and dinner is at six. There's plenty to do in the area, if you'd like to get out and about, but I'm sure Megan can give you the rundown."

"Thank you, Katarina," Rose said, then gave her attention to her daughter. "We'll get settled in later. First, we want to hear everything."

A lead ball sank to the bottom of Megan's gut. She didn't want to relive everything over again, but at least this way she'd only have to go through it one more time.

"Okay, follow me."

She led them to her bedroom, and waited while they found seats. Mikayla and Rose claimed the bed, while Mark and Clarissa sat cross-legged on the floor, and Joe took the desk. Megan joined her mother and sister, wishing she could climb under the covers and pull the blanket up to her chin, but she didn't want to look any weaker than she already did.

Inhaling a lungful of air, she opened her mouth, trying to figure out where to start. A hand wrapped around hers, and she glanced down. Mikayla squeezed, and sent her a smile that said they were all here for her.

"Take your time, sis."

Tears welled in Megan's eyes. She had the best family ever. "I love you guys."

Without further ado, she launched into her story, telling it as dispassionately as possible from beginning to end. Mikayla kept a hold of her hand, and she used it to anchor herself in the moment, and to remind herself that she was safe now, with people who cared about her. When she finished, no one spoke for a long time.

Finally, Mark slammed his fist on the ground and swore. "When I see that bastard next, I'm going to—"

"When you see him next, he'll be across a courtroom," Mikayla interrupted. "Isn't that right, Mum?"

"Damn straight it is," Rose agreed.

Megan stared. She'd never known her mother to utter anything remotely resembling a curse word.

"Oh, don't look at me like that," Rose continued. "My baby girl has been hurt by a horse's ass. If I have my way, he won't see the outside of a prison cell for years." She reached over and rested her hand on Megan's knee. "Show me your affidavit, honey."

Megan disentangled herself, went to the desk drawer and withdrew the paper she'd written her statement on. She handed it to Rose and waited while she read.

"Good," Rose said after a while. "You'll need to sign it in front of a Justice of the Peace, and then leave it to me. I'll file the documentation, then they'll notify Charles of the proceedings, and all you have to do is appear in court at the appointed time."

A cold shiver rippled over her skin. "I have to be in court at the same time as him?"

"I'd strongly recommend it."

"Okay." She bit her lip. This wasn't a surprise, but it was something she'd rather not think about. Fortunately, a knock on the door drew everyone's attention away from her.

22

Sterling entered, and he and Mark embraced, then Mark drew back, hands on hips, lips pinched together. "Why didn't you call me the moment she arrived?"

Sterling's expression didn't waver. He seemed to have been expecting the question. "She used a false name, and it took me a while to recognize her."

"Oh." An awful silence descended as everyone in the room contemplated how messed up she must have been for that to be true. Mark swallowed. "Wow, okay."

Frantically, Megan searched for a topic to distract them. One that didn't involve the beating she'd received from Charles. "Sterling, Mark, what does it take to join a business?"

Both men turned to her, sporting identical frowns.

"Sorry, what was that?" Mark asked, apparently having trouble processing her words.

"If I wanted to join an existing business," she said more slowly, "what would I need to do?"

He rubbed his temples, brows knitting together. "What does that have to do with anything?"

She hurried to explain. "One of the locals asked me to partner with her, but I'm not sure what it would involve."

"And you're seriously considering it?" Joe asked in his deep baritone. "Are you sure it's a good idea to be thinking of such a big change so soon after everything you've been through?"

"I think it's a brilliant idea," Rose said, shooting Joe a warning look. "And it just so happens you've got a very qualified roomful of people to talk to about it."

"Yes," Mark said, warming to the topic. "Joining an existing business is different to starting one from scratch. I could easily draft a partnership agreement for you to discuss with your new friend. What does she do?"

"She owns an ice cream parlor."

They all made appreciative sounds.

"I'm happy to give you an overview of what you'd need in place to manage the business," Sterling said.

Mark clapped him on the shoulder. "Thanks, man." To Megan, he said, "Clarissa would also be able to help talk you through running a business. Between the three of us, we've got you covered." He smiled at his girlfriend, his eyes crinkling at the corners, and something within Megan softened. She wanted a man who looked at her that way.

"I'm happy to help in any way I can," Clarissa said. Megan thanked her, even as she was enveloped by envy. Clarissa was so self-assured. She had her life together, and what did Megan have? A big old mess.

"Shall we move our bags into our rooms?" Clarissa suggested. "We've overwhelmed poor Megan, so let's give her a moment to herself."

Megan silently thanked her as her family shuffled out. But Mikayla stayed.

When the door closed, her sister asked, "So what's going on between you and the hunk?"

"Huh?"

"Aw, come on, sis. He's super-hot and clearly into you." She leaned forward, wearing a cheeky grin. "Has anything happened?"

"I only just broke up with Charles." Even to her own ears, the words sounded hollow.

"And?" Mikayla asked. "That's never stopped anyone before."

Megan fiddled with the edge of the blanket and reminded herself that this was her sister, and she could trust her with anything. Though she may have a sharp tongue, Mikayla would never betray her.

"I like him," she confessed.

Mikayla pumped her fist. "I knew it!"

"But it's not just because he's hot." She ducked her head and lowered her voice. "He's very sweet, great with his dogs, and he stood between Charles and I when he tried to take me away."

Mikayla's eyes flashed. "Then he has my vote. Especially if he's the reason you finally came clean with us."

"He is." She would have gotten there anyway, but he'd certainly sped the process along.

"That man is a keeper."

Megan's smile softened. "I hope so. We're taking it slow, though. Trying not to jump into anything too quickly."

In fact, she got the feeling, during some of their quieter moments, that he was trying to keep an emotional distance for some reason. But then he'd see her watching and smile, and everything would feel right again.

"Good for you." Mikayla shuffled over until they were side by side and wrapped an arm around her shoulders. She was tiny, and the hug didn't provide much comfort, but Megan appreciated the sentiment. "Just don't let him slip through your fingers because the timing is crap."

"I won't," Megan promised, and she meant it.

TIONE DIDN'T SEE Megan after her family swept her away, but he was happy for her. She'd been through a lot and it was important that she be around people who cared for her. Unfortunately, he hadn't gone this long without seeing her for a while, and it felt wrong. For more than half a day, she'd been shut away with her family, the sound of their chatter coming through the walls. He was starved for the sight of her, but he doubted she'd tell anyone what was happening between them—hell, he wasn't even sure what it was himself—so he'd stayed away.

He was lying in bed, reading by the light of his lamp, Pixie tucked into his side, when something crunched outside. His muscles tensed. A few seconds later, a knock came at the door. He padded across the wooden floor and opened it. Megan stood on the other side, her hair damp over her shoulders, smelling of shampoo and woman.

She smiled up at him. "Hi. I hope I didn't wake you."

"No, I was reading." He stepped aside to let her in, and she brushed past him. Closing the door, he turned, only to find her right in front of him, her face level with his chest.

"I wanted to see you." Her hands landed on his hips, and she shuffled closer until only an inch separated them. His jaw clenched. If she tilted her face up, and he lowered his head, they'd be kissing. He ached to do exactly that, but reined it in. The last thing she needed was for him to crush her to his body and kiss the hell out of her the way he wanted to.

He cleared his throat, and studied her face. The delicate nose, the amber eyes, the upturned mouth he ached to taste. "How is your family?"

He'd hoped the question would remind him that her family probably wouldn't approve of him. They were lawyers and business owners and executives. They wore suits and expensive watches. Even though Tione had enough money in the bank to buy and sell them all, he was still a tattooed cook who lived in a two-room cabin and wouldn't know a dessert fork from a steak fork. Alas, despite all of this, he still yearned to kiss her.

"They're good." She demolished the distance between them, her soft, perfect body rubbing against his. Resting her cheek on his chest, she wrapped her arms around his waist and relaxed into him. The affectionate gesture touched his heart, which swelled with happiness. He hugged her back.

"I'm sorry for all the craziness," she said. "It's so good to see them, though."

"I'm glad they came through for you," he murmured into her hair, wondering if it was her shampoo that smelled fruity, or her body lotion. He'd become familiar with her scents, and this was a new one. Perhaps her sister, the pint-sized brunette, had brought products from home. "It's important for you to be surrounded by people you love and trust."

She snuggled closer, burrowing into him, and he felt like he might overflow with warmth and tenderness. Her breasts flattened against him, her hips rocked, and the mood of the embrace subtly changed. His dick started to stiffen. She felt so good, and his body wanted to bury itself in her, regardless of how inappropriate that might be. He tried to shift back, to hide his condition, not wanting to make her uncomfortable.

"I'm in a good place right now, and that's thanks in large part to you." His shirt muffled her voice. She tilted her face up to meet his gaze, and he could have drowned in those gorgeous golden irises of hers. "Whatever happens between us, I trust you, and it means so much for me to be able to trust a man."

He went rigid as one thought struck him with absolute certainty: he didn't deserve her trust. God, he wanted it—wanted *her*—but he didn't deserve her. He wasn't worthy of the gift she was giving him. There were things she didn't know, and if she did, she'd revise her opinion of him pretty damn quickly. He opened his mouth, determined to speak the truth, but the admiration in her eyes stopped him. He liked the way she looked at him. If he was honest, would she still gaze at him so openly?

It didn't matter. Not really. He knew her truth, and he owed her his in return.

"Megan," he began. "There's—"

She stretched onto her toes and kissed him. All thought of spilling his guts exited stage left. Her lips were gentle on his. Hesitant. And then they weren't. The pressure increased, and he wasn't sure which one of them initiated it, but the kiss deepened. Her lips parted, and a sigh escaped as he slipped his tongue inside and tasted her the way he'd been craving. He was careful not to be rough. Instead, he explored her mouth with painstaking slowness.

Gathering her close, he got the sense that no matter how tightly he held onto her, or how well he kissed her, he could never get enough. One of his hands cupped her chin and the other caressed a line down the center of her back. In return, her hands clutched at his shoulders, and she leaned into him, giving him her full weight.

On and on the kiss went, growing deeper, more desperate as their tongues tangled and breath came in puffs. All the sweet kisses they'd exchanged over the past few days had nothing on this. He wanted more, more, *more*.

23

THERE WAS a good chance that her emotions were unbalanced from everything that had happened lately, but Megan felt like she was a dinghy being tossed by a violent sea and the only thing anchoring her in the storm was Tione. She couldn't give words to the belief, but she wanted to let him know how she was feeling in whatever way she could. She wanted to embrace that elusive spark of attraction she'd never thought she'd experience again.

She reveled in the slide of his lips on hers, and the glide of their tongues over each other. He kissed her like kissing was the end game, not a precursor to anything else. Charles had rarely kissed her. He'd been an in-and-out kind of guy. She'd bet her last meal that Tione would linger over a woman as he made love to her, and savor every last moment.

God, she wanted that. Her body was a whirl of hormones and pent-up lust. Every brush of his torso along the length of hers set her nerves alight, and she wanted nothing more than to strip him off and have her wicked way with him, but she didn't. However turned on she might be, it was too soon. Nevertheless, she ached for him to fill her, and that made her so goddamn happy.

Trailing her hands down his sides and around, she rested them on his tight butt. His hips rolled forward, sending a jolt of heat sizzling from her core outward. She moaned.

He raised his mouth from hers. "Fuck, you're so damn sweet." She tried to kiss him, but he backed out of reach. "It's too early for us to go all the way. You know that, right?"

Drawing her lip between her teeth, she nodded.

"Good." He said it more to himself than to her. "I want to give you pleasure. To remind you how good a man's touch can be when it's done right. Is that okay with you?"

Being the subject of his intense concentration unsettled her, but at the same time, she gloried in it.

"Yes." She wet her lips. "More than okay."

If possible, his eyes darkened. "You won't regret it."

Then he was moving away from her. She blinked, grabbing the wall to steady herself. He opened a cupboard beneath the sink and withdrew a packet of dog treats. Her gaze flew to the dogs lined up on their beds against the wall, and her cheeks heated. She'd forgotten they were there, and they'd nearly gotten quite a show. They watched, ears pricked, until he called them over. He tossed a handful of treats outside and closed the door after they scuttled out.

"Will they be okay out there?" she asked, concerned they might wander off.

"They'll be fine. They won't go far." He set the bag

down and moved toward her with predatory grace. "On the bed."

She blinked, confused. "Huh?"

He swallowed, his throat rippling, and she couldn't help but stare at the taut cords of his neck, fascinated. "I want you on my bed."

"Oh." Her knees went weak, and she didn't realize he'd backed her to the bed until the mattress hit her thighs. She sat.

"Take off your jeans.

She undid her zipper, and shimmied out of them. Embarrassment churned her stomach when she remembered she'd left all of her nice underwear behind at the apartment she'd shared with Charles and, in a fit of defiance, had only brought comfortable granny panties with her.

"Keep going," he croaked, and it took her a moment to realize he wanted her to strip off the underwear, too.

Feeling shy, she did as he asked. "Like that?"

"Mmm." He made a sound of approval deep in the back of his throat, and if she hadn't already been wet, that sound would have done it. "Lie back."

She did, and he sank to his knees before her, spreading her thighs. She squeezed them together, and he chuckled.

"This isn't going to work if you don't open for me," he said. "Do you want me, or don't you?"

"I do." She eased the muscles of her legs, feeling exposed.

He wedged his shoulders between them and she rose up on her elbows to watch as he lowered his mouth to her. His tongue flicked out, touching her sensitive flesh, and she gasped, her hips bucking. His forearms landed heavily on her legs, pinning them down.

"Easy," he soothed. "Easy."

Dropping her head to the bed, she sighed as the flat of his tongue stroked down her center. She stared at his inked forearm where it contrasted with the luminous white of her skin, and for some reason, seeing those swirling lines, being reminded of exactly who it was that had his mouth on her, made her want to scream with joy. So she did. His lips curved against her, and she shivered. But then she promptly forgot about anything except the sensation of his beard on the inside of her thighs, and his mouth as he loved her.

He wound her higher and tighter, encouraging her with gruff sounds of need as he gave her what she desperately wanted. Her back arched from the bed, and the way she pressed herself to him should have embarrassed her, but she was beyond that. He'd turned her into a senseless puddle of desire, and she adored every minute of it. She'd never been able to let loose like this before. Not with Charles, not with anyone. Tione brought out the vixen in her, and she raked her fingers through his thick hair, relishing the way his entire body shivered in response.

Then he slipped a finger inside her, and she was lost. Pleasure pulsed through her, unlike anything she'd ever experienced. She sobbed aloud, her hips collapsing to the bed, spasms wracking her body.

"Omigod," she whispered, wondering why her cheeks were wet. "Oh. My. God." The heaving of her chest slowed as she caught her breath, and she wiped the moisture from beneath her eyes and grinned at the ceiling. "I think you've ruined me for all other men."

The bed dipped, then his face appeared above her. He was smiling crookedly. "In a good way?"

She kissed him, unsure what the protocol was when a man had just given her the best orgasm of her life. "Yes, in a good way." She released a heavy breath. "Phew, I'm exhausted."

One of his eyebrows shot up. "*You're* exhausted?" he teased. "Who do you think was doing all the work here?"

He settled onto his elbows, and she couldn't take her eyes off him. Where was the sullen guy she'd met that first night? This man smiled down at her as if he'd like nothing more than to gather her in his arms and keep her there forever. Her heart gave an extra thump.

"You shouldn't look at me like that," she murmured. "You'll give me ideas."

He brushed her hair back from her forehead, and kissed her temple. "Maybe I want you to have ideas."

Her heart lodged in her throat. Was he saying what she thought he was? She felt a crinkle form between her brows.

"Stop thinking so much," he told her, kissing the tip of her nose. Perhaps it was the afterglow from her orgasm, but the simple sweetness of it nearly undid her. She bit her lip, and tried not to cry. That would be a sure-fire way to ruin the mood. "Climb into bed," he continued. "I'll let the dogs in, then I'll spoon the hell out of you."

"But—" Surely she ought to do something in return. The massive erection brushing her stomach hadn't gone unnoticed. He was turned on, and needed relief.

"No buts." His tone brooked no argument. "I'll be back in a moment."

Climbing off her, he sauntered to the door, stopping

to adjust himself, most likely when he thought she couldn't see. Then he summoned the dogs, and petted them as they passed. Taking a bag from beneath the counter, he dropped a treat in front of each bed and watched fondly while they gobbled them up. Meanwhile, Megan's ovaries sang with happiness. If he was like this with pets, how amazing would he be with actual babies? God, she didn't think she could handle the sight of him with a tiny human. Her ovaries might explode.

He crossed to the bed, drew back the covers, climbed in, and she shuffled over to him. He switched off the light, then drew her tighter into his embrace, resting his forearm over her belly, his chest to her back. She could feel his heart thudding against her, and she counted the beats. She couldn't recall a time she'd ever felt so at peace. And when a scrabbling sound interrupted the moment, and a wet nose touched her cheek, she laughed and let Pixie burrow into the bed with them.

For once, she felt truly content.

Megan woke Tione with a kiss. She touched her lips softly to his, and watched him come awake. When he gripped her hips and returned the kiss with more pressure, she knew he was fully conscious, even though his eyes didn't open.

"Good morning, sleepyhead," she said, drawing away and smiling in a way she hoped didn't look half as goofy as it felt.

"*Morena*," he murmured, his hand going to the back of her head to pull her in for another kiss. She snuggled closer, safe in the circle of his arms, and poured all of the feelings she wasn't ready to voice into the kiss. Their tongues met lazily, slow and deep, as though they had nowhere else to be and nothing else to do, despite the fact that he would need to leave for the kitchen soon.

She buried her face in his broad chest and stayed there while he stroked her hair with one hand and held her with the other. Finally, his alarm blared, and he eased away and threw back the covers.

"Will I see you again this morning?" he asked as he yanked on a pair of jeans.

"I hope so," she replied, enjoying the ripple of muscle as he shrugged into a black t-shirt. "I'm not sure what my family's plans are, but they'll definitely want breakfast."

"Good." He bent to drop a kiss on her forehead. "Wish I could stay."

So did she. But he needed to work, and she had to sneak back to her room before her family rose and realized she was missing, although she doubted their first thought would be that she'd been doing the dirty with the tattooed hunk they'd met yesterday. Well, other than Mikayla. Her sister could read her like a book.

"I'll see you soon."

He vanished into the bathroom before heading out. When the door closed behind him, she flopped back against the pillows. Being bad felt so damn good. She rolled over and inhaled the scent of Tione that was imprinted on the sheets. Was she weird for doing so? Definitely. But there was something to be said for the way the man smelled. Maybe it was pheromones. She wasn't scientifically-minded enough to know.

She stretched, then climbed out of bed, trying not to topple Pixie, who was perched on the edge. Tione had let the other dogs out when he left, and after she dressed, she grabbed a handful of doggy treats and tossed them on the lawn as she crossed it.

When she reached the foyer, she turned the handle as slowly as possible, wincing when the latch clicked. She let herself inside and padded barefoot down the hall. All of the bedroom doors were shut, bar one. Mikayla sat at the desk, tapping on her computer. As Megan passed, Mikayla gave her a conspiratorial wink.

Sisters. Had to love them.

24

TIONE TOOK his cock in his hand. It was hot and hard and heavy. He stroked it, his forehead resting on the bathroom wall in his cabin, and summoned the memory of Megan as she'd come apart under him last night, whimpering and writhing, so fucking sexy. He'd denied himself then, and it had been the right thing to do, but now he worked his hand over his length, imagining that she was on her knees in front of him.

A groan tore from his throat, and his hips pumped faster. In his fantasy, Megan licked the bulging head of his dick. She petted him like he was her plaything, lips and fingertips grazing him, bringing him closer to the edge. His other hand massaged his balls, and they drew up tight to his body. He squeezed his eyes shut, wishing more than anything that he'd open them and see her exactly as he'd pictured.

Another few strokes and he gritted his teeth, unable to hold back any longer. Just as well nothing had happened with her last night, or he wouldn't have lasted more than two minutes. His hips jerked, pleasure concentrating at the base of his spine, then he grunted, and pulsed into his hand.

He stayed there for a few moments while he caught his breath. Then he wiped everything clean, tucked himself back into his underwear, washed his hands, and headed back to the lodge. He'd finished readying the breakfast service early, and had considered visiting Megan, but decided it was a better idea to get his rocks off so he wouldn't overwhelm her the next time they were alone together. She was recovering from a difficult relationship, and she didn't need a horny guy getting up in her grill. Besides, she'd probably be with her *whanau*.

When he reached the dining hall, he found the Talbots clustered around a table, eating breakfast. He caught Megan's eye and smiled, then felt his balls shrivel as her stepfather eyed him. He hoped the man couldn't sense what he'd been up to. He hated to think of how that conversation would go.

Excuse me, young man, were you jerking off to fantasies of my daughter?

Yes, I was. Do you have a problem with that?

He must have looked guilty because the guy's gaze sharpened. He tried to remember his name. Jack? James? *Joe.*

"Tione!"

He started at the voice, searching for the source of it.

Megan's sister, Mikayla, waved to him. "Grab some breakfast and join us. There's plenty of room."

He'd rather not, especially considering the way Mikayla appraised him as he stacked waffles on his plate and drizzled sauce over the top, but he had to eat and he couldn't see a polite way out. He squeezed into the space beside the pretty blonde, Clarissa. She wiped her mouth with a napkin and shuffled over to make room.

"You look like you need a coffee," Mikayla said, more cheerily than the situation warranted. She turned to Megan. "Doesn't he look like he needs a coffee? Must have been a rough night."

Something about Mikayla's cheeky grin and dancing eyes made him think she knew exactly how he'd spent his night. But far from being suspicious of him, as he'd have expected, she seemed delighted, especially when her sister's cheeks flamed red. Her delight contrasted with the expressions of every other person at the table. Megan's mother studied him curiously, Clarissa completely ignored the subtext, and the two men glowered like he'd deflowered her right in front of them.

"He looks fine," Megan said, apologizing to him with her eyes. He shook his head to indicate she shouldn't worry about it. At least he had her sister's vote of confidence. There weren't many people he'd dated seriously, but experience told him that women put a lot of stock in their sister's opinions.

"What is it that you do, Tione?" Megan's mother asked, spearing a piece of banana from the fruit salad he'd made earlier.

"I'm the in-house caterer for the lodge," he said, waiting for the disdain that was bound to follow. It didn't come. Huh. Most people tended to look down on him once they learned his occupation, either because it wasn't manly or because it was low-brow.

"Are you responsible for this delicious breakfast?"

"Yes, ma'am."

"Fabulous." She smiled at Megan. "There's something about a man who can cook, isn't there?"

"Charles never cooked," Mikayla added. He was getting the feeling he'd been ambushed. The Talbot women were clearly trying to send some kind of message. "He'd have Megan slaving in the kitchen for hours for one of his fancy dinners, and wouldn't lift a finger to help her. Isn't that right, sis?"

"Why would he waste his time helping? He needed to primp and practice his jokes in the mirror."

Everyone fell silent, gaping at Megan. Tione didn't know what had happened. Then, as one, they burst into laughter.

"That's the first time they've heard her say anything derogatory about him," Clarissa murmured, for his benefit. "She's always been very tight-lipped about their relationship, or so I understand."

"Thank you," he said, grateful for the explanation. He dug into his waffle stack, glad the attention had been diverted away from him. A foot knocked against his under the table and he glanced up just as Mikayla winked at him, and mouthed something. He didn't bother trying to interpret, just focused on his waffles.

"You're a local?" Joe asked, and it was the first time the man had spoken since he'd sat down. Megan's stepfather-to-be was a big guy, broad-shouldered, with a shaved head and one of those faces that seemed to look the same regardless of his mood.

"Yeah. Didn't grow up here, though. Moved to the bay about three years ago. One of my cousins knew Kat and arranged for me to stay here with her." He didn't mention the part where his cousin had feared Kat was mentally unstable after the car crash that killed her husband and wanted someone to look out for her. Even Kat didn't know that detail.

"You'd be able to steer me to the best fishing spots, then? I brought my rod with me."

"Joe," Rose exclaimed, clapping her hand to her mouth. "We came here to be with my daughter, and you brought your fishing rod?"

Joe shrugged, unperturbed by her outburst. "I didn't think Megan would appreciate having all of us around twenty-four seven. Forgive me, doll?"

Megan's lips curled up into an adorable smile that made Tione badly want to kiss her. "Forgiven."

"See." He smiled smugly at his fiancée, who swatted him on the shoulder. "So, Tione. Where should I set up?"

Tione had never been much of a fisherman, preferring to net flounder or catch eels, but no one could live in the area without knowing the best places to find trout. "Head up that little creek you crossed over just before the lodge. It doesn't look like much, but don't let that fool you. Best fishing around."

He nodded. "Thanks, man."

"No problem." Putting his cutlery down, he glanced at the clock. He needed to make a start on cleaning up.

Mark spoke before he could move. "You said you moved here three years ago. Where were you before then?"

He frowned. What did his whereabouts have to do with anything? "I was living in the United States."

"On an O.E.?" Mikayla asked, using the shorthand for "overseas experience," an international working trip that many young Kiwis embarked on.

"Something like that."

"Which part of the States?" Mark asked, regaining his attention.

"California." And he didn't intend to say anything

more on the matter. Not until he'd confessed the whole story to Megan. Guilt sat heavy in his stomach at the omission. "I have to get back to work. You have a great day." He tipped his head to Joe. "Let me know how it goes."

With that, he stood, collected his plate, and strode to the kitchen. When the door closed behind him, he leaned on it and sighed. He needed to tell Megan the truth, before things between them got any more complicated than they already were. But shit, he didn't want to. Every muscle in his body rebelled at the idea. Why did life have to be so complicated?

"PROMISE YOU'LL CALL us if you so much as catch a whiff of his cologne," Mark insisted as he hugged her goodbye.

"I promise," Megan said. "But I'd say he's gone. I haven't seen him for days, and he's not the type to hang around without making a move."

Charles may be a manipulative bastard, but he wasn't a lazy one.

"I'll file the paperwork for the restraining order tomorrow," Rose said, lining up for a hug.

"Thanks, Mum." Perhaps it was silly to feel so relieved, considering how ineffective restraining orders could be, but she felt like she was taking a step in the right direction, and that, more than anything, gave her control over her life. Rose kissed her cheek, squeezed her one last time, and climbed into the car.

Joe enveloped her in his arms. "Bye, doll. Stay safe. Remember the moves I showed you."

Earlier on, he'd drilled both her and Mikayla on self-defense maneuvers they could use against a larger opponent. In another life, Joe had been a lieutenant in the army, and now he taught boxing to at-risk youth. He tousled her hair as he moved away.

"Take care." Clarissa's embrace was light and swift.

"Thanks for coming, Riss." Megan knew how busy she was, establishing the new wing of her bridal empire in Auckland.

"Any time."

Finally, everyone had loaded into the car except Mikayla, who took her hand and drew her further away. "Are you sure you're okay if we leave you here?"

Megan swallowed, her throat suddenly tight. While she loved Haven Bay, having her family around had been reassuring. "I'm sure."

Mikayla held her gaze for an uncomfortably long time, then said, "Okay. I believe you." She threw her arms around Megan, and rested her chin on her shoulder. "I love you, sis. Tell me everything that happens between you and Tione. I need to live vicariously through you. I spend too much time working to meet men."

Megan laughed. "Would it matter if you did?"

Her sister had been hung up on her boss for as long as she could remember. Megan got it. The guy was handsome, suave, successful, and a bona fide genius, but he was also never going to settle down with a woman, especially not the one responsible for ensuring his life ran smoothly. He needed to keep Mikayla around, and if he burned her, she'd accept one of the other numerous job offers she got every year.

Mikayla rolled her eyes. "Shut up." The rebuke held

no heat. They'd had this conversation a number of times before.

Megan pretended not to hear her. "Love you too. Bye, now."

Mikayla winked, then hopped into the last empty seat in the car. Megan waved as they drove off, calling farewells out the open window. When they were gone from sight, she rubbed her upper arms, the air feeling chillier than it had, and headed inside.

She reached her room, only to find the door to the hall ajar. She stopped, her hand flying to her chest, and edged back, poised to run, but a familiar voice called, "Megan. That you?"

Her shoulders slumped as the tension left them, and she shoved the door open. "Tee, you scared the bejeesus out of me."

He lay on her bed, head resting on her pillow, nose in a book, which he set aside as he glanced up. "*Arohamai.* I wasn't thinking." He patted the spot beside him. "Come over here."

A deep yearning pulled in her belly, and she closed the door and went to him, lying alongside him, close enough to feel the heat from his body but far enough away that they didn't touch. She leaned on one elbow and tilted her face toward his. "What are you doing in here?"

"I missed you."

Her heart danced a tango. "You did?"

"Yeah." He dipped his head until his mouth touched hers, ever so slightly. As he exhaled, their breath mingled, and her eyes fluttered shut. How was it that they weren't even kissing, yet this was more intimate than she'd ever been with Charles? She shifted, and her lips brushed the silken skin of his. He stiffened. She got the impression he was trying to restrain himself, holding back because he didn't want to overwhelm her, but she was reclaiming her life and she wasn't some delicate rose who'd be crushed by the force of his passion.

She kissed him.

It hadn't escaped her notice that she was the one initiating contact between them nearly every time they were together, but perhaps that was a good thing. For too long, she'd been a passenger in her life, and he'd put the power squarely in her hands. She liked it.

He groaned deep in his throat. His palm flattened against her lower back and he hauled her to him. Her senses were electrified, consumed by the feel of him, the scent of him, the taste of him, and the sound of his labored breathing as he kissed her like his very existence depended on it.

She couldn't look away. It was weird as hell to be staring at him while he kissed her, but his features were so harsh they could have been cast from bronze, and his eyes burned back into hers. He was fierce, scorching hot, and in this moment, he was all hers.

Primal satisfaction swelled within her. She didn't understand why he wanted her. He was thoughtful, protective, and a magnificent specimen of manhood. She was just… her. A woman who'd made too many mistakes, and would no doubt make many more. But when his slumberous gaze skimmed down her body, followed by his hands, then—dear God—his mouth, she was a seductress. One who moaned and whimpered and pressed ever closer.

Gradually, their kisses slowed, changing in temperament from desperate to tender. Their tongues danced, mouths mated, and after a long while, he just held her, positioning her head on his chest. She relaxed into him, listening to his heartbeat.

"Not yet," he murmured, kissing her forehead. She didn't know whether he was talking to her, or to himself. "We'll get there. For now, let's take it slow."

Her body was alight for him, and her core throbbed with the memory of his face buried between her thighs, but she nodded and counted off the thuds of his heart. He stroked her hair, and held her like he never wanted to let go. She was on board with that. She'd be happy to stay here in his arms forever. But was that really a possibility?

25

THE MORNING SUN filtered through the clouds, warming the top of Megan's head as she played in the garden with Zee. She'd been teaching the dog how to navigate Bella's seesaw, and while progress was slow, it was very rewarding, especially when she'd managed to lead her over it successfully while a couple of children watched, buzzing with excitement. Zee was still not fully grown, and she was too exuberant to follow directions for long.

Megan lobbed a ball and watched her race after it. A breeze stirred the air, and she tugged the sleeves of her jersey down to cover her hands, poking her thumbs through the holes in the cuffs. She'd never have gotten away with wearing something so scruffy when she lived with Charles. Not even to sleep in. Now, she relished it. Being inside the secondhand jersey felt like being in a warm embrace. She tucked her chin into the collar and rolled her eyes as Zee picked up the ball but refused to bring it back.

"Megan?"

She glanced over her shoulder at the sound of Kat's voice. "Hey."

Kat held up her phone. "Your brother is on the line."

"Oh." She hadn't been expecting a call, and less than twenty-four hours had passed since her family left, so she accepted it with a little trepidation. "Hi, Mark, how are you?"

Kat went back inside to give her privacy.

"I'm okay." He sounded distracted. "But Meg, there's something you need to know. You might want to sit down."

"Give me a moment." She let herself in through the foyer, gestured to Kat that she was still using the phone, and paced down the hall to her room. Once inside, she locked the door and settled on the bed. It was unusual for Mark to be so serious, and she didn't want their conversation to be interrupted. "I'm sitting down. What's wrong?"

He sighed, and she pictured him raking a hand through his hair as he often did when he was distressed. "You're going to be upset, so I'll open with the best of the bad news."

Her pulse seemed to speed up and slow down simultaneously. "What is it?"

"After you called Mum last week, I hired a private investigator to look into the Wentworths."

Finally, she allowed herself to breathe. That wasn't so bad. Perhaps she'd let herself get worked up about nothing. "Oh?"

"She found plenty to hint that the family is involved in shady dealings, but there's no concrete evidence she could nail them with."

Megan deflated, but wasn't surprised. The Wentworths were careful. Especially Charles Senior, whose prominent position in the legal community made him a tempting target for blackmailers and criminals. "I guess it was too much to hope that they'd have slipped up somewhere."

"Yeah." He didn't sound any more at ease than when he first called. "It gets worse. When we visited you, I called the P.I. and asked her to run background checks on Katarina Hopa and Tione Kingi to see if anything popped." His words started to run together. "I just wanted to make sure you were safe. I didn't expect her to find anything."

Dread settled in the pit of Megan's stomach. "But she did."

"Yeah, she did."

She rubbed her forehead, her fingers cold against her skin, and tasted something sour. "What?"

"Kat got a clean bill of health."

She tried to swallow, but her mouth was too dry. "And Tione?"

Mark was quiet. Seconds passed, but they felt like minutes. Finally, he said, "I just want you to know I'm sorry. I know you like this guy, but you're my sister, and I've done a shitty job of keeping you safe. Better late than never, right?"

She noticed she was shaking her head, and stopped. "What are you on about? Get to the point, please."

"Okay." He exhaled shakily. "Have you ever heard of Michele Franklin?"

"No." But she couldn't help wondering what the woman had to do with Tione. Was she an ex? Jealousy gripped her, shocking in its intensity. Of course he'd have exes though. What grown man wouldn't?

"Who is she?"

"She's the person who's dead because of him."

The words fell like bombs in the silence between them, each one of them detonating in her head and piercing her like shrapnel.

She pressed a fist to her mouth. "No. No, no, no. You must be wrong. Tell me you're having me on, Mark. This is some sick joke."

He sighed. "I wish I could, but it's true. He's the reason a woman is dead."

"But... but..." Head spinning, she lowered herself fully onto the bed. "If that were true, he'd be in prison."

"Not if he made a deal with the prosecutor." Mark sounded disgusted. "I'm sorry to tell you this over the phone. God, I wish I was there with you."

"Wait. Hold on." She tried to make sense of what he'd said and came up short. "He killed someone?"

"Not directly, but he was responsible for it."

"How?" She needed to know. "I don't understand any of this. Can you start at the beginning?"

"Yeah, okay. If that's what you need." She heard him moving around at the other end, probably making himself comfortable. Meanwhile, she felt like she'd never be comfortable again. She wanted to crawl out of her skin. She just couldn't fathom the idea of Tione as a killer—it was wrong. It had to be wrong. He may be gruff, but he was gentle and kind. He wouldn't hurt anyone... Would he?

"Here's the rundown. A few years ago, he lived in Silicon Valley. While he was over there, he designed an app that sold for a lot of money. We're talking multi-millions. It was basically blind dating for dogs. You enter in your dog's details and they're matched with others in the area for play dates."

Well, that was cute, but what did it have to do with a woman's murder? Besides, they were talking about a technophobe here. His phone was ancient, and he didn't have a single piece of computer-based technology in his cabin. The thought that he was a sophisticated software developer was, frankly, ridiculous, and so was the idea that he had millions of dollars stashed in the bank. He was up at dawn every morning, seven days a week, to work. Why would a Silicon Valley tech millionaire be making sandwiches in a lodge in Haven Bay?

"That can't be right," she said.

"I'm sorry, but it is. Here's where it gets worse."

She swallowed a lump of fear, not wanting to hear whatever turn his story was about to take. She wanted to hang up and pretend they'd never had this crazy conversation, but she needed to listen to everything he had to say before going to Tione, who'd no doubt tell her he was mistaken.

"Tione wasn't only a software designer. He was also a hacker for hire."

The other shoe dropped. "You're having me on." Relief hit her with enough force to knock the air from her lungs. "Not cool, Mark. There are times when it's okay to joke around, but now isn't one of them." She patted her chest, feeling it decompress as she managed to breathe again. "I can't believe you did that."

"I'm serious."

She scoffed. "Yeah, sure. Tione—the man who probably doesn't even know what Bluetooth is—used to be a hacker for hire. A likely story. I can't believe you'd make up something like this. I don't need this kind of crap right now. Just because you don't approve of him—"

"I'm telling the truth," he snapped.

She shook her head. Screw him. How dare he mess with her emotions right now.

"Mark—"

"Just listen," he interrupted. "He was hired by a tech company CEO to report on his wife Michele's activities. Shortly after Tione hacked into her accounts, she was murdered. He testified against her husband in court in exchange for immunity, but he chose to leave the country after the case closed and the husband was convicted." He paused, as if waiting for her to say something, but she couldn't. Her throat was tight, and her eyes prickled with tears. Why was he doing this to her? It couldn't possibly be right. It had to be lies. All of it. Otherwise, she was a stupid fool with monumentally poor taste in men.

"Meg," he said cautiously, "the guy is bad news. You can't trust him. He may not have killed that woman, but he certainly played a central role in her death. Please come home. Move in with me and Clarissa. Let us take care of you."

"No." Pressure sat heavy on her chest. "Stop messing around. It's not funny."

"I'm not messing around." His tone was somber. "I wish I didn't have to do this—"

"Then don't," she retorted. "I don't believe you. It can't be true. That's not the man I know." She had to talk to Tione. To hear him say Mark was mistaken. "I have to go. We'll talk later."

"But—"

She didn't wait to find out what he was going to say. She hung up.

Tione could tell something was wrong the minute he got back from running the dogs. Megan was sitting on his porch, cheeks flushed, eyes wild. She stood as he approached, and her hand trembled as she tucked a lock of hair behind her ear. When she spoke, she wouldn't look him in the eye.

"What happened in Silicon Valley?"

He froze, one hand on the clip to release Bella, and his blood turned to ice. He could have sworn he'd never told her which part of California he'd lived in. With unsteady movements, he forced himself to unclip each dog, and Trevor bounded away to sniff a clump of grass.

"Tee?" she prodded. "I need to know."

Wiping his palms on his shorts, he straightened and threw his shoulders back when what he really wanted to do was drop to his knees and beg her not to pursue this line of questioning. To accept him as he was, the way she had been since they met. But even while he wanted that, part of him knew this had been coming all along. It was inevitable. He wasn't good enough for her, and someone had finally clued her into that fact.

He answered her question with one of his own. "Who have you been talking to?"

Her eyes narrowed. "Mark."

For a moment, he didn't understand, but then he realized. Her brother was finally pulling his weight, and doing his bit to protect her. He'd looked into Tione's past and told her everything. He studied her face anew. Was she disgusted by him? Did she wish she'd never had the misfortune to meet him? His limbs felt heavy, his throat clogged, and his knees wanted to give out. Sighing, he dragged a hand down his face.

"Come in," he said. "Sounds like you know all about it, anyway." He led her inside and settled on the stool, letting her take the comfortable chair, and wondering if this would be the last time she'd want to be in the same room as him.

"I need to hear it from you." Her eyes searched his, seeking reassurance. She wanted him to say it was all a big misunderstanding, but he couldn't do that. He couldn't give her what she wanted. Not this time.

"What would be the point?" Whether she heard it from his mouth or someone else's, the end result would be the same. She was too pure and decent for him—always had been—and now she'd know it.

Her expression took on a hint of desperation. "I want to hear what you have to say."

He looked at his hands, knowing what she really wanted was for him to maintain the carefully constructed web of lies that made him who he was, but it was time she knew the truth.

"Fine. You want the whole story? Here it is." He launched into a retelling without pausing to think whether this was what he really wanted to do. The faster the ugliness was over, so he could hide in his cave and lick his wounds, the better. "When I was young, I thought I was a fucking genius. I moved to Silicon Valley with the dream of designing the next big piece of computer software and becoming the Maori version of Steve Jobs. Turns out, I was good, but nothing special compared to all the other aspiring entrepreneurs there."

Megan paled and glanced around the room. "I

thought you hated technology." Her voice was small. "Your phone doesn't even have wi-fi."

"I do hate it," he said. "Now. The point is, I wasn't the instant star I expected to be, so while I was developing an app, I signed on to do subcontracted work for a private investigator. I had to pay the bills somehow."

"Hacking?"

"Yeah." He swallowed. "Nothing big though. I found evidence of affairs when people were going through divorces, or tracked down embezzlers, that sort of thing. Once my app sold, I didn't need the extra money anymore, so I quit."

"It was legal employment?" she asked hopefully. "Within the law because you were working with an investigator?"

He snorted. Of course she'd like to think that. But he wasn't the hero of this story. Far from it. "Not strictly, no. It was moral, and that's how I justified it to myself."

"Oh."

Yeah, *oh*. Just wait until she heard what came later.

"The trouble was, I hadn't realized what a high I got from hacking. I missed it. Even though I didn't need the money, I struck out on my own, pimped out my services again, but this time without anyone to act as the middleman." He rubbed his temples and looked at the ground. "I was a dumb shit. I took a job that I thought was like the dozens of others I'd done during acrimonious divorces, but Michele was different. I dug into her life, and couldn't find any dirty laundry. She was a good person, faithful to her husband—although God knew he didn't deserve it. She donated to charities and volunteered for a few of them as well, and she was smart. So damn smart."

Megan stared at him. "It sounds like you..." she trailed off.

"Had feelings for her?" he suggested. "I did. Or at least, I thought I did. The more I learned about her, the more I liked her. I actually started to believe she'd be better off without her husband. He was an ass, and I..." Squeezing his eyes shut, he wished beyond anything that he could go back and correct this mistake. "I considered fabricating evidence of an affair so they'd separate. I didn't, but I thought about it. How awful is that?"

She didn't answer.

"In the end, it didn't matter. I told him she was clean, he accused me of lying—said I was screwing her myself—and then he... he..."

"He killed her," Megan whispered, her tone full of horror.

"Yeah." It was the first time he'd spoken the words since he'd been on the witness stand, in front of a jury of people who wouldn't have hesitated to prosecute *him* if they'd had the chance. "And it was my fault. If I'd vetted my clients more carefully, she might still be alive."

"I..." She blew out a breath. "Wow."

He let a wave of self-loathing crash down on top of him. If it suffocated him, that was no less than he deserved. Finally, he forced himself to look her in the eye, hating the doubt he saw there, and the despair that had arisen from discovering he wasn't the man she'd believed him to be.

He could relate. He wasn't the man he'd thought he was, either.

"Mark is right," he told her. "You shouldn't trust me, and you can't rely on me."

She took his words like blows, jerking back as each

one landed. “You haven’t done anything to hurt me,” she said. “You protected me from Charles. You’re not that guy.”

“Haven’t I hurt you?” he asked, standing to pace the length of the room. “How are you feeling right now?”

She didn’t answer, and he kept his back to her, unable to bear seeing her look at him with the disgust she no doubt felt. He had to get her out of there.

“You should leave Sanctuary and let the professionals protect you. I have no place filling that role, and they’ll do a better job than I ever could.” He scrubbed a hand over his bearded cheek. “I’ve already proved I bring nothing but trouble.” Coming to a halt, he stared at the wall, waiting to hear the swing of the door as she left. It didn’t come.

“I don’t understand,” she whispered. “You don’t have a computer, and your phone wasn’t built this decade. I’m not even sure it was built last decade. It can’t be true.”

His shoulders slumped, but he didn’t turn around. “It is. Everything you thought you knew about me was a lie. Accept it, and move on.”

There was a reason he didn’t have top-of-the-line technology. He couldn’t be trusted with it. Technology was his vice. Like an alcoholic, he couldn’t resist imbibing if it was around, so he kept it far away.

He could tell from her silence that she was finally getting it. The last pieces of the puzzle were dropping into place. That didn’t make it hurt any less when the silence stretched out. He touched the spot above his heart. It ached for her. With every beat, it yearned for her to come to him, wrap her arms around his waist, and tell him it didn’t matter. When he finally turned, the expression of utter betrayal on her face slammed into him as effectively as a brick wall.

"You want me to leave?" she demanded. "You want me to let the police handle things?"

He swallowed, torn between wishing he could erase the pain from her eyes and wanting to push her away so she didn't get hurt.

"Yes," he said. "I think that would be best."

"Okay." She wrapped her arms around her waist. "I guess this is goodbye, then."

Every step she took toward the exit put another crack through his heart. When the latch clicked softly behind her, he told himself it was just as well she'd learned the truth before they got in too deep. But he felt broken inside. Shattered. Torn apart.

I miss her. I want her.

She's better off without me.

26

Leaving Tione's cabin, Megan felt oddly detached, like a bird hovering above her body, watching her actions but feeling nothing. Everything was numb. Her skin, her feet —as she tripped over a root—and her heart. She weaved between the gardens and crossed the lawn on autopilot, her mind replaying the conversation that had ended moments prior. Tione hadn't denied a thing. She'd actually believed that she'd found someone to trust, but she didn't know him at all.

She was a fool. A naïve little fool.

What was wrong with her that she only chose men who hurt her? Her judgment must be fundamentally flawed. Not only could she not trust *him*, but she could no longer trust *herself*. Choosing the wrong man once was a mistake, but twice was a pattern.

She ripped the foyer door open and stalked to her bedroom, anger simmering beneath the surface. She'd been so close to moving on, and now this. One thing was for certain, she'd never be able to believe in a man again.

She'd be alone for the rest of her days, all because she couldn't tell the difference between a knight in shining armor and a black-hearted knave.

It was only when she reached her room that she noticed Pixie trotting behind her. The Chihuahua tried to follow her inside, but she closed the door between them. She couldn't handle any reminder of Tione right now. She needed to leave. To be gone. To put distance between herself and the man in the cabin. All of their kisses and touches and promises had been lies.

A paw scratched on the other side of the door.

"Go away!"

The scratching didn't stop, so she threw a sneaker, which hit with a thud. Through the wood, she could hear feet scamper off.

"Good," she murmured to herself, tossing her belongings into her bag. She went to the bathroom and collected her toothbrush but left the travel-size tubes of soap, shampoo, and conditioner behind. They weren't hers to take. Finally, she dragged the bag down the hall to Kat's apartment, and hammered on the door.

"What's up?" Kat asked as she leaned on the doorframe.

"I'm checking out," Megan said, hating the flash of concern that passed over her face. "It's time for me to get back on my own two feet, but thank you so much for letting me stay here with you."

Kat's hand went to her chest. "It sounds like you're telling me goodbye. Are you going back to Auckland?"

"No." She exhaled, the tension leaking from her shoulders. She was never going back to Auckland. Not to live. She couldn't be there without remembering things best forgotten. "You'll see me around. I just need..." She trailed off, unsure how to finish the sentence. What did she need? Time? Space? A place to call her own? "I need to work out some things."

Kat touched her arm, her fingers warm against Megan's chill skin. "Is this about Tee? Did something happen?"

She shook her head, then kept shaking it, seemingly unable to stop. *Get a grip, girl.*

"It's just time."

Kat's fingers traveled down her arm and slipped around her wrist, holding firm. "But it's not safe out there."

"We haven't seen Charles for days, and the police would have let me know if he was around. He's gone, Kat. And if he's not, then I can handle myself. He won't do anything stupid, because there are some things not even his parents can sweep under the carpet, and I'm not the timid girl he remembers. I'm not going anywhere with him. Not now, not ever."

That, at least, she was certain of. Because finally, after all this time, her fury outweighed her fear. She'd been quiet for too long, and hiding from her past hadn't helped. Tione had been right about one thing—she needed to start living again.

World, meet Megan Talbot, version 2.0.

She dropped her bag and hugged Kat tightly. Something about the other woman grounded and reassured her. She hoped they could stay friends. She didn't have many, and the few she did were precious.

"I'll see you around?" she asked, withdrawing. Kat's eyes were glossy with emotion, and Megan had to battle not to yank her into another embrace.

"Too right, you will." Kat kissed her cheek. "Be safe,

beautiful. And buy a cell phone, so we can talk. I want to know you're okay."

Megan smiled tremulously. "I will. Bye, Kat."

Then, before she could change her mind, she hauled the bag out of Sanctuary, loaded it into her car, and drove into town.

MEGAN DROVE three full circles around the town center before she made up her mind about where to go. She parked a short distance from The Shack, jammed her fists into her eye sockets to hold back the tears for a while longer, then walked to the ice cream parlor. It was busy, with a line to the door, and she waited until the customers had all been served before approaching the counter. Faith took in her expression with a single glance.

"Aww, buttercup." She came around and hugged her. Megan's tear ducts threatened to go into overdrive, so she patted Faith on the back and extricated herself. "What do you need? Tell me, and I'll make it happen."

"Do you really mean that?"

Faith frowned. "Of course. Anything that's in my power."

Megan took a deep breath. "I need a place to stay."

Faith's frown deepened. "Did you leave the lodge?"

"Yes, but I'd rather not talk about that right now." She couldn't handle thinking about Tione for a while.

Faith nodded and moved closer, taking her hand and squeezing it. "You can stay at my place." Her lips curved up. "On one condition."

She struggled for breath. Couldn't she just get a break with no strings attached? "What?"

"I want a dozen of your fabulous cupcakes to sell here every day." Faith's lips parted in a crooked grin, her teeth white against the red of her lips. "Consider it your rent."

Megan relaxed. She'd been expecting... Well, she wasn't sure exactly what she'd expected, but it hadn't been that. "Absolutely." She offered a hand. "Deal."

Faith rolled her eyes and pulled her into a hug even tighter than the previous one. "No shaking hands. We seal our business deals with hugs around here. If you're going to live with me, you might as well get used to the fact I'm a very hands-on person. Is that a problem for you?"

"Not at all."

"Great." The door pinged as a customer entered, and Faith reached into a pocket sewn in her skirt to retrieve a key, which she pressed into Megan's palm. "I live at 26 Rata Lane. The spare bedroom comes off the lounge. Make yourself at home."

"Seriously?" she asked. "Just like that?"

"Just like that," Faith confirmed. "I have to serve this gentleman, but help yourself to anything you like from the pantry, and I'll be home a little after six. See you then."

"Bye."

Dazed, Megan wandered out of The Shack and back to her car. She'd been afraid to hope for too much, and the ease with which the other woman had offered her home filled her with warmth, but also gave her a head rush. This shouldn't be so easy. In Auckland, no one went out of their way to help a virtual stranger, but everyone she'd met in Haven Bay had welcomed her with open arms, hefty baggage and all. Their kindness blew her mind.

Realizing she hadn't gotten directions and had no means to find Faith's house, she stopped and asked an old lady she'd never met for directions. The woman obliged and wished her a good day, but it was her parting remark that stunned Megan.

"Don't worry, lovey, we've got our eyes open for that no-good scoundrel. He won't get anywhere near you."

After recovering her voice, Megan thanked her and left, her thoughts spinning wildly. How did that woman know who she was, and why would she care about Megan's problems?

Did everyone around here have to be so wonderfully good?

She followed the woman's directions to Faith's house, but didn't notice much of anything as she unlocked the door and searched for the spare bedroom. Then she threw herself onto the bed and let the tears of pain, confusion, and gratitude finally fall.

HE WAS AN ASSHOLE.

An untrustworthy, mean asshole.

An asshole who deserved all the shittiness the world sent his way.

He shouldn't have pushed her away like that. He'd felt like a cornered dog, and he'd lashed out like one, cutting her deeply. He should have taken a few deep breaths and talked to her about his past. Taken the time to explain why he'd done the things he'd done rather than throwing it all in her face and expecting her to handle it.

But he wasn't reasonable. Not where Megan was concerned.

Should he have tried to convince her to stay? As it was, he may as well have handed her a one-way boarding pass to Sweden. He was never going to be allowed to touch her again. To kiss her again.

But he couldn't forget how she'd looked at him. Her eyes had questioned and condemned simultaneously. She was right to have looked at him that way. He'd revealed his underbelly to her, and it wasn't pleasant. The truth was, he shouldn't be responsible for caring for a woman—any woman. He'd fuck it up eventually. If she'd stayed with him, he'd have let her down sooner or later. That was what he did.

The cabin door crashed open, and Kat lurched through, uttering a stream of expletives. When she let up, she crossed her arms over her chest, and glared at him.

"You complete and total ass. I hope you're happy with yourself."

He stared at her, baffled.

"Megan left," she said in a tone that implied he was thick. "I don't know what you did to her, but she flew out of here like a *taniwha* was on her tail."

His stomach roiled, threatening to throw up the eggs he'd eaten for breakfast, and he covered his mouth with a hand. She'd gone. Just like that. It hadn't even been ten minutes since she left his cabin.

"Did anyone go with her?"

Kat's lips formed a thin line. "No."

God, he felt sick. Goddamn furious, too. How could she be stupid enough to leave the safety of the lodge without any protection?

Had he driven her to put herself in danger?

Bile rose, but he swallowed it down, taking perverse pleasure in the burn of acid in his throat. He deserved whatever pain the universe saw fit to heap upon him.

"Fuck."

"Exactly." Her pupils were pinpricks, her spine ramrod straight. He'd rarely seen her this way, but he recognized the symptoms of rage.

He whipped his cell phone from his pocket and dialed Elliot. The call went to voicemail. Swearing, he tried again.

"Tee," Elliot said when he answered. "To what do I owe the pleasure?"

"Megan just left Sanctuary," Tione replied. "She's alone. Has there been any sign of her ex in the area?"

"No reported sightings," Elliot said. "He's not staying at any of the hotels, but that doesn't rule out B&Bs."

"It's a good start." He thought fast. "I don't know where she's going." He turned to Kat, whose glare had lessened. "What do you think?"

"She wasn't leaving town." Kat seemed reluctant to offer more, and he reminded her that Megan's safety might be at risk. "Try Brooke or Faith," she suggested.

He relayed the message to the policeman. "Call Brooke and Faith; one of them might have seen her."

"Will do." Elliot cleared his throat. "Don't panic, Tee, the whole town is on the lookout for this guy. Once I track your girl down, I'll arrange a patrol to check up on her every few hours. We've got this under control. That bastard won't lay a finger on her."

Tione prayed he was right. "Thanks, Elliot." Hanging up, he turned to Kat. "The police are onto it. They'll do a better job of watching out for her than we possibly could."

She just shook her head, her upper lip curled in disdain. "Get over yourself."

He took a step back, shocked by her vehemence.

"Don't pretend you don't know what I'm talking about," she snapped, and he was glad for once that none of the dogs were inside with him, because they'd have had their hackles up, prepared to defend him. Kat looked ready to take a swing. "You're being a self-pitying sack of shit, and I've had enough."

She advanced on him until the bed hit the back of his knees and he sat. He had to crane his neck to see her face, but he immediately regretted the action because her eyes were like lasers searing him to the soul.

"You've made mistakes," she continued, fully into her rant now. "So what? That's not who you are anymore. But if you continue to let them rule your life, you'll lose her, and you know what?" She knelt in front of him so he couldn't avoid her gaze. "It won't be anyone's fault except your own." Her tone softened. "You don't want to go down this road. Trust me, I've been there. Regret won't keep you warm at night, and all the regret in the world won't reverse what happened." She patted his cheek, surprisingly gentle, and stepped away, giving him room to slump onto his back and stare at the ceiling.

Was she right? Had he changed? He wasn't so sure. And yeah, he knew regret wouldn't keep him warm at night, but he didn't deserve to go to bed with a woman he loved. He deserved to pay for his crimes. The justice system had never held him accountable, so the job was left to him.

"It's time to move on," she said, and he heard the door open. "Think on it."

27

MEGAN HAD KNOWN LEAVING Sanctuary would be difficult, but she wasn't prepared for how hard the loss of Tione's rare smile and gruff laugh hit her. Baking helped, though. Her first day in Faith's commercial kitchen felt strange, like she was trying to wear a shoe that didn't fit anymore, but by the second day she'd fallen into a routine of mixing batter and swapping recipe ideas.

She stayed in the back, away from customers, not ready to expose herself to them, but she listened to the buzz of conversation and tried to tell herself she could easily join in if she wanted. She wasn't broken, just weary. Apathetic. At least, she was until the first reviews of her cupcakes started to surface. People came back for seconds. Some asked for an entire box to take away with them. By day three, she was filling orders for dozens at a time. Her apple martini and pina colada cupcakes were crowd favorites. One woman even asked if she could supply cocktail-themed cupcakes for a wedding, in lieu of a cake.

With every bit of positive feedback Faith whispered

in her ear, she felt more and more like her old self—the one she'd been before she had the misfortune to meet Charles Wentworth Junior. Unfortunately, despite her success, her heart ached with loneliness when she collapsed into bed late at night after giggling with Faith over stories of kitchen experiments gone awry.

She sighed, and rolled onto her side. At least she seemed to be safe. Surely if Charles were in the area, he'd have made a move by now. Perhaps he'd decided to cut his losses. She tried to be comforted by that thought, and to ignore the fact that Tione had also let her go—well, more like he'd pushed her into letting *him* go. But no amount of mental gymnastics could help her come to terms with his past—although she did feel for him, because he seemed devastated by it. Once or twice, she couldn't resist the urge to use Google to learn more, but afterward she just felt sordid, so she put it to the back of her mind and assured herself that she was better off without him. She had Faith, and her new friends, and that would have to be enough.

"Hey," Faith called the following day, turning to catch Megan's eye across the kitchen. "That's the last of the Malibu cupcakes. Would you mind whipping up some more?"

"Sure thing," she agreed, going to the refrigerator where a generic batter waited to be flavored. "One dozen, or two?"

She heard Faith say, "Better make it two," and then someone grabbed her from behind, holding her arms tight to her sides and stuffing a cloth that smelled sickly sweet over her mouth. She tried to break free, or cry out, but the crushing grip didn't let up. Her head started to swim, her senses dulled, and then she lost consciousness.

"We've got a problem."

Ice pierced Tione's heart at the unexpected statement coming from Elliot, and a cold shiver raced through his body. Something must be horribly wrong. Elliot was the king of understatement.

"What happened?"

"A little under an hour ago, Megan Talbot vanished from The Shack."

"She what?" he demanded. He couldn't be hearing this right. "How could that possibly happen?"

Behind Elliot, wind whooshed in the background. "We don't know."

Before he'd even made the conscious decision to move, Tione was at the table with his keys in his hand. He clenched his fists, the keys digging into his palm so hard it hurt, and forced himself to focus on the call.

"Go back to the beginning."

"Not sure if you're aware of this, but Megan has been working at The Shack and sleeping in Faith's spare room," Elliot said.

Tione's heart squeezed. He had known that, but only because Kat had made sure to tell him, so he knew she was safe. "I know."

"The girls ran out of cupcakes this morning, so Megan was in the kitchen, making another batch. When Faith hadn't heard from her after half an hour, she went to check on her. Megan was gone, but nothing seemed to be out of place." He was quiet for a moment, and Tione wished he'd hurry along, but Elliot worked at his own pace. "Faith called the station immediately. She's hysterical, poor girl. We've gone over the kitchen, and visited her home, but there's no sign of Megan." He made a sound of frustration in the back of his throat, and Tione clutched the phone tighter to his ear. "I've walked the road between The Shack and Faith's place myself, and there's no trace of her anywhere."

"That's not good enough," Tione barked. "How can there be no trace? She must have gone somewhere. Women don't just disappear without their purses in the middle of a working day." Not unless they were taken against their will—something he seriously didn't want to consider. "Where's her car?"

"Parked at Faith's house. Apparently they've been walking to work."

"*Damn*. That little idiot." She should have known better than to make herself so vulnerable.

"Hey, now," Elliot warned. "Don't you talk about her like that, and there's no need to panic. There's a good chance she wandered off to one of the shops and forgot to let Faith know, or headed down the beach for a stroll. Faith tells me she wants to learn how to surf. We've checked the beach, but we could have missed her."

Tione shook his head, and started to pace. He knew in his soul that she wouldn't leave without saying where she was going. She wasn't like that. Something had happened to her. The whole town was on the alert, the police were looking out for her, and something bad had still happened.

"For God's sake," he growled, stomping his feet and

taking comfort in the dull ache that throbbed up his ankles. "You were supposed to be watching her. She was supposed to be safe." She was supposed to be better off without him.

"Don't you take that tone with me, young man." In the space of a second, Elliot morphed from friend to authority figure—into the man who'd picked Tione up out of the gutter more than once when he first moved to the bay, and who had no patience for his crap. "A patrol has been going past every hour, as I promised. If someone has been watching her, they probably waited for a window of opportunity between the patrols."

He couldn't argue with that logic, although his skin crawled at the thought of someone spying on Megan as she went about her life, completely oblivious. Sweat broke out on his upper lip. This wasn't Elliot's fault, it was *his*. He'd pushed her away in a bout of fucking self-pity. Yeah, sure, he'd told himself he was doing her a favor, but the horrible truth was that he'd been waiting for the other shoe to drop, and as soon as it showed any sign of doing just that, he'd given her the shove she needed to strike out on her own.

He should have kept her close. He should have protected her, whether she wanted him to or not. His life would be worth nothing if his actions caused harm to another woman, especially Megan.

Megan. His heart seemed to echo her name with every beat. *Ka-thunk* became *Meg-an*. Every godforsaken pulse of blood in his veins screamed for her. *Megan, Megan, Megan*. What was he without her? Nothing. He'd let her down, just as he'd feared, and just as he'd tried in vain to avoid.

"What can I do?" he asked. "I'll do anything, Elliot. Where are you? I'll be there in two minutes."

"Stay where you are," Elliot ordered. "The most useful thing you can do is keep your cool and try to track her down. I can't mount a full-scale manhunt. Not until she's been missing for forty-eight hours. But if you see something suspicious, I have reason to call for reinforcements."

"You're shitting me." They weren't looking for her? He couldn't be serious.

"I'm sorry, Tee. My hands are tied."

"Fuck that. I don't give a damn about your government bureaucracy, Elliot. You and I both know something is wrong here, and she could be on the other side of the country by the time forty-eight hours are up. She could be *out* of the goddamn country."

Elliot sighed. "I'm doing all I can. I'll be out looking for her, and so will every other policeman in town. Haven Bay isn't big. Someone must have seen something, and we'll find them, then we'll find her. We'll get your girl back, Tione."

"We'd better."

28

MEGAN'S MOUTH WAS DRY, and her head pounded. She tried to draw in air, but her tongue was thick and clumsy, blocking the way. Instead, she breathed in through her nose, ignoring the stinging sensation around her nostrils, and immediately inhaled the scent of seawater and fish. Gagging, she bent at the waist and expelled warm vomit onto the floor between her knees. The sour smell of it made her retch again, but her stomach had been thoroughly emptied. She hung her head, feeling the rasp of rough linen over her skin. A blindfold.

She stilled, paralyzed by terror, and took stock of her situation. Her wrists were bound in her lap so tightly her fingers had swollen, and when she wiggled them, they tingled. Tensing her calves, she felt rope looping around her ankles, securing her to a chair. She tested the knots. They weren't budging.

Where was she? Why had she been brought here?

She remembered arms around her, being tossed over someone's shoulder like a sack of potatoes, and then... Nothing. What had happened?

Hinges creaked, and she heard footsteps. Instinctively, she loosened her muscles, went floppy, and pretended to be unconscious, but she was too slow.

"Good, you're awake."

She'd know that smooth, slimy voice anywhere.

"Charles," she croaked, as though she hadn't spoken in months.

The steps stopped. "God, what is that foul smell?" He must have noticed the vomit because he clucked his tongue. "You're quite revolting sometimes, do you know that? I mean, really, was that necessary?"

She tried to answer, but her tongue refused to cooperate. With what brainpower she could summon, she took stock of her situation. She was alone with a man who wouldn't hesitate to hurt her if he thought he could get away with it.

Without warning, something slapped her hard enough to snap her face around. A searing burn at her temple told her the skin was split. He'd probably reopened her old wound with the same signet ring that had injured her the first time around. Rough fingers grabbed the blindfold and tore it from her, taking several strands of hair with it. Light flooded her eyes, so bright she could scarcely stand it. She tried to squeeze her eyelids shut, but Charles dropped the blindfold and held them open.

She cursed and her voice echoed between them, giving her an idea. She opened her mouth to scream, so someone would hear her, but he clapped his big hand over her mouth. She bit him, tasting blood, and spat it out just as he backhanded her hard enough to overbalance the chair, sending her crashing to the ground.

He kicked her, but she was expecting it and curled

into a ball to protect her damaged ribs. "Bitch! You don't do that to me. Have you forgotten who's boss, Meggie? I *own* you."

"No, you don't," she panted, breathing through the pain and refusing to be cowed. "I'm not a piece of property." She spat again, trying to get rid of the awful taste in her mouth. "Nobody can own me."

He laughed like a crazy man. "That's what you think? Haven't I taught you anything?" He strode away, and while his back was turned, she took the opportunity to study their surroundings.

They were in an old wooden building that measured perhaps six meters by five. The roof was low and rotting, with several boards missing. There was nothing to clue her in as to where she was. No furniture, other than the chair she was tied to, and no personal items. She battled to quieten her breathing so she could hear noises outside. The low hiss of surf over sand suggested they were near a beach, but she couldn't make out any other details before Charles was back, waving a sheet of paper in her face. She squinted, trying to make out the letters on the page.

"You filed a restraining order against me?" he demanded, and kicked her shin. She hissed with pain, but was strangely relieved to know what this was about. "You're nothing without me, you backward little bitch. Did you think I'd let you ruin me like this?" He strode to the wall and slammed his fist into it. She flinched, but at least he'd chosen not to rain his fists down upon her. *Yet.* She held her tongue, hoping to delay the inevitable.

"If this ever got out... fuck." He kicked her other shin, and she bit her lip hard enough to draw blood. "If this shit ever got out, my chances of making partner at the firm would completely vanish." He squatted, looming over her, his face close enough for her to make out the red streaks in the whites of his eyes, and the blackheads on the tip of his nose. "You know, I thought about moving on, Meggie. However much Glenn likes you, there are other women out there who would make him happy and not act like such an entitled slut. But you had to go and do this. I won't let you spread your vitriolic lies. It's time to shut your mouth, come home, and tell everyone this was a big misunderstanding. Do you hear me?"

Megan's eyes fluttered shut, and for the length of a heartbeat, time seemed to stand still. She was hovering over a precipice, her future hanging in the balance. If she did as he asked, she'd never escape him, and everything would get exponentially worse. If she didn't, and he'd truly lost it, he might kill her and toss her body into the ocean. Either way, she was screwed, and damned if she was going to bow to him ever again.

Her body trembled, every nerve coming alive, every muscle twitching with raw energy. It was impossible to straighten her spine when she was tied to a chair and lying on the ground, but she raised her head and looked him in the eye.

"No."

His eyes bulged, and his mouth fell open, his breath incongruously minty. "No?"

"No," she repeated, then she whipped her head back and smashed her forehead into his.

He stumbled, clutching his face, swearing colorfully.

"I won't back down this time." Strength rose from somewhere deep within her. She needed to say these words. Had needed to say them for quite some time. "You can do whatever you want to me, but as long as I'm alive, I'm never going to stop telling people what you are."

She was weightless, her chest so light that she could have floated away if not for the binds holding her down. Finally, she'd done it. She'd become a person she could be proud of. Whatever he did to her, he couldn't take that away. It was priceless. Eternal.

"Yes, you damn well will back down." He let go of his head, and she could already see a lump forming, the skin turning blue. No doubt she looked worse, but she didn't care. That bump was a sign that she was a fighter, and she could fight this. "I'll cut your tongue out and feed it to the sharks," he blustered. "I'll put a fucking bullet in your brain. You won't be telling anyone anything then, will you?"

She held his gaze, her own steady and unflinching. "And how will you explain that to Glenn?" She could mention the police, but his boss had always been his weakest point. "You're all talk, Charles, and you may as well give up now because the only way I'm going anywhere with you is in a box."

At that moment, Charles's phone rang. He snatched it from his pocket and barked into it, "What do you want, Seeley?" He was silent for a moment, apparently listening to Seeley on the other end, then shook his head. "I don't care what you think of the plan." He strode over and kicked a wall. "Fuck you." Then he hung up and met her eyes again. "It's just you and me, Meggie. Good old Seeley is on his way out of town. You sure you don't want to change your mind about that box?"

"FUCK," Tione growled, hanging up from his conversation with Betty, who'd mobilized the town's senior citizens. Despite searching for two hours, no one had seen her. Stalking to the intersection, he hauled in a breath and tried to calm himself. He'd walked the streets, checked out the beach, looked in the library, the cafe, the pub, the gym, anywhere he thought she might have been. Every dead end he reached only made him more certain that she'd been taken against her will. Even with the crowds of tourists, someone would have seen her if she was around.

He drew a sheet of paper from his pocket and moved to the next name. Hugh MacAllister, the town's council representative. Tione doubted Hugh had seen or heard anything, but he was methodically working his way through a list of anyone who might be tuned in to what was happening in the bay. When Hugh had no information to share, he hung up before he could say something he regretted, and fought the urge to smash the phone on the pavement.

He wracked his brain. There had to be a better way to find her. A more efficient way. Wentworth was a guy with resources, which meant he might have enough money and connections to hide Megan somewhere out of reach of the locals.

A thought niggled at the back of his mind, taunting him. If he embraced his old skills, he could find a clue no one else had. He could find *her*.

But in doing so, he'd risk losing himself—and what if things ended as they had last time? What if he inadvertently made things worse for her? He couldn't live with himself. But he didn't think he could live with himself if he sat back and did nothing, either.

What was he worth without her? Nothing. Even if he went down the rabbit hole and never came back out, it wouldn't matter because he'd have done his best to save her.

Decision made, he ran to his car, fired the engine, and raced to Sanctuary, skidding over the gravel to park at the entrance. He sprinted up the ramp, down the hall, and threw open the door to Kat's living quarters. She wasn't there, but he'd already known she wouldn't be. She was out searching, as was Sterling. Tione found her computer, powered it up, and muttered impatiently under his breath as it came to life.

The screen asked for a password, and he entered it, and waited. His fingers were jittery on the keyboard, his knee rocking up and down as the homepage loaded. He found Wentworth's employer's intranet website, uploaded his personal hacking software, and prayed to God it still worked as well as it used to. With a few keystrokes and a bit of luck, he was into Wentworth's email account. He scrolled, scanning for anything of interest. When he found nothing, he ventured into the man's browsing history and struck gold. The history had been deleted, but not erased completely, and the most recent web page was an article about the historic boathouse located on the beach outside Anderson Gray's property.

Gray's place was on the edge of town. Tourists stayed away because they didn't know it existed, and locals stayed away because Gray was an ass. He was also, by and large, housebound. If a person were to find his way to Gray's beach without cutting through his property, the guy was unlikely to know they were there. It was an ideal spot to hide a terrified woman. No one would see her, and no one would hear her scream.

Tione called Elliot and wasted no time explaining himself. “Send someone to check Gray’s boathouse. I think that’s where he’s taken her.”

“Huh,” Elliot said. “That would make a lot of sense. Is this a lucky guess, Tee?”

Tione swallowed. “It’s better than a lucky guess. I can’t tell you anything, but you need to go and look for her.”

“I’ll send a team as soon as I can, but Gray’s not going to like this.”

29

Tione hammered on the door of Anderson Gray's renovated villa, hard enough to bruise his fist.

"Gray!" he yelled. "Open up, you sullen son of a bitch. Get your ass out here right now."

The door swung inward, and Tione stumbled. He would have fallen on his face if the bulk of Gray's body hadn't prevented it.

"Get off my property, fuckwit," Gray grumbled in his American drawl, shoving him away and then jamming his hands in his pockets. In years past, Gray had been a Hollywood heartthrob, and Tione supposed he was still a decent-looking man, although his hair was unkempt and his clothes looked like they'd been balled on the floor and recycled a dozen times without being washed. "What's up with people not leaving me the hell alone today?"

His words sent sharp jabs of both fear and exhilaration through Tione. "What do you mean?"

Gray wrinkled his nose, taken aback. "What's your problem, man? Calm the fuck down."

"I will *not* calm down," Tione said, low as can be. "Tell me what you meant."

Gray shrugged broad shoulders, then cracked his neck. "Some jerk is out on my beach and won't leave. Gave him a piece of my mind, but he's a stubborn shit."

Adrenaline rushed through Tione's veins. He was right. Wentworth was here.

"Here's how it is," he said, his tone brooking no argument. "That man on your beach has kidnapped a woman. You need to call the police and tell them to get here yesterday. Got it?"

"Are you playing with me?" Gray asked, dubious.

"No," he gritted out. "Call the police. Right. Now. I have to get down there. She might be in trouble." He didn't bother asking Gray to go with him.

"Wait." Gray spoke quickly now, ushering him into the house. "Take this." He thrust a hunting rifle into Tione's hands. "I'll call the police, and then follow you down."

"Sure." No way was that going to happen, but he'd let the man have his pride.

"Go out the back door, and take the path through the woods. They won't see you coming."

"Will do." Clasping the rifle tight to his chest, he ducked out the exit and darted into the cover of the trees that grew down to the edge of the sand. The gun made him uncomfortable. He'd only ever used one at a firing range in Silicon Valley when he was trying to impress a potential investor, and that had been a long time ago. Today he was taking far too many trips down memory lane.

Pretend it's a paintball gun.

Reaching the edge of the trees, he spotted the dilapidated boathouse no more than thirty yards away. The wall facing him had no windows, and he dashed across the sand, dropping to his knees nearby. He crawled around the building until he found the window, and rose up into a crouch, peering above the windowsill.

The gloom inside made it difficult to see anything, but when his vision adjusted, he could make out Megan bound to a chair on the floor. Blood streaked her temple and dribbled down the side of her face, her lip was fat, and one of her eyes was swollen. Fury washed over him. He'd seen her like this before, and he wanted to strangle the monster responsible. His hands squeezed around the cool metal of the rifle, and he amended the thought. Forget strangulation, he'd be happy to shoot the man.

Charles Wentworth had his back to Tione, and was speaking in a low voice. Then, without provocation, he struck Megan's torso with a steel-toed boot. She screamed, and Tione tensed, wanting nothing more than to bust through the window and throw the bastard on the ground, but he might have a gun or a knife. He ground his teeth together. He had to be patient, and wait for the right time to make a move, but as Megan pressed her lips together to keep from screaming when another kick landed, staying still was the hardest thing he'd ever done.

"COME HOME." Charles punctuated the words with a kick. "And tell everyone," *kick*, "you were mistaken, and you're marrying me." *Kick*.

Megan's teeth ground together because if she allowed her jaw to loosen, she feared she'd give in and do whatever he wanted to make the beating stop. He was wearing her out, and with every kick, the whites of his eyes bulged wider, more spittle flew from his mouth, and she wondered if she'd ever be safe. Even if she got away from him, could she actually keep him away from her? Or would he always come looking?

Staying optimistic in the face of his relentless rage proved challenging, and seeing him now, she didn't know how she'd ever been fooled into thinking him charming. He was a brute, plain and simple. She must have been willfully oblivious.

A flash of movement in the window caught her attention, and she tried not to react. If someone had found her, she didn't want to give them away. The top of a dark-haired head appeared, then a bronze forehead, and finally a pair of the most gorgeous dark eyes she'd ever had the pleasure of gazing into.

Tione. He'd come for her.

A wave of relief washed over her. She wasn't going to die in this ancient shack, and Charles wouldn't escape justice. With Tione here, it was two on one, and she'd yet to see any sign that Charles was armed—he'd always preferred the hands-on approach—so she liked their odds. But first, she had to make sure Charles didn't notice him. Her ex was deranged, and she was afraid of what he'd do if cornered.

"Hey," she called, her voice wavering. "I'm not going home with you, and you know what? You were a terrible boyfriend."

It worked. He dropped to his knees, grabbed the collar of her shirt, and jerked her toward him. "You want to say that to my face?"

She did. She *really* did. "I lied when I said my family liked you. They hated you from day one."

His hand wrapped around her neck in a way that might have been considered loving if he hadn't done this exact thing once before, and then proceeded to choke her.

"Shut the fuck up. You're not in charge here."

She sucked in a deep breath. He wasn't holding her tightly enough to cut off her air supply yet. "You're bad in bed," she choked out. "You're not funny, and you're a sexist pig."

His hands tightened around her neck, crushing her larynx, making her see spots. "Shut. Up."

The door slammed open and Charles's whole body jerked in shock, but his hands stayed where they were. Megan shoved her chin down to loosen his grip, and gasped for breath.

"Let her go, or I'll shoot." Tione's voice shook, but from what she could see of him, his hands were steady on the trigger of a shotgun.

Charles tensed, then slowly released his grip on her. Cool air rushed into her lungs, and she coughed.

"You won't shoot me," Charles said, and then laughed. He was cracked. Truly cracked. "If you shoot me, you're going to look like the guilty party."

Tione didn't waver. He aimed the rifle directly at Charles's head. Megan wondered whether he'd ever shot a gun before. Something in the way he held it made her think he wasn't particularly familiar with them.

"The police are already on the way," he said, his gaze flicking to Megan and narrowing as he cataloged her injuries. "Why don't you come in easy? Don't make this worse for yourself."

"I don't believe you." Charles stood, ignoring her like she no longer mattered. "Do you know who I am?"

Tione's jaw worked. "You're an asshole who hurts people weaker than you. A bully."

"I'm a Wentworth."

"Maybe that means something in Auckland, but out here, it sure as hell doesn't." An ominous click sounded as his finger moved. "Get on your knees, and put your hands behind your head."

Charles started to obey, and Tione gave his attention to Megan. It was only for a moment, but it was enough for Charles to lunge forward, catching Tione around the waist and knocking him down. The men wrestled for the gun. A shot went off, and she screamed, thrashing against her bindings, trying to break free. The knots around one ankle loosened and she yanked her foot out, not caring as the rope ripped her skin and pain blazed through her limb as circulation returned to the extremities.

Using her free foot, she shuffled around until she had a clear view of the men, then cocked her knee, and rammed her throbbing foot into Charles' back. He howled, and lashed out at her. Pain surged through her anew, but as she'd hoped, her move gave Tione the chance he needed to pull the rifle clear and drag himself away.

Before he could stand, another shot rang out, and a chunk of wood exploded out of the wall opposite the window. They all ducked for cover as policemen in black outfits stormed the building, forcing Charles to the ground and cuffing him before escorting Tione from the room and talking in low voices that she couldn't understand.

"Miss Talbot." A face appeared above hers. A face with ruddy cheeks, wisps of gray hair, and worried eyes. It was the kind policeman who'd taken her statement. Officer Elliot. "You hold still now, little lady," he said in the tone one might use with a skittish dog. "We're going to cut you free, okay?"

"Okay," she whispered. Though she'd been full of fight mere minutes ago, all of the energy seemed to have drained from her, and she felt tender and limp. Her ribs ached, her lungs burned, her throat was raw, and every inch of her was battered and bruised. She longed to soak in a warm bath, and then be put to bed by her mother. She wanted to be held, and to be told that everything would be all right.

The policemen finished cutting her leg bindings and she sagged onto the ground. They untied her wrists last, and she winced as the blood flow returned to them, then rubbed at the deep grooves imprinted on her skin. It occurred to her that she should probably get up, but she wasn't sure her legs would support her weight. Charles had kicked her so many times she wouldn't be surprised if he'd broken something.

She shifted, testing whether she could sit, and whimpered when a hot lance stabbed her side. A hand landed on her shoulder. Tione? She looked up so fast she almost gave herself whiplash, but it was only Elliot.

"Don't move," he said gently. "We've got a stretcher coming for you. You'll be airlifted to Waikato Hospital. I'll come, too. The doctors will help, and we'll need to take your statement and collect evidence so we can nail that bastard in court."

She nodded, but what she really wanted was to see Tione.

“Tee?” she asked, hoping he’d understand.

The thunk-thunk-thunk of helicopter blades and the blast of air through the open door signaled the arrival of the medical chopper.

Elliot turned away from her and called, “Bates, find Tione.” To Megan, he said, “We’ll get him, sweetheart.”

Two paramedics entered, carrying a stretcher between them. One of them, a woman with a tight braid and a friendly but detached expression, knelt beside her. “Hey there,” she said. “I’m Debbie. What’s your name?”

“Megan.”

“Nice to meet you, Megan.” Her partner moved to Megan’s feet and palpated her legs. She tried not to make a sound, but damn, it hurt. “Sara and I are going to lift you onto the stretcher, okay? You don’t need to do anything. It might be painful, but we’ll be as careful as we can. Do we have your permission to do that?”

“Yes.” Talking hurt. Her throat had been bruised in the assault.

The two women supported her back and legs, and heaved her onto the stretcher. Megan gasped, but bit her tongue so she didn’t swear at them when they were only trying to help.

“Tee?” she asked again, to the room at large.

“Bates!” Elliot yelled.

Officer Bates stuck his head in the door. “No sign of him, boss. Desta says he was taken to the station to give a statement and discuss whether he’d face any charges.”

Panic spiked through her. “Charges?” She reached for Elliot, but fell short. “Why would he face charges?”

Bates didn’t seem to sense her distress. “Unlawful possession of a weapon. Assault with a deadly weapon.”

“But he was protecting me!” Her inflamed throat

protested as she spoke louder, but she went on. "Please, don't do anything to him. I want to see him. Can you—"

"Don't worry yourself," Elliot soothed. "We'll work it all out. You just focus on healing, and answering questions. I promise you'll see him again soon."

Megan's chest tightened, and her skin heated. She wanted Tione. Why had he left? Why wasn't he here?

Lying back on the stretcher, she stared up at nothing as the paramedics began to move her to the helicopter. Perhaps he didn't know how much she wanted him with her. Perhaps he thought she hated him. She wished that everything would just make sense for once.

30

At Waikato Hospital, Megan was X-rayed, photographed, poked and prodded to the edge of sanity. If not for the pain medication, she'd have begged them to leave her alone hours ago. The doctors reported that her ribs were broken, but would likely heal on their own. Otherwise, none of her injuries were serious. She'd bruise like hell, but Charles hadn't done any permanent damage. She could have told them as much. The only permanent damage was to her peace of mind.

She talked Elliot through the events of the day, and he recorded the interview, then she repeated the entire story to Faith, who'd driven from Haven Bay. Now, Faith sat beside the bed, holding her hand, while Elliot jotted notes on a notepad. Faith had been crying. Eyeliner ran down her cheeks, her nose was red, and she'd apologized a million times.

"I'm so, so sorry," she moaned. "I should have checked on you sooner. I can't believe I let this happen."

Once again, Megan squeezed her hand to reassure her. "It wasn't your fault."

"Tell that to my conscience. I feel responsible." She plumped Megan's pillow and fussed with her blanket, drawing it up to cover her shoulders. Megan wasn't cold, but the actions calmed Faith, so she didn't say anything.

Elliot tucked his pen into his pocket, and Megan asked him the question that had been on her mind since they began the interview. "How did you find me?"

The officer cleared his throat. "A tip from Tione."

"Oh." That raised another slew of questions. "How did he know where I was?"

Elliot gave her a pointed look. "I don't know, and I'd rather not ask, if you get my meaning." With that, he stood and strode to the door. "Take care, Megan."

Then he left them alone in the hospital room.

Faith raised a quizzical brow. "What do you suppose he meant?"

Megan made herself shrug. "No idea."

But she did know. At least, she thought she might. Tione used his old hacker skills to find her. The ones she'd condemned him for because of how he'd messed up in the past. But he'd used them to save her, even though hacking had resulted in what must be the worst experience of his life, and even though he'd clearly said he didn't like the person he became when he did.

That wasn't the act of a bad person, it was the move of a selfless man who cared for her. Even loved her, maybe.

Her stomach sank. She'd screwed up. He'd tried to push her away the moment she learned about his past, and she'd let him, but she should have stood her ground and asked more questions. He was a decent man, and she should have trusted her judgment when it came to him. After all, a lot of people had shady pasts, or periods of their life they weren't proud of, but he wasn't like that anymore. He was good to his core, and she needed to let him know that. He couldn't keep carrying around the guilt.

"Faith?"

"Yeah, cutie pie."

"When they discharge me, can you take me to Sanctuary? There's something I need to do."

TIONE KICKED A SOCCER BALL, picturing Charles Wentworth's face, and sent it flying across the yard. Trevor, Bella and Zee raced after it, and Pixie ran behind them on shorter legs. Zee won the quarrel over the ball and brought it back, dropping it at his feet. He kicked it again, breathing heavily, his shoulders rising and falling. His struggle with Charles earlier should have worn him out, but instead he was jittery, as though he'd drunk ten coffees and washed them down with a Red Bull. He'd thought the cool evening breeze might help, but so far it hadn't done the trick.

"Tee?"

He whirled around, his breath catching in his chest when he saw Megan silhouetted against the foyer doorway. He took a step forward, then stopped himself. He wanted to run to her, take her in his arms and kiss her all over, but he didn't want to hurt her, and he didn't know where they stood. Did she blame him for not being there to protect her?

Bella nudged his foot, and he shooed her away.

"You're here." His voice was hoarse.

"So are you." She traced the patches of lawn between the garden, making her way to him. She walked with a limp, and one arm curved protectively around her middle. His dogs—Pixie included—dropped the ball and raced over to greet her. She bent, wincing a little, and patted each in turn.

"Hi, sweethearts. It's so good to see you." Pixie jumped up, her paws landing on Megan's knees, and she petted the Chihuahua affectionately. He watched her movements, marveling in the difference between their reaction to her now compared to when she'd first arrived, and wishing she'd touch him that same way. Finally, she straightened and addressed him. "You didn't come with me."

He swallowed, a lump working its way down his throat. "I had to give a statement, and I wasn't even sure if you'd want me there."

"I did." She stopped in front of him, and his heart banged at the sight of her battered face. Her cheek was blue and purple, the wound on her temple taped shut, her eyes swollen as he'd noticed earlier. He didn't realize he'd reached for her until his hand touched hers. He pulled away, but she twined her fingers firmly between his. "Thank you for saving me."

He moistened his lips. The way she was looking at him... Did she know what he'd done?

"I wish I'd gotten there sooner. In fact, I wish I'd never left your side. That I'd kept you safe."

"Tee." His name was soft on her lips. He ached to hear her say it again. "I know what you had to do to find me, and I know how hard it must have been."

Her statement was a scythe to his soul and a benediction, all at once. She knew, but she was still here. She wasn't looking at him with revulsion, or shoving him away.

"I was crazy with worry," he confessed. "I'm sorry I let him get his hands on you." Misery tasted like iron in his mouth. "I'm sorry I let you down."

"You didn't let me down," she murmured. "You were there for me when no one else was."

He dropped to his knees, keeping his hands in hers. He'd stay on his knees forever if it kept Megan in his life. Fighting his feelings for her was futile. He'd been an idiot not to see the truth: he was already in love with her. He had been for a while now. There would never be anyone else for him, but he didn't know if he could repair the damage he'd wrought on their relationship.

"I should have told you about my past," he said, sitting back on his heels, holding her gaze and willing her to see the truth in his eyes. "You were too good to be true, and I guess I was scared that if I told you, you wouldn't be able to see past it. I'm not the person I was back then, but I know how important trust is to you, and I should have come clean." With the utmost care, he wrapped his arms around her waist, his hands hovering over the surface of her lower back, and rested his head on her stomach. "I hope you can be a better person than I am, and find it within yourself to forgive me."

EMOTION SWELLED in Megan's chest, stronger than anything she'd ever experienced. She could scarcely grasp what was happening. This man—this wonderful, fierce, protective man—was on his knees for her. He was handling her as though she were the most precious thing he'd ever had the privilege of touching, and he'd embraced a part of himself he loathed because her safety meant more to him than his own.

"You're a good person, Tee." She could hear the passion dripping from her words, and hoped he could, too. "Everyone has made mistakes they'd rather others not know about." She threaded her fingers through his hair and cradled his head against her belly, grateful for the painkillers she'd been given at the hospital, otherwise even touching like this would probably hurt. "Look at mine. They literally came back to beat the crap out of me."

"It's not the same." His lips moved on her tank top, and heat skittered up her spine in response.

Her hands journeyed lower, stroking his cheek, rubbing the line of his jaw. "Your past mistakes don't define you, and I shouldn't have ever believed they did. I certainly don't need to hear them all, although I'll be around to listen if you ever want to talk."

He tilted his chin up. "You will?"

"Yes," she confirmed, learning the contours of his face with her fingers. "I might not know every little thing you've ever done, but I know who you are inside, and that's enough." She closed her eyes and let him ground her in the moment. Today had been exhausting, but she'd gained her second wind. "I can see that you're sincere. I care about you, and I hope that you care about me, too."

"I do. So much, sweetheart. I love you." He pressed a kiss softly to her belly. "We may not have known each other long, but that doesn't change how I feel about you. I love you so damn much it hurts."

Her lips lifted, and so did her heart. "Truly?"

"Truly."

She laughed, despite the ache of her throat. "Good. Because it may be early days, but I want to take a risk on you, Tione Kingi." She didn't think her heart had ever hammered as furiously as it was now. She was putting everything out there, and hoped to God he wouldn't let her fall. "I love you, and if you're prepared to deal with the mess that is my life, then I want us to be together. What do you think of that?"

A grin split his face, and his teeth gleamed in the moonlight. "I think you're crazy if you honestly believe there's any possibility I'd say no."

"So that's a yes?" she teased.

He stood, cupped her face between his palms, and gave her the gentlest kiss she'd ever received. Their lips hardly brushed, but that light touch conveyed a depth of emotion so powerful her eyes filled with tears, and she had to blink them back. She wanted to lean into him, to be absorbed into his big, strong body until they were one.

"I will never deserve someone as good as you," he rumbled, his face not even an inch from hers. "But I'll try every day to make sure you never regret choosing me." He bent his forehead and bumped the tip of his nose to hers. "Come inside with me. The dogs have missed you." He skimmed another butterfly-soft kiss over her hair. "*I've* missed you. Come back, Megan."

Wordlessly, she took his hand and followed him into his cabin, knowing as she did so that his invitation wasn't only into the cabin, but into his life, and his heart. She went gladly, offering up the same in return.

Her old life had burned down around her, but from the ashes had arisen the promise of something new, and so much better. For as long as she lived, she would never let that go. Tione was her safe place now, and Haven Bay was her home. Finally, she belonged.

EPILOGUE

THE DAY HAD ARRIVED, and none too quickly. Megan studied the letter from her doctor that declared her officially healed. Hearing Tione's voice outside the cabin, she stuffed the letter in a drawer and positioned herself on the end of the bed. She crossed her legs, then uncrossed them. Which was sexier? She settled on crossing them, and leaned back on her elbows, striking a seductive pose—she hoped.

The door opened, and paws skittered over wood as Pixie darted inside. Tione's head was turned away, his attention on something behind him, but the second he swiveled around, he stopped short and stared.

"Holy shit." He looked her up and down, then his tongue peeked out between his lips, and he moistened them. A choking noise came from the back of his throat. "Is this..." He trailed off. "Are you..."

"Clean bill of health."

She couldn't have hoped for a better reaction. He scrambled to grab Pixie, thrust the dog outside, slammed the door, and dropped his pants.

"Fuck," he breathed, crossing the distance between them, the bulge in his underwear already thickening before her eyes. "Look at you."

He yanked his shirt over his head, leaving his torso bare, and she couldn't tear her gaze off the tattoos across his chest, the ridged abdomen, the meaty biceps she wanted to bite into.

"Where'd you get this?" he demanded, gesturing at the tiny lace corset, panties and garters she wore. "No wait, don't tell me. I like the mystery." He swore. "God, you're hot."

"Are you just going to look at me?" she asked, her courage faltering.

His eyes rose to hers, dark and intense. "No fucking way. I'm going to make you come so hard you can't remember your name."

She swallowed, and he watched the delicate movement of her throat, riveted. "Oh."

"You'll remember mine, though," he growled, and then he dropped to his knees and tore at the corset with his hands. "Shit, how do I get this off?"

"Laces," she breathed. "At the back." Rolling over to give him access, she pushed her butt into his crotch and rubbed against him like a cat. His fingers fumbled with the delicate strings, but then he jerked them wide and lifted the corset over her head.

She turned over and wriggled back on the bed, giggling nervously when he hauled himself onto it and crawled over her. His tongue flicked the bead of her nipple, and she gasped.

"So pretty and pink," he muttered. "I want to see your other pink parts." His hands went to her thighs and separated them, exposing the damp fabric of her panties to him. "Mm." He made a sound of contentment, then buried his face in her lap, his mouth latching over her.

Her back arched off the bed. "Oh, God," she panted.

This wasn't what she'd expected. She'd thought he'd head straight to the main course, but he didn't seem to be in a hurry, and she didn't intend to stop him. Clutching handfuls of his hair, she rode his tongue until her hips were bucking and every muscle of her body was quivering.

TIONE HAD NEVER SEEN anything more beautiful than Megan when she came. Her whole body clenched, her skin flushed, and she thrashed as if she were in agony and he was her only salvation. He knew she was getting close, but he drew back, refusing to give her the little push she needed to go over the edge.

"Tee," she moaned, her head tossing from side to side. His dick hung hot and heavy between his thighs, so hard it hurt and pre-cum oozed from the tip. He wasn't proud of it, but he'd been humping the bed ever since he started plundering her with his mouth and tongue.

She wanted to come? Well, so did he, and this time, he wanted to feel her spasm around him as he thrust into her. He wanted to own her, body and soul, the way she owned him. He wanted it all.

He drew back, notched himself into her entrance, and rocked back and forward, teasing her. Teasing himself, too. She'd gone on the pill shortly after Charles was arrested, and he couldn't wait to feel her silken walls surrounding him, with nothing to keep them apart. She bit her lip and pressed onto him, forcing the head of his dick into her warm, wet channel.

He swore. "I'm trying to take this slow, babe."

"Forget slow. We've been slow enough." She ground into him, rotating her hips in filthy little motions that had him sweating and cursing and grabbing them to hold her still.

"You do that, and it's over."

He eased back, then plunged into her.

She sighed, her eyes fluttering shut, fingers digging into his shoulders. "Again, Tee."

She clenched around him, already so close to coming, but he wanted to draw this moment out forever. He slid in and out, feeling the glorious heat of her all around him. He gritted his teeth and lodged himself deep within her, nice and slow. But then her hands were gripping his ass, hauling him to her, and a savage roar tore from his throat.

He tried to slow down, to regain his agonizing rhythm, but every slide of their bodies made him crave more. Faster, harder, deeper. Lowering his head, he bit into her shoulder to keep from shouting again, then eased her legs further apart and shuddered when she stilled beneath him, staring into his eyes, her own wild and struggling to remain open as she came for him. He drilled into her, willing her to keep looking at him. Nothing in his life had ever been as incredibly intimate as holding her gaze as she mounted a crescendo of pleasure and crashed over the other side.

Then he was coming with her, jerking inside her, unable to resist her pull for any longer—and frankly, not wanting to. Stars exploded behind his eyes, and his vision clouded as he gave her everything he had. Then he dropped onto her chest, out of breath. Her arms came around him, her hands resting on his lower back. She turned her face and her breath tickled his ear as she spoke.

"That was well worth the wait."

He laughed, utterly drained, and raised himself up to kiss her. Not with the passion of a few moments ago, but with all the tenderness that resided in his heart for her. "I love you."

She grinned, and nuzzled him back. "I love you, too."

And then they breathed together, content to simply exist in each other's arms. At least, until they regained their energy for a second round.

THE END

IF ONLY YOU KNEW - PROLOGUE

MICHAEL BRIGGSTON'S heart hammered in his throat as he tucked a bouquet of wildflowers—Bex's favorite—under his arm and approached the door to the home she shared with his brother Wesley. For two years, he'd done his best to ignore the way he felt about Wesley's girlfriend, and instead be satisfied with her friendship, but he couldn't do it anymore. He was in love with her. Completely. Irrevocably. And he couldn't help thinking that if she'd met him first, she'd have been his from the beginning. They fit together so much better than she did with Wesley. They were even closer in age, with him being thirty-one to her twenty-three, versus the full ten years between she and his brother.

He'd intentionally come by on an evening when he knew Wesley would be out. His brother's position as an up-and-coming politician meant he attended meetings and community events many nights of the week. Bex, an artist, wasn't a fan of the political scene and didn't always join him. He stopped at the door and knocked.

"Hang on a moment," she called from within. He hadn't told her he was coming over, so she wasn't expecting him. He'd been afraid he'd lose his nerve and not show up. After all, what he was about to do could ruin his relationship with his older brother and their parents, and Bex might not feel the same way. There were no guarantees. They were close, and he knew she saw him as an ally inside a family where neither of them truly belonged, but that didn't necessarily mean much. She was a good person. Loyal to Wesley. She'd never given him any indication that she thought of him as anything other than a friend, but that hadn't stopped him from dreaming.

The door swung open, and Bex greeted him with a vibrant smile.

"Michael! It's such a surprise to see you." She threw her arms open and he caught her just as she launched herself at him, a floral scent from her hair tickling his nose as one of his arms enclosed around her while he held the flowers to the side so they wouldn't be crushed. For the briefest of moments, he allowed himself to envision this as his future. Coming home to a warm greeting from her every night. It would be a dream.

She stepped back, and flicked her dark hair over her shoulders, and her gaze latched onto the bouquet. "Are those for me?" She beamed. Joy radiated from her every pore.

Michael smiled tentatively. Things were looking good. Perhaps he had a chance.

She took the bouquet and inhaled deeply. "So good. I can't believe you remembered my favorite."

"I remember everything about you."

"Oh, I get it." Her eyes lit up. "Wesley told you. I didn't realize he'd spoken to any of his family yet."

"Told me what?" he asked, his heart sinking.

"I'm pregnant." She hugged the flowers to her chest. "We're having a baby."

"Oh." Michael's world crashed down. All of his hopes evaporated in an instant. If Bex was pregnant, he couldn't ask her to leave Wesley for him. He wasn't a monster. Especially not when she was so clearly thrilled about it. "Congratulations."

Her brows knitted together. "You didn't know? Then what were the flowers for?"

"Don't worry." His fingernails dug into his palms as a sense of loss threatened to swallow him whole. "Was it planned?"

Her face fell momentarily. "No, and Wesley was a bit shocked, but I know he'll come around."

For her sake, he hoped so. But despite that, Michael wasn't sure he could handle seeing her at every family event for the rest of his life without being able to touch her. He supposed he'd just have to suck it up and suffer in silence. There would be no happily ever after for him and Bex.

"I'm sure he will." He kissed her cheek, determined that it would be the only time he'd ever allow his lips to brush her skin. "He'd be a fool not to."

His brother was many things. Opinionated. Arrogant. Self-centered. But not a fool.

"Thank you." She took his hand and squeezed. "I'm so glad you're the first to know."

Gently, he disentangled himself from her. Even though he knew she didn't mean anything by it, all physical contact between them needed to stop. It fed the tangle of tender emotion knotted in his chest.

"Me, too," he lied. The first blatant lie he'd ever told her. The heaviness in his heart said it wouldn't be the last.

ALSO BY ALEXA RIVERS

Haven Bay

Then There Was You

Two of a Kind

Safe In His Arms

If Only You Knew

Pretend to Be Yours

Little Sky Romance

Accidentally Yours

From Now Until Forever

It Was Always You

Dreaming of You

Little Sky Romance Novellas

Midnight Kisses

Second Chance Christmas

Blue Collar Romance

A Place to Belong

ACKNOWLEDGMENTS

Some books hit you harder than others. Safe In His Arms was one such book. I loved it, I hated it, and I cried over it in turn. I knew that I was looking forward to writing Tione's story, but I didn't know who his heroine would be until I remembered Megan Talbot, Mark's sweet but quiet sister from Dreaming of You who'd been in a bad relationship. As soon as I thought of her, I knew in my heart they'd be perfect together, and I hope you agree.

Because writing and editing this story was such an emotional journey for me, I especially need to thank my lovely and talented editors, Kate and Serena, who encouraged me and helped me make it the best story it could be. I appreciate you more than you know. I also need to thank my sister, the first person to read this book in its very rough state, who told me that Tione was her favorite of my heroes yet. Thanks, Sis. To Mum, who reads all of my books—even the acknowledgements—and is my last checker for typos or grammatical errors after the proofreader, thanks for being so supportive and faithfully reading each and every one. Love you.

Thank you to my husband, Mr. R, for being my biggest cheerleader. XO.

Thanks to the crew at Deranged Doctor Design, for this gorgeous cover—you outdo yourselves every single time, and to my advance readers and support team who help make every launch special. I'm so thankful for you all.

XO, Alexa

ABOUT THE AUTHOR

Alexa Rivers is the author of sexy, heartwarming contemporary romances set in gorgeous New Zealand. She lives in a small town, complete with nosy neighbors, and shares a house with a neurotic dog and a husband who thinks he's hilarious. When she's not writing, Alexa enjoys travelling, baking cakes, eating said cakes, cuddling fluffy animals, drinking copious amounts of tea, and absorbing herself in fictional worlds.

You can keep up with Alexa at:

alexarivers.com/subscribe/
www.goodreads.com/author/show/18995464.Alexa_Rivers
www.facebook.com/AlexaRiversAuthor/
www.instagram.com/alexariversauthor/
www.bookbub.com/profile/alexa-rivers
twitter.com/LexRiversWrites/

Made in United States
North Haven, CT
21 February 2022